ECLIPSE

THE SEVERANCE: BOOK 2

SUZANNE HAGELIN

CONTENTS

CHAPTER 1

Circuit Broken

*A careless word echoes long
in the corridor of silent years.*

Glimmering far over the ground, with faint threads of sparks and lightning along its filigree, the solar power web known as the Reticulary stretched in a band around the planet.

Sedate, silent, steady.

Far below, a stealthy threat rumbled unseen on the Earth's surface.

Above, Reticulary Technicians and their machines hummed and purred, busy with their routines beyond the atmosphere, harvesting massive amounts of solar power to feed the planet. Working and residing in efficient stations stretched out along the Reticulary, scattered sparsely along thousands of kilometers of wiry netting, they lived with a glut of freedom and breathtaking views. They loved their work, and their positions were coveted.

Beneath them, on the planet surface, heavy vehicles rolled down barren roads in the darkness. Muted boring drones gouged tunnels under walls and fences. Armored troops shifted by handfuls into hundreds of strategic places near key facilities, ports, harbors, airports, spaceports. Bus, train, and air taxi stations.

Over the Earth, the community of techs and their families went about their day blissfully unaware of the impending cataclysm down planetside. They were getting ready for summer, vacations on the surface, summer intern programs, orbit tourist hub visits.

On the dry land…enemy forces of the Jagged Edge gathered in the darkness.

Warm family scenes played out kilometers above sea level.

Destruction assembled in the wings below, preparing for invasion.

←↑↓→

"Reticulus work is for older people with skills and talent," Pitch shot over her shoulder, adding a good dose of ridicule to her tone. "Not obnoxious pests who can't even keep their stuff organized…"

Thump! A wadded-up towel hit her in the back of the head, knocking her slightly off balance.

She made no attempt to soften the look of fury in her eyes as she turned to glare at her brother. Eleven months younger was too close—had always been too close, as if he were not just on her heels all the time, but scraping them with the toes of his shoes, no matter how fast she ran.

"You are insufferable!" she screeched before yanking the decibels down to a grating hiss. "I can't wait to get out of this space-locked dump and into the wide, electric nets out there, where you never have to stay in a station longer than you wish. Where there aren't any annoying little *Breakers* with incandescent eyes and… and…" Bending over to pick up the towel, she shook it at him.

"Yeah?" he challenged her, his dark, not-at-all-incandescent eyes widening. He was either angry, or something else, but she didn't feel like figuring out what exactly. She just curled her lip and sneered at him. He sneered back. "What?"

Pitch straightened as if she had just remembered she was older and dropped the towel on the floor. Her face assumed what she considered a sophisticated, bored look. "Well, so much for goodbyes," she said, swiveling back to face the door.

She would be interning with several Reticulary Tech families in orbit, while the rest of her family went planetside for the summer; except for her sister, Tenna, (short for antenna), who was already apprenticed at the 120°W Station. It wasn't *actually* summer, since there were no seasons in orbit, but the RT residents in the Northwest Quadrant had a calendar patterned after lands below them on Earth.

"Wait…" Fuse said. Even the nickname he had wanted was lame. She had recommended Diode, or maybe Ion, but he had hated her suggestions. Fine. Let him be Fuse to everyone else, and she would call him Breaker. It fit him perfectly.

All the kids of the Reticulary Force used nicknames among themselves inspired by the work their parents did. It was useful when tourists were around. It was like a club outsider kids couldn't get into.

"Well?" Pitch snapped, throwing her pack over her shoulder. She was going multi-kilometers away for an RT monitor internship, the first stage in becoming proficient at her parents' vocation. And one thing she wouldn't miss for the next nine months was a pesky brother with a penchant for throwing things when he couldn't think of a good retort.

"What if you don't come back?" Fuse's voice was gruff. "What if I never see you again?"

She turned halfway back, puzzled and skeptical. She knew he was as glad to be rid of her as she was to be away from him. Why did he have to say something like that? "No such luck, El," she said casually, the childhood name adding a touch of affection. "Not in this universe."

Pitch hadn't learned yet that an almost fifteen-year-old like herself didn't know enough about the universe to make a statement like that. Turning away again, she almost missed the one tear in his eye. In fact, she did miss it at the time.

It didn't register until later.

Fuse gritted his teeth, as though willing himself to be strong, as if some emotion was about to overwhelm him. His face contorted, and for a moment she thought he was going to say something like he was sorry for being a pest, or ask her if she would miss him, or maybe ask for a hug. But something stifled the words, and he swallowed instead.

Pitch shrugged and was through the airlock with the seal engaged without another word being spoken.

She could have at least said, "Goodbye."

Why hadn't she done that?

←↑↓→

Running the wheel at the X-Qrtz station hub wasn't as exhilarating as she had imagined, but Pitch caught the hang of it quickly. The dashboard she worked at had a wide glass window she could see the cables through as she rolled them. The Reticulary used multiple duplicates of every cable so that they could execute the constant maintenance that was needed to keep them free of space dust and static. The wheels rolled each cable, whirring it through a sweeper, smoothing, cleaning, and straightening it. Each station tested the tension as well, making micro-adjustments in its elevation to maintain orbit stability.

The wires soaked up solar rays and fed the accumulated electric power to hubs that spat them to the surface in regular intervals, but it wasn't, and couldn't be, a uniform process. With so many kilometers of cable, traces of static residue collected unevenly along its length, attracting cosmic dust. Sometimes this was minimal, but at other times, it was enough of a nuisance to be a problem, adding weight and resistance to the net.

Pitch liked this hub. It was one of the newer models that had gravity fields, and she didn't have to worry about getting enough hours in the spinner to keep up her health. She didn't mind living like that, in fact, it had gotten to where she hadn't even noticed going from weightlessness to centrifugal weight or vice versa several times a day. But steady gravity was far better, almost like being on the planet.

Not quite so left out of the family vacation.

"Under-cable 23 rotation cycle complete," she informed her mentor over the com.

"Looking good," Helena responded encouragingly, "two more this shift and you're off for the rest of the day." She walked in from the portside door at a quick pace. "I have some programming glitches to work on..." She was a trim, muscular woman with a stiff chin that looked like she must grind her teeth when sleeping, but her eyes were gentle.

Pitch swiveled her chair around to face her. "Uh... what kind?" She had been hinting at a chance to help with this sort of thing.

Helena pressed her lips together thoughtfully, staring out at some swirling storm clouds over the Pacific Ocean. "Hmmm," she hesitated.

"Hackers?" Pitch really wanted to get better at identifying and countering hacking. At home, she had been improving a ton. At least her parents had told her so.

"Not sure," was the answer. "Something is going on." Helena was thoughtful, not worried.

Pitch leapt to her feet. "Let me help," she said with an artificial calm, restraining the burst of excitement she felt. "I can help."

"I know," Helena said softly, dropping her eyes to the screen she held in her hands, "you've mentioned it before."

"I'm really good. Really, really good," the girl added, shifting her weight off her heels onto her toes and raising her eyebrows. *Don't say too much!* She was learning that could have the wrong effect on mentors. They thought *they* should decide what she was ready for.

"Well..." the woman crossed her arms, tucking the screen under an armpit. "One thing you could help me with is..." She stopped herself with a sharp look at

Pitch, scanning her as though reminding herself that she was young. "But…"

"I am happy to help," Pitch forced herself to breathe and wait, and not beg for whatever it was that she might be too young for.

"I don't have anyone else available at the moment, and I really need to check on a malfunctioning node. I can't get any data from it. I don't even know if it's fried or functioning normally and just off-grid or what." Helena caught her gaze and seemed to read her eagerness. Narrowing her eyes, she asked, "You have some skating skills, of course?"

Pitch nodded. Skating the cables was required training before beginning an internship.

The woman shifted her screen out to tap and scroll through something. Nodding and murmuring, she finally said, "I guess you should be okay for this."

Pitch nodded slowly in response, afraid to speak—because it might come out in a shriek. She was about to be given a *real* task, like a legit Reticulary Tech!

"Alright," Helena decided. "Suit up, grab the tools, and skate west till you get to this node here." She pointed to a spot on the screen. "Scan it, check the fuses and breakers, dust levels, the usual, and report back. You're coming straight back. No exploring and no fancy skating tricks."

"Of course," Pitch nodded once with a sharp drop of the chin and the appropriate measure of respect.

"Nothing but normal business." Helena leaned her head sideways and raised one eyebrow—almost as if she knew how much Pitch wanted this.

"Nothing but normal business," Pitch echoed soberly as she whipped around and sped down the hall.

She was surprised to hear a faint chuckle behind her.

The equipment she strapped on belonged to the station, but Pitch's suit was her own. It had a wide clear visor that gave her a full range of vision and some high-tech radiographic scanning along the lower rim. This was to help her determine distance better. There was no atmosphere to bounce and soften light and shade, and the stark cutouts in space could trick the brain. A massive object far away could just as easily be a small object close by, and there was no way to tell just by looking. The faint aura of color on the lower edges of the objects she saw was built into her eye gear and its hue indicated distance. Red, further away. Blue and purple, close.

Poised outside the airlock, Pitch knelt at the edge of the gravity field and stared over the side down at the Earth. It gave her a brief moment of vertigo, tugging her downward. But she knew that once she was away from the hub, she would be weightless, and that confusion would pass quickly.

She ran through the checklist and made sure every item was accounted for. Clipping the skating tether onto a guiderail, she unclipped herself from the station and jumped off the side. One moment she was heavy and the next she was a free agent in space, soaring westward over the wires.

Flying.

"Nice takeoff," Helena said via com, and Pitch felt proud, wondering if she had done better than other interns.

That first leap took her nearly two thirds of a kilometer before she began to deviate and had to reel herself down to the guiderail. Touching it with the toes of her boots, she let the magnetic pull draw her heels down to connect. Without hesitating for more than a few seconds, she leapt again. She would cover less distance this time without a gravity assist.

Skating was about building up forward momentum and tapping against the rail periodically just enough to keep moving in the right direction. Every tech had to find their own stride, their own rhythm. Some of the fastest skaters were beautiful to watch and when she was practicing, she mimicked their movements. Some weren't artistic or athletic but were fast anyway. It wasn't like on the surface of the planet where the wind caused drag and speed skaters had to learn to lean into it. Out here, it was about finding your center of balance according to how your muscles worked together and how you positioned your body with that foot tap.

Pitch sketched arcs and vectors in her mind as she skated, trying to find the perfect bent at her waist, the perfect angle to lean her body, and whether a curve with abdominals tightened or a long horizontal with a straight back was better. One had a sense of rolling to it, the other felt like being a projectile.

Tap, snap the legs straight, lean into it, breathe. Arms lengthen behind. Body elongates, stretching the muscles, almost relaxing them. Then roll the fingers into fists, tighten the core, lower the chin, and pull the knees in. Descend for the next tap and kick off.

The way she pictured it in her mind was elegant, but the reality was clumsy and slow. But that was fine. Just being out here, skating in the dark over brilliant swirls of white and blue, was exhilarating. It was her first skate without a tutor or a co-skater to watch over her.

Slowing down was not just a reverse of the skating process. It had its own technique. For now, she just tightened the tether to brake.

She had reached the node before getting even one smooth kick in but that couldn't dampen her joy. "Well done!" she told herself aloud, landing on the malfunctioning node, clapping gloved hands in soundless applause.

You can't hear that in space, right?

Her feet felt unsteady. Or maybe the node had shifted. Why did her brain think there was a sound she couldn't quite hear? She clapped again to confirm what she already knew that sound would not carry through the emptiness from her hands to her ears. The vibration would travel through her body but that wasn't the same thing, and her brain knew that.

The node wasn't vibrating. But had it resonated when she landed?

"Time to find out what's going on," she muttered and slung her pack down by her feet. It was magnetized like her boots and would stay where she put it. The diagnostics pad was soon clamped to her arm, and she was rotating the dial that opened the panel. Most problems could be identified from this spot, and she shouldn't need to crawl into the node. In fact, if she did go in, she wouldn't have the skills—well, at least, not the experience—to fix it. "I can figure the problem out though," she reassured herself. "I know enough for that."

The node moved again as she was plugging in. Strange. This was not like the long oscillations that rippled when the Reticulary was hit with solar flares. It was confusing. She crouched and clung to the node with one hand as she turned around to scan the vastness of space.

The next time she felt it, she knew it wasn't her imagination. She could see a reddish tinged spark lighting up the filigree in the distance. As if localized flares were hitting points on the web and jostling it…

…like vibrations that alert a spider that something is caught in its threads.

Pitch crawled to the edge of the node to look over and stare down at the planet. In the distance, over the nearest land mass, there were bursts of color and cloud, dark orange, glowing yellow. Sharp blue flashes. And black circles that seemed to bleed strips of wispy charcoal. As if fireworks were no longer used only for holidays but for interplanetary displays.

She stared at it silently in astonishment. Those cloud swirls over the sea that she had noticed earlier were riddled with unusual strands of color and their motions made no sense—no meteorological sense.

"What?" Helena's voice crackled over the com. "This malfunction must be wider spread than we realized…"

Her last words were startlingly bland.

"Are those numbers righ…?"

The hub erupted into a spectacular explosion of fire and debris that almost instantly went dark, hardly visible as a crinkle of metal in the distance. The rolling shock that hit the node was unmistakable.

It was instinct that made Pitch flatten herself against the outer skin of the node. Whatever debris had been flung her way would be there any second and the frail field around the node might help deflect it.

She heard nothing, but felt a patter of thumps in the metal under her body as the refuse of the explosion pelted the node.

"Helena?" she whispered, knowing there was no one to answer. "What is happening?"

Turning her head over, she looked beyond, further east and waited for what she wished wouldn't come. But it did.

There. Another blast, then, so distant it was hardly a speck, she saw another and she knew it would be followed by another and another. With each one, the evidence rippled in her direction through the cables. Like thunder after lightning.

And it went on like that for hours.

Opening the hatch and descending into the node was her only choice at the time but she wasn't aware of making the decision. She just went through the motions and once inside, found herself checking all the equipment.

Emergency supplies. Check. Monitors activated…warnings flashing and scrolling. Check. Life support activated. Check. She was taking off her helmet and pulling herself into a chair without choosing to do so, strapping herself in; an open, untasted ration bar clutched in her hand. Staring out a porthole at the surface of the planet.

The Earth had become a living canvas painted with moving streaks and whirling blobs of abstract blacks, greys, and stabs of color.

Graffiti over nature.

Watching and waiting, salty drips trailing down her cheeks, Pitch sat motionless, time moving forward without rhythm. Minutes. Hours. Longer.

There were no clear thoughts. Just cold silence.

And a massive block of numbness in her heart.

CHAPTER 2

Invasion

Twenty years to spread deception
Five years to provoke unrest
Six months to train the troops
Seven days for invasion
—Severance communique to
the Jagged Edge strategist

The explosions in the night were like vast fountains of fireworks bursting and flashing across the horizon on every side. Brilliant sprays of silver white and gold, sometimes tinged with red and purple, seared the darkness again and again.

"This is my moment," the elderly man uttered in a monotone. His lukewarm eyes flashed with echoes of the distant battle and his knobby knuckles bulged, gripping the armrests tightly. Excitement coursed through his veins.

General Dedic was not the ordinary, milk-toast man he appeared to be.

Seated at the view window of his airship which rested on a bluff overlooking the valley, he could see the darting of the drones and hear the blasts of laser fire. He could imagine the screams of the people as the troops poured down the streets.

"Why do they resist?" he murmured, savoring the words. He had imagined saying those very words for so many years. They tasted sweet. "The end came long before this night."

He had sketched out the initial draft of his master plan to conquer the earth and rule the human race when he was barely seventeen years of age. And he hadn't wasted a day since then, fleshing out the details, building the deception, putting all the pieces together. Money, of which he had inherited a great deal, had been crucial in the beginning, but he had soon found that the people themselves loved and chased after all the tools he needed to control them.

They were sheep. Fools.

"I am no longer your master," he said to no one in particular, "I am your god and your devotion." He had spoken these words often to himself. His attendants were so used to hearing him murmur them that they thought nothing of it. They had long since accepted that his final victory was unavoidable.

The Earth was fighting an alien invasion.

But the 'alien' soldiers had been recruited from among their own people.

Dedic laughed. It was a long, raspy, empty sound that his lungs weren't ready to perform. But he had promised himself he would laugh, and nothing would keep him from it. Besides, the old, frail chamber he inhabited would soon be abandoned for a better, younger version that he had chosen and groomed for the purpose.

At his left elbow, the new chamber sat smiling. Corso, a young eighteen-year-old male snatched from his home as a toddler to be cultivated for the purpose: educated to develop the brain, fed well to make him healthy, physically trained to make his body limber and strong. Nothing had been lacking in shaping him into a remarkable specimen. He wasn't particularly handsome—this mattered little to Dedic. He was capable and smart, and he was exactly the *type* Dedic had wanted.

"Rounding up the survivors…" came the report from somewhere in the air.

Dedic nodded with a savage grin.

"The last ones have surrendered," the voice informed. "We are ready to eliminate them all according to standard procedure. Awaiting your command."

Dedic knew the commander that spoke considered himself human—not alien. He had been trained and shaped into a freedom-fighter of sorts, one that believed he was fighting aliens. He was convinced that none of the people they had corralled were human. They were facsimiles, imposters. They had to be exterminated in order to reclaim the world.

"Stay," he instructed.

Turning to his right, he pressed a switch. He liked switches as symbolic gestures and had had this one installed for this very moment, his moment of triumph.

"Engage," he said to another commander, leader of another group of forces. He was grinning so fiercely his face hurt but he couldn't help it.

A stream of ships descended out of the skies screeching like banshees, sinking down all around the original forces that had just conquered the last city in the final battle, that were waiting for the order to wipe out the last survivors. One after another landed and disgorged its complement of white armored troops that came out blazing, firing weapons, steamrolling down the streets, knocking over everything in their path.

"I made dystopia," Dedic said to the window. The young man at his side turned to look respectfully at his mentor. This was familiar and he knew what would come next.

"Now," the old man said. "NOW, I am giving them Utopia, and they will LOVE me for it. They will LOVE me and sing to me for all eternity." He pushed himself unsteadily to his feet and stretched out his arms on either side.

Corso rose to his feet and gazed out the window as well. It wasn't easy to see what was happening, and there were several displays they could turn to if they wanted details. But the window felt more real.

Dedic grew suddenly impatient. He was tired of this old body and anxious to put on the new one. He hadn't intended waiting this long, but the last child he had groomed as a replacement had failed miserably, and he had had to wait another fourteen years—not wanting to settle for something less suitable.

He didn't know if Corso knew what his destiny would be. He had gone to great lengths to keep it a secret, giving him a lot of responsibility as his assistant, hinting at his permanent value as a personal assistant. The boy was smart, but he was naïve, too.

"The aliens are defeated!" came the announcement in the air. The man that spoke was full of elation. "We arrived just in time to save these inhabitants!"

"You have answered the Noble Call," Dedic told the commander of the second force. "It's a joyful reward, isn't it?"

"Yes!" he answered, his voice trembling with emotion.

"Welcome to Earth," the old man greeted him. "You are the saviors of the world!"

"Conciliator!" he cried out, his voice breaking with emotion.

Dedic flicked the switch cutting off the effusion that came next. "Commander?" he called to the dark forces that had been sent to execute the inhabitants. "Commander, report!"

A few staticky clicks were the only answer.

Dedic began to chuckle. "I knew it would work," he explained to Corso who stepped closer to take him by the arm to steady him. "They were primed, not by me; by others who went before me. But I saw the opportunity and seized the day. Heh, heh, heh…" He was wheezing as he walked from the view window to another room in the ship, leaning on the young man's arm.

"Yes, Master," Corso nodded.

Dedic wondered briefly what thoughts passed unspoken in the youth's mind but didn't care enough to ask. And soon it wouldn't matter. "I planned an alien invasion. They all knew it was coming. They all expected it. They had all kinds of high-tech gear ready to combat it. I just preempted the aliens and staged one myself. And it wasn't hard. It wasn't hard at all."

He stopped and turned a piercing stare onto Corso, digging his nails into his arm. Corso froze and looked back at him.

"Do you know?" the old man gritted his teeth as he glared at him. There had been enough cruelty in Corso's training to make him afraid of that look and he quailed before him. "Have you figured out the steps I have not told you?"

Corso shook his head.

"I used their own forces to conquer them," the old man spat out. "And while the invasion was moving across the world, continent by continent, I harvested new recruits from among them. They gave me their freshest resource, their children, and I raised them to be aliens, Corso."

It was unusual for the old man to use his name and Corso blanched.

Dedic stared at him, waiting for a response.

"Yes," he whispered. He had heard the plan many times.

"They became the heroes, you see. That's why they were willing to turn on their own people. Because they believed the lie. They all believed what they wanted to believe, and it was all a fairytale that I didn't write—but I told again and again and again. Until this day. This night, that is."

There were two chairs in the Transfer Lab. Dedic often sat in one and broadcast his mind elsewhere, engaging with his commanders around the world. Corso would stand by and keep watch. This time was different.

"Have a seat, Corso," Dedic said calmly, pointing to his own chair. "It's your turn to celebrate."

"No, thank you," he demurred.

"I insist," Dedic's voice had an edge of steel.

The sheer force of the old man's will pressed down on Corso's face, heating it up, tightening his throat, and he found himself sinking into the chair, heart pounding. "Master," he said, "I'm not sure I can do this… I really can't… I don't think…"

Dedic sneered. He had sought out a docile personality in the specimen, though it was something he despised. But he was glad at the same time because it made it much easier to go through with the plan. Any faint misgivings he had were washed away by the wimpy little complaint.

With a grunt, Dedic shoved Corso's head back into the socket that connected him to the transfer framework and locked his body into place. This was the tricky part because he didn't want to find himself stuck once he had transferred into his new chamber. He had to time the locks just right, holding this body in place until the moment when the old body needed to be restrained. He had rehearsed it in his mind many times.

"One, lock him in," he mumbled to himself. "Two, suction his head. Three, climb into the secondary seat. Four, initiate the transfer but *don't rest the head yet*. Five, set locks to close. Six, unlock the other chair…" He was puttering around tapping details into the display and adjusting levers.

"Two and a half… a little celebratory drink…" he said, pouring a shot of whiskey and tapping some powder into it. Stirring it with his finger, he gulped it down, licking his thin lips.

Corso's eyes were wide as he watched him move around. "What are you doing?" he gasped when Dedic leaned over in front of him and loosened his shoelaces.

"Don't worry about it," the old man snapped at him. But he was humming. He wasn't angry at all.

"One, done," Dedic mumbled, "Two, done. Three…" He climbed into the secondary seat across from Corso. He was laughing. "This is beautiful!" Pausing to sneeze, he went on. "Three, done. Four…"

"Don't do it!" Corso cried out.

"So, you do have an idea, do you?" Dedic curled his lip and glared at him with a sideways tilt of his head.

Outside, the sound of marching grew louder and louder. The heroes, shining in white armor could be seen in the distance, filling the street as they marched toward their Conciliator's ship. A faint vibration began and grew as they drew closer.

"They're coming, Corso," Dedic shook his head reprovingly. "No time for whining." He reached out and swiped the panel in front of him. "Four, engaged." The two seats began to hum, and Corso's head was sucked back tightly into the socket. "Five, done," Dedic said as restraining belts tightened around his waist, arms, and legs. "Six, engage…" he added.

All the restraints on Corso's body unfastened, but the young man didn't move. His eyes were rolled back into his head.

"Now, Corso…" Dedic, the old man, spoke for the last time in an old man's voice. The marching had grown louder, and the ship was shaking with each pounding step. "Welcome to your destiny."

Dedic let his head fall back and the suction took him into its grip, and the old eyes rolled into the old head. A loud crashing sound coinciding with one of the marching steps reverberated through the room and with a bright flash of blue light, the machine died down.

"Well," Corso's mouth said as he opened his eyes and sat up. "This is nice, very nice."

The old man was moaning and pulling weakly at his restraints.

Corso—actually Dedic now—jumped to his feet with a loud exclamation. "Ha, HA!" he cried out, somewhat absurdly, stretching his arms to the sky, flexing his fingers, relishing the power and youth in his limbs.

The old man opened watery eyes and stared at him in horror, understanding for the first time what his purpose had been. The rejection pierced him. Dedic had never valued anything about him except the body he inhabited… used to inhabit.

The un-Corso swiveled around still stretching and moving in exaggerated gestures and tapped the release button on the old man's chair. He was laughing and humming, dancing clumsily and sweeping his hips side to side. "Oh, yes," he chuckled. "I am god now."

The old man creaked and groaned as he rose to his feet. "Master…" he whispered with a swallow.

"Call me god," the un-Corso said with a malevolent grin, pointing at him for a second before turning away again and continuing his victory dance.

Dedic had been powerful in his aged shell, in spite of all its weakness, by sheer force of will. *What would he be now in a young and healthy body?* The soul of Corso wondered, his breath catching as he straightened in the aged body, and a sharp pain pierced him in the left side. He couldn't bring himself to call the thief 'god'.

"You took me… you took my…" the old man floundered in confusion, unaccustomed to the sluggish brain.

"Oh, Master Dedic!" The un-Corso cried out in mock concern, pressing a hand to his chest. "Are you alright? Are you unwell? I've tried so hard to take care of you as your loyal servant—so hard!" He grinned fiendishly and leaned into him, in his face, so that even a whisper would be loud. "You are too good to me…" The words came out gravelly.

The old man fumbled with his hands, looking for a place to rest them and relieve his shoulders of their weight. Pockets. He found them and thrust them in. The shock began to diminish as fear and anger set in, each fighting for dominance.

"I am Corso," he croaked, twitching his hands in the pockets trying to warm them.

"Master Dedic," the un-Corso replied twisting his face into a semblance of sorrow. "You are rambling again. It's gotten so much worse of late, hasn't it?"

There was something in the old man's pocket. He felt it and puzzled over it, staring off into the distance. Groping it brought a picture to his mind. It was one of the master's many tools for survival.

"I am humbled. No, moved to tears, by your generous, lavish gift to me," the un-Corso was twisting again as if about to break into some more dancing. "Dare I even call you, *Father*?"

The old man glanced at him, bewildered. "What?"

"You chose *me*? *ME*? I had no idea!" The un-Corso tipped his head back and laughed. "I will do you proud, Father, when you are gone..." He swiveled away again, humming and snapping his fingers.

He never expected the old man to attack. Dedic had lived in a weak body for a long time that was no match for younger body's power and had assumed that would be obvious to Corso. When the old man leapt onto his back and wrapped an arm around his neck, he reacted instinctively, flinging his limbs and knocking himself over onto his face.

He didn't know how to fight.

But the old man did and even in an aged body, he was a force to be reckoned with.

The un-Corso yelled in rage and wrestled to throw off his attacker, but not before the plunger in the old man's hand had been slammed into his neck, the needle snapping off under the skin.

"What have you done?" the un-Corso bellowed, scrambling to his feet and clawing at his neck to scratch the broken needle out.

Elite guards of the Jagged Edge poured in the door, tackling the young man and pinning him to the floor as he screamed and thrashed, spewing insane orders and demands at them.

"Master!" some of them cried out as they lifted the bruised and bleeding aged man off the floor. "Are you alright?"

"Not him!! ME!!" the younger man hollered, then fell to his knees and started seizing. The guards jumped away from him in disgust.

"He was like a son to me…" the old man wheezed, wiping a tear from his eyes, as two guards lifted him gently and set him in a chair. "I don't understand what happened…"

"Surely he's not a traitor. He loved you, Master," one of the guards said as the younger man's fits increased, and he thrashed on the floor. "It is some terrible disease, perhaps a final alien weapon unleashed against you in your moment of triumph."

"Perhaps you are right," the old man's eyes gleamed as he looked into the guard's eyes and took a deep, rasping breath. "I fear…" he added, wincing in pain.

"Master," the guard uttered reverently, eyes glistening, wrapping an arm around his frail body as it sagged in the chair.

"… it has succeeded…" the old man's eyes lost focus, he sucked in and held a breath, longer than anyone imagined he could hold it, his lips working as if to speak one more time.

"You will rule in my…" the jaw released and wouldn't shape sounds. The breath exhaled and did not return. The eyes blackened, and the body surrendered.

The young man on the floor, gasping for a moment between fits, shrieked and uttered incomprehensible words, eyes fixed on the old man's body.

"He was poisoned," another guard said. "Look." He held up the old man's glass where powder swirled in the dregs.

"Vilar, did he just put you in charge?" a third looked at the one who held the lifeless body, "How in the master's name do you expect to do that?"

The un-Corso writhed on the floor, growling, foaming at the mouth.

"I have no idea," Vilar answered. And turning to glance at the young man that looked like Corso, who was once again seizing, he pulled out a gun and shot him through the head.

"But I'm not doing it alone," he added, spreading his lips in a thin grimace.

The others nodded. They were the General's elite personal guard, the highest tier of the Jagged Edge and the bond between them was strong.

"I guess that makes me Vil-Darad now… Conciliator," the new leader said thoughtfully.

The troops were amassing in the lawns out the window, awaiting the instructions of their deceased god.

"Does anyone know what the next part of the plan was to be?" he asked calmly, glancing around the room. Each one sensed the unspoken pact and entered into it without question. Someone else had plotted to take over the world—but they would rule it.

"No one must ever know that this was *not* the plan," Vil-Darad hissed.

"We don't have the codes for the machine," one objected, gesturing toward the console by the seats.

"This hand is still warm," the new Conciliator snarled as he yanked on the old man's arm and pulled it toward the colored glass dome on the console. It lit up when the hand touched it. "Authorize Vilar of the Jagged Edge as Conciliator with full privileges and access," he commanded.

The band around his wrist grew luminous with rolling waves of green and blue light.

"It won't give you everything," someone said.

"It will be enough."

They saluted as he placed his own hand on the dome and began to address the army outside in a victory speech.

CHAPTER 3

Tick Tocking

*To be alone is to be already dead
but one voice can bring life.*

Tick, tick, tick. Tock...tock...tock.... Tick, tick, tick.

Quiet filled the node, a quiet so deep it felt as though sound had been leached out through the hull, as though sophisticated dampening effects rendered it null, as though death had robbed Pitch's ears of their intended skill.

Except for that ticking sound.

Tick, tick, tick. Tock...tock...tock.... Tick, tick, tick.

At first, she had been frantically trying to figure out how to set up communications with hubs, stations, and other nodes. The instruction books—there were always hard copies as backups—were confusing and she could hardly think straight. But by the time she had figured it out, she had become afraid of what would happen if she tried to send a message.

What if the enemy, whoever it was, heard and identified where she was hiding?

Then she had tried just listening, and the cacophony of messages coming over the wireless was distressing, confusing, and overwhelming. She could make no sense of them yet listened to them for hours and hours. Dozing and waking, in lucid dreams, in nonsense dreams, in a stupor, in a feverish panic.

And she was alone. All alone.

A kid shouldn't have to be alone at a time like this, she was sure.

Except… she was a kid no longer. There was nothing left of the childhood she had left behind when she walked out on her brother without saying goodbye. It had been a few weeks, but it might as well have been years ago. In another universe.

Tick, tick, tick. Tock…tock…tock…. Tick, tick, tick.

She wasn't sure when she turned off the radio. For a while, her heart had sounded like a throbbing drum, pounding in her head at varying paces as the hours went by. Then the sound of whimpering and sometimes sniffling arbitrarily caught her off guard and startled her. After a few days, even that stopped. Silence filled the node, and she settled into a numbness. She wasn't even belted into a seat anymore and just drifted around the interior.

There was nothing but empty air, air that didn't ripple when she moved, or hum when she opened or closed…or opened…or closed her eyes.

Or her hands.

Or her mouth.

Tick, tick, tick. Tock...tock...tock.... Tick, tick, tick.

Now and then, she had to make an audible gasp for breath to be sure she was breathing because it seemed like death.

It *was* death.

Had she eaten? Her mouth was dry, but there was a water hydration tube hanging loosely nearby as if she had left it out to sip whenever she felt like it. There were several wrappers floating. And a few crumbs. And the odd glistening drop of water... Water? No, they were salty.

Don't think about that.

Tick, tick, tick. Tock...tock...tock.... Tick, tick, tick.

"Just shut up," she murmured, speaking more softly than she had intended and, at the same time, startling herself with the noise of her own voice. The words resonated up close, bouncing off the walls at her, mocking her. Death shouldn't be so loud.

When had the ticking started? A long time ago. A few minutes ago. They both felt possible.

It didn't matter.

Tick, tick, tick. Tock...tock...tock.... Tick, tick, tick.

The sound was soft, but the pattern was annoying. Somebody had really bad rhythm. No sense of timing. It was like it was meant to be irritating. It nagged at her brain as if it meant something and as if she alone could decipher it. She didn't *want* a mystery to solve. She just wanted to fade into nothingness and never think again.

And she didn't want to think about her parents and what they had taught her—about *that* sound—that CODE!

"Screaming sparks!" she shrieked suddenly, flinging all four of her limbs out. "That's an old Mayday SOS if I ever heard one!" She had never heard one before, but the shock of identifying a message with human intent behind it sent her into a massive adrenaline rush. Her lips began to tingle, and her hands and feet felt like prickling electricity were zapping them. And the throbbing was back in her head with shades of blue pulsing in her vision.

Her fingers trembled as she pulled herself into the command chair, strapped in, and started searching the main console for clues.

"It's coming through the Reticulary weave," she muttered audibly. "That means it's not an enemy because only techs know about that."

She hoped.

In between every cycle, the sender had left a blank space so an answer could be sent. Pitch decided to wait till after the next SOS to respond. The how-to was simple. The triggers they used to thump each cable were tapped a few times each 24-hour period to identify issues with the tension. It was an automatic process but there were switches the techs could use to test it as well. Identifying which cable the sender had chosen was easy.

Tick, tick, tick. Tock…tock…tock…. Tick, tick, tick.

She selected cable 16 and pounced on the tension test switch.

Tick, tick, tick. Tock…tock…tock…. Tick, tick, tick, was her answer.

For a moment nothing happened. Then the signal came again, three times without pausing, ticks and tocks representing letters in the alphabet.

—SOS, SOS, SOS

Pitch repeated the pattern in response.

>>*SOS, SOS, SOS*

This time a new message came over the cable. Decoding the Morse was going to be slow. What was the symbol for '*hang on*'? The computer had a record function, so she taped it, only missing the first few clicks.

"There's probably a decoding tool in this computer," she told herself. "But no time to look for that now. Pretend it's a game." A stab of sadness hit her in the stomach because game = childhood = family = her brother she didn't say goodbye to.

Shove that thought away.

After a few moments of wrestling with her memory, she put this together: *HOW MANY SURVIVE.* That's what the person beyond was asking.

Now she recognized that she had subconsciously noticed the difference in the sounds all along. The staccato *ticks* were alternated with resonant *tocks*, simulating dots and dashes. Ticks and tocks. The tocks had a longer wavelength and duration than the ticks.

Tick, tock, tock, tock, tock, she replied. ONE.

Another pause.

—*YOUR LOCATION*, the next message prompted.

She gave the exact longitude of the node. As an afterthought, she considered that if an enemy actually were on the other end, it could be bad for her. But it didn't seem so scary now. Anything was better than being the only person left in space.

—*YOUR CALL SIGN*, was the next request.

Techs had call signs. Their kids just had nicknames.

"Well, the techs around here are all gone and I'm all that's left," she explained to the empty air. "I'm an honorary tech now and my code name makes a great call sign."

>>PITCH, she transmitted back.

The response was garbled, and she was unable to make sense of the ticks, tecks, tucks, and tocks that came back with no clean distinction between them. "What's wrong with you?" she barked without hostility. There was no one to hear her and she needed to expel some of her inner turmoil. "That's as good a call sign as any!"

The cables grew still, and she waited. What was she supposed to answer to that gibberish?

Finally, it started ticking again and for the first time she wondered how far it had to travel from its origin.

> *—PITCH*, the signal said clearly, *ARE YOU PITCH.*

She began trembling and her hands shook so badly she wasn't sure they would work when it was her turn to answer. Did the person at the other end know her? Had her mentor escaped after all? Or maybe the hub where she had trained for a couple of weeks in the winter had survived.

> —PITCH STOP ARE YOU PITCH

The word 'STOP' confused her for a moment, even though she knew its purpose. It was like a period or a comma.

>>YES, she tick-tocked.

She could hardly decipher the reply. *Tock. Tick. Tock, tick. Tock, tick. Tick, tock.* As she stared at the console, the sounds came again. *Tock. Tick. Tock, tick. Tock, tick. Tick, tock.*

—T E N N A

It looked so familiar. Was she shaking or was that the chair? A strange gasp, like a choking sound, came from her throat, and she realized she was clutching at her chest. A low moan came from her lips.

"Tenna," she mumbled, rocking from side to side as if her whole body was saying, No, No, No. "Tenna, Tenna, Tenna…"

Her sister.

She hadn't dared to hope that her sister was alive.

She started tapping out the name over and over as she was murmuring it. After about twelve repetitions, it occurred to her to pause and wait for an answer.

> —*PITCH*, Tenna tapped back, YOU ARE ALIVE STOP IS IT REALLY YOU STOP ARE YOU ALIVE.

"I'm here, I'm here!" she shrieked painfully, scrabbling at the console looking for the radio. A brief blip sound showed she had found it. She jerked around looking for the manual and pulled it out, roughly shoving through pages in search of instructions on how to send a verbal message.

> —*NO RADIO*, Tenna messaged. She must have heard the blip. *ANYONE CAN HEAR STOP DANGER.*

> \>\>TENNA, Pitch tapped back, WHERE ARE YOU I NEED YOU I AM ALONE I AM

SCARED EVERYONE IS GONE I THOUGHT YOU WERE DEAD.

It took a long time to send all that and she was sobbing by the time she was done. She kept wiping the tears from her eyes and they would blur over again, and her fingers were slipping on the keys.

—I AM HERE

>> WHERE ARE YOU I NEED YOU WHAT ARE WE GON TO DO

—I AM WORKING ON IT

>> HELP ME HELP ME HELP ME

—YOU ARE OKAY NOW STOP WE ARE OKAY NOW STOP WE HAVE EACH OTHER

>> I WILL COME TO YOU

—NO STOP NOT YET STOP NO MOVEMENT

>> I AM ALONE

—YOU ARE NOT ALONE

The conversation took a lot longer than the simple words imply since neither one of them was very good at encoding or decoding. By the time they had covered this much, Pitch had begun to calm down and a different kind of quiet had settled on her.

—WE WILL TALK AGAIN IN A FEW HOURS, Tenna said.

>> OK

—TRY TO GET SOME REST AND EAT

>> OK

—I LOVE YOU

>> I LOVE YOU TOO

The cables stilled and silence returned to the pod. She was ravenous now and dying of thirst. "There's got to be more than just emergency rations," she said aloud, unbuckling and pushing herself across the open room. Opening and closing several cabinets, she found and extracted a long container. "Ah!" She pulled out several packages, tucking some under her arm, scanning others. Spaghetti and meatballs, ice cream, veggie juice, coffee.

Biting open the juice she chugged it down, thinking it had never tasted so good. Soon she had polished off the spaghetti and ice cream as well. And deciding that it was about time she became a coffee drinker, she guzzled two tubes of it.

Then an exhaustion descended on her so heavy that she could hardly keep her eyelids open, and she barely managed to tuck herself into the cocoon on the wall before falling into a deep sleep.

Her lips were mouthing, *thank you, thank you,* as she slipped into slumber.

←↑↓→

Few knew that the invading alien forces were controlled by the very leaders who also backed the desperate defense the world mounted. And the rolling tsunami of battles across the globe left numerous political wastelands filled with governmental refuse and debris.

In places where the earth forces survived, they had no leaders. And where the aliens had won, there were no structures in place to take over. Chaos and anarchy reigned and even in that, no one stepped into the power vacuum.

Vil-Darad had no idea what General Dedic had intended to do next and was unable to locate the plans for this stage of conquest, if they even existed. They must have existed. And how had he stayed in communication with all his leaders? Whatever implant he had used gave him a unique ability that no surviving scientists could explain, let alone duplicate.

The new Conciliator had to improvise. New implants were devised, and transfer stations were ordered so that meetings could be called. In his own ship, he set up robots to be the recipients of his leaders' psyches or souls or whatever their consciousness was when it traveled, and that was how they met in the early stages.

They needed new recruits, fresh agents to take up the mantle of governance under his leadership. Brainwashing wasn't difficult if he used the right approach. And persuading the world to accept them would be even simpler. People were longing for safety. The problem was where to find these agents—and the solution was clear.

Children were malleable. And many were already parted from their families. Others could be easily separated for their own 'protection'. The central AI was complex enough to manage their training and maintenance once they were converted. Once they had forgotten who they were and where they came from. Once their loyalties and love had been appropriately redirected. Their very longing for home would make them zealous to watch over the new utopia he was building.

The Jagged Edge had accomplished its task and the Severance was complete.

The Order of Peace would be founded.

A new race of creatures would bring peace to the world, and he, the Conciliator, would be the Father of All.

Pitch internalized Morse code practically overnight and became so proficient at it she sometimes dreamt in code, tapping instead of speaking. It became the main form of communication for the surviving Reticulary Techs, unnoticed by onboard computers or anyone monitoring them on the surface. But making a digital record of any kind was unwise so messages had to be understood and remembered, stored in human brains.

It was amazing how much Pitch's brain could store verbatim now that it was crucial to do so. They had no way of knowing who controlled the Reticulary AI and couldn't risk contact with it.

Tenna instructed her how to build a simple telegraph and attach it to one of the guidewires used for skating. There were no computers attached to that part of the structure and no chance the AI would identify them.

She was now part of a network of survivors and joined the labor of finding other techs who hadn't died. Since tick-tock signals decayed along the wire without electronic boosting, because of course, that would be an indicator of active human involvement, people like her and Tenna had to retype the messages. Both sending maydays through the cables with the tension test switch and passing on telegrams became a major part of her life.

Pitch wished they could stop calling themselves survivors. Names were a big deal. And she knew they needed something to bind them together and make them feel less helpless. RTs didn't feel right since many of them, like herself, were merely apprentices.

When the attack had begun, the enemy had had no intention of destroying Earth's main power supply and while it had seemed to Pitch that all the living stations and hubs had been wiped out, only about every third one had been completely destroyed. Many of the others had been attacked with computer code that temporarily wiped out life support, suppressing oxygen and heat until the people inside were dead.

Survivors on those sites had managed to climb into spacesuits and either skate or escape in repair modules to empty nodes, which was standard emergency protocol. The nodes were lifeboats, equipped to help people survive until they could be rescued.

Some of the older stations were uninhabited and had been ignored. The enemy, presumably, intended to send up their own techs to run the power grid once they had established themselves below.

Food stores in the nodes would run out at some point. And resupplying from earth was out of the question. The survivors would have to go back to some of the remaining hubs and reacquire them so they could access the farms there. Maybe they could find a way to stay. Or maybe just live in hiding and come back to tend the gardens and lab-farms and restock supplies.

More than getting by, though, they needed a plan. And who would come up with it?

Someone would be bound to take the lead, right? Once they had an idea of what they were working with?

>> IS SOMEONE BUILDING A CHART OF OUR PEOPLE OF WHERE WE ARE ON THE R

Pitch was telegramming her sister. They had resorted to using initials for commonly repeated words. The 'R' was the Reticulary. And they were getting used to no punctuation.

— *MAYBE,* Tenna answered.

>> WHAT IS THE PLAN

— I DONT KNOW

>> HOW ARE WE GOING TO FIND A SAFE HAVEN

— SOMEONE IS WORKING ON IT

>> WHO

This wasn't the first time they had had a discussion like this one. Tenna thought things were being handled but she didn't know exactly how or who was taking care of them.

— ARE YOU PASSING ON LOCATIONS

>> YES OF COURSE

— THAT HELPS

>> WHO IS COLLECTING THEM

— SOMEONE

Pitch could tell her sister was getting annoyed, but she couldn't help the pressure she felt to get things moving. She needed to know who was collecting the location data and what they would do with it.

In fact, she was already collecting it herself and wanted to be a part of the next step. She had been penciling it on edges of the manuals as well as memorizing the GPS coordinates. All you really needed was longitude because the Reticulary was a thin band with individual locations stretched along its length.

>> WHO TOLD YOU

— ABOUT WHAT

>> OF THE PLAN

There was no answer.

That's when it suddenly became crystal clear to Pitch. Sometimes, everyone is looking to everyone else to take the lead, to get something started, to stand up and make the first move. And people with no idea where to start are looking around for *someone* to get things going.

Making a map, identifying intact stations and hubs, figuring out how to move from one node or station to the next, formulating a plan for what to do about connecting with people, about finding out what was going on planetside, about how to keep existing without going insane…

What if…if a plan was going to be set in motion…

What if it was up to her?

>> OKAY STOP I WILL MAKE A MAP

There was no immediate answer.

>> AND YOU FIND OUT HOW MANY REPAIR MODULES WE CAN LOCATE WITHIN

She paused to consider what would be realistic.

>>FIFTY KM ON EITHER SIDE OF YOUR LOCATION

There was still no answer from Tenna.

>> I WILL COME TO YOU SOON STOP TOMORROW

— TOO DANGEROUS, Tenna messaged.

>> NECESSARY

— BUT WHAT IF YOU ARE SEEN

Pitch was tired of that what-if. Even though she had seen firsthand how dangerous it could be at the stations, she wasn't convinced anyone below was even looking their direction anymore.

>> I WILL BE OKAY STOP GET ME THE LOCATIONS

Tenna's response was so simple, but it was like the universe shifted and Pitch's world had changed forever.

— OK

Her older sister accepted what she had said? "Does this make me the rebel leader?" Pitch asked aloud.

She could be okay with that.

CHAPTER 4

From the Surface

When hope survived extinction
the peril avoided was forgotten.

Pitch skated deftly along the guidewire stretching into the distance. Above and around her, stars glutted the black emptiness of space, like hundreds of thousands of diamonds poured over black velvet. Beneath her feet, the earth turned, luminous in the dark where clouds and continents and oceans hid in the night, and city sparkles traced the outlines of human habitation.

She was untethered.

Without the tether, the slightest vibration of a cable under her feet could toss her into the night sky, casting her down to burn like a meteorite in the mesosphere. Her boots were held to it by the barest hint of magnetism. Moving along safely required a sliding, skating motion, barely lifting each boot five centimeters from the cord as she swept the leg forward and tapped it to anchor it before sweeping the other. It was crucial that she keep the momentum going in exactly the right direction along the cable.

It was risky but skating with a tether made her far more vulnerable to solar flares. And it was much faster. Once she got going, she raced across the wire like a bolt of lightning.

And felt no fear.

"Crossing marker-113.92W," she said, broadcasting through her helmet. Short-range coms between Specs—that's the name Pitch had chosen for the space survivors—was possible once they had linked in person. Most of their inter-spec communications, though, took place via telegraph.

"Can you go any faster?" Tenna responded, "There's a flare coming."

Pitch leaned forward and lengthened her stride, huffing in a rhythmic pulse. She couldn't keep this pace for too long, but it would be enough to get her to the next node before the flare hit. Solar flares could be dangerous if she were touching the Reticulary weave when they hit.

"How far?" she gasped.

"23 seconds till it gets here," Tenna said, "Less than that till you hit the next intersect if you can speed up just a hair… Come on, Pit!"

Pitch pressed harder counting on her innate sense of motion, allowing herself an edge of carelessness that could slap her off the cord if she made the slightest miscalculation. She thought only of the 'shooshing' sound of air through her teeth as she raced.

There. She could see the ring-shaped intersect glinting. *Too far,* she thought, despite what Tenna had said. And the solar flare was about to hit.

If it hit her while her feet touched the cable, she would be fried, crisped like a fly in a bug zapper.

She felt the tug in her gut, as if space were distorting around her body, the aura before the blast, and bent her knees, slapping her feet away as her momentum continued to carry her forward. The solar flare arced through the cables lighting up the spidery weave stretching as far as her eyes could see.

Crrrruuusssstzzz!! That low-pitched sound in her suit was unmistakable. She was being magnetized, and it would be hard to say how it might affect her movement.

Punching her fist forward, she ejected a grapple targeting the intersect and closed her eyes instinctively. It latched on and held her as she swooped past it, was yanked back, and swung around, flailing. She shrieked in frustration as the line reeled and drew her in, flapping her back and forth, till she could grasp the ring and cling to it panting. Several rhythmic throbs shook her as the node absorbed her magnetic charge.

"Graceful," Tenna commented, her tone giving away the anxiety she felt. "We got a pretty good charge off of that one," she added as the power surges registered in the instruments.

Pitch's heart was pounding and her fingers throbbing, her face, leaning against the inside of her visor which was pressed against the cold metal casing of the ring. It felt like it was vibrating. She always thought that, though they always told her she was imagining it.

"Yeah," she panted, holding on tightly as she turned and placed herself into a sitting position, an illusion in a weightless realm.

The wire structure was designed to circle the earth, creating both a communication network and a power generator unlike any the world had ever seen before, protecting against excess solar radiation and damaging flares, controlling weather, and more. They didn't know what all it had been intended for because it had never been finished, and the system was only partially functional.

Pitch fumbled at the controls and opened the intersect's main panel. It was flashing the message "RESET" in green letters. She plugged in the drive she carried, tapped quickly on the keys, and overrode the original code. This would reflect dummy messages to earth when triggered and allow it to be controlled by her people.

Her space rebels.

"That was close," Tenna said coolly, as though her calm would be soothing. It wouldn't. Pitch knew when her sister was freaked, but she appreciated the effort. In the early days, she kept shrieking in the com when Pitch did anything, absolutely *anything* risky. She had to beg her to stop because her panic echoed in Pitch and drove up her anxiety levels, which were normally not a problem. Pitch was pretty good at keeping a level head when she needed it.

So, actually… the calm tone *was* helpful.

Smiling as she waited for her heart rate to slow down, Pitch took a few sips of water from her suit's hydration tube. It was good to have someone to watch out for her. And nice to have someone to take risks for.

A reason to live and a purpose to fight for.

"We got a message from Faraday," Tenna said. Three Specs lived there, two of them real RTs. "There's been some interest in that station, and they are worried the aliens are thinking of doing a sweep or maybe even sending up agents to reestablish control there."

'Aliens' was what they were calling the enemy because that was how they had presented themselves during the conquest. Of course, they must be human since no aliens' ships had ever appeared from beyond, but the label had stuck.

Faraday Base was one of the major Reticulary stations the enemy hadn't destroyed and it had been built to house several hundred people. Fully equipped with gardens, labs, recyclers, medical supplies, and entertainment, it had been a village in space. There had been festivals and 'market' days and community meetings there. RTs and their families from many kilometers away on either side would gather there, sharing life together.

Now it was a ghost town with only maintenance bots keeping it clean and functional, running the systems, tending the gardens, harvesting the food. And three people who slunk around its interior like space rats, careful not to leave enough evidence of their presence to catch the attention of the people below. They had walled off a small sector from the AI and the station's units where they lived undetected in relative comfort.

But a living person would be able to recognize the cheat if they came looking.

"Is that an immediate concern?" Pitch asked, rolling onto her stomach, and pulling herself to the edge of the intersect to gaze down at the planet. She never tired of the view.

Oxygen 40%, her suit warned, flashing yellow in a lower corner of her visor.

"Uh… not sure," Tenna replied. "I'll find out."

"I'm going on to Needle Post Node," Pitch said. "No point in changing plans until we know there's a problem." She had some arbitrary names for nodes that she was having trouble getting the other Specs to adopt. It made her feel like she was traveling along a known highway with pitstops and campgrounds.

Tenna groaned. She could never remember which node Pitch was talking about.

"If you traveled more, you would like my names," Pitch reminded her.

"We can't both travel at the same time. Someone has to run communications and be ready if there's an emergency."

"Yeah, yeah, yeah." Pitch rose to her feet and stared into the distance. Only thirty kilometers to the next stop. She could make it in twenty minutes if she didn't use the tether, but the danger of flares was over for the time being and she was getting tired. In fact, the last flare had scared her more than she cared to admit, and she didn't feel like taking any more unnecessary risks.

Clipping the tether to the guidewire, she launched herself in a graceful arc out across the cabling, soaring effortlessly for a long time before having to touch down. Then in smooth sweeps, she skated at speeds she had only dreamed about before the crisis. Like an eagle in flight, soaring high in the sky, lifted on powerful wings, beating forcefully every now and then just for fun.

Needle Post came faster than she had expected, and she wondered if she was still increasing her maximum pace. *I would so win those races*, she thought, *if they ever do them again.* Yanking on her tether, she pulled her feet down to the guidewire and let the boots clamp down. Then tightening on the strap, she flipped around, skidding with her body almost horizontal to the wire, using the drag forces in her feet and the tether brake to slow herself down. She considered engaging her legs this time, wrapping them around the cable as she didn't like overshooting the node. It was sort of like wiping out while surfing (she imagined), getting thrown and jolted and crashing into the structure.

Dropping one knee against the guidewire, just for a second, she stopped with flawless precision. But the suit went crazy with alarms and warnings about possible suit damage. She shrugged and gulped at the same time.

One tiny breach was all it would take to *decommission her forever.* One little tear or crack, and her life's breath would be hissing out into the dark, probably faster than she could get into the safety of the node. '*Maybe it didn't break this time, but it's weaker now,*' she could hear her mom's voice in her head warning her. These days, suits had several layers resistant to tears, but they couldn't prevent all damage.

Never, never, never risk the integrity of your suit.

Yeah, I know, she thought, with a tinge of both guilt and sorrow. *Sorry mom… wherever you are.*

Climbing into the node, she sealed the hatch and took off her helmet. The air wasn't as stale as she had expected, which was nice. In fact, the whole place was tidy. Whoever had been there last had cleaned up after themselves. *Probably wasn't me,* she chuckled to herself.

With a few taps on the console, she powered up the radios as she often did to see what she would pick up from earth. Scanning the various stations, she heard the usual stuff. Music, announcers talking about how well everything was going, propaganda for the Order of Peace and the utopia they were building, praise for the Sentinel aliens who had come from another planet to protect the survivors of the invasion—except there had been no aliens, neither invading, nor coming to protect anyone, so…who the bolts knew what they were talking about.

One signal was new. And it was so faint she had to narrow the reception band so it could pick it up.

"What's this?" she wondered aloud, sitting back in the command chair.

"…ansfer incomplete… *skktttzz*… power reserves dwindling… unable to reestablish link…"

"You aren't alien," she said, straightening and stretching herself as if she could heighten her hearing, like a cat turning its ears toward the sound. She fiddled with some settings and finetuned the signal until she could hear it clearly.

The transmission went on for some time, talking about some power crisis and imminent failure of some system. It must not be referring to the radio broadcast because though weak, it didn't show signs of dissolving.

"Tenna," Pitch whispered, clicking on her coms, not wanting to miss anything the earth station said. "We've got non-aliens planetside."

"What?" her sister replied after a brief pause.

"REBELS LIKE US!" she shouted back. This was something she talked about sometimes, postulating that there was a rebel underground, a group of survivors on the surface that were working to overcome the aliens and win their freedom.

It was more than wishing to be a part of something exciting. More than longing to be free of the difficult and lonely life they were leading. More than wanting to see an end to the so-called Order of Peace and its double layers, utopia for some and work camps for others.

It was the desperate hope that her loved ones had survived and were down there somewhere, doing their part to overcome the nightmare and reunite the family.

She dreamed about it a lot.

"What do you mean, rebels like us?" Tenna had that tone in her voice that meant, *Here we go again.*

"They're transmitting, but it's such a weak signal that I think the alien stations on the surface can't pick it up. We've disabled their access up here so they wouldn't be able to hear what I'm hearing."

"Real people?" Tenna allowed a little excitement in her voice. "You can hear real people talking? About…. About what?"

"About power running out and what to do," Pitch shot back. Her heart rate was accelerating with excitement. "Tenna, we've got to do something."

"We can't broadcast back," her sister warned. "Anything we transmit will be picked up by the Order."

"Not if it's coded in a normal power burst," Pitch countered, lowering her voice to communicate the conviction she felt. "We have to find a way to connect with them."

"Don't do anything stupid!"

"I'm not!" Pitch almost allowed herself a screech but caught it just in time. "I'm not," she said again, evenly. "I'm going to send out a net-wide alert to all the Specs—"

"I wish you wouldn't call us that," Tenna interjected.

"…to all the Specs," Pitch continued, "per high urgency protocol."

"…which you also named."

"It means top priority, extremely important," Pitch gritted her teeth. "You can name the things you establish."

Tenna didn't respond to that.

"Here's the message we need to broadcast:

POCKET OF EARTH REBELS DISCOVERED ON THE SURFACE STOP THEY ARE IN DIRE NEED OF POWER STOP WE MUST DO THREE THINGS STOP ONE IDENTIFY THEIR POWER HUB AND SEND SUPPLY STOP TWO SET UP PLAN FOR COVERT COMMUNICATIONS WITH THEM STOP THREE ENSURE THESE OPERATIONS ARE NOT DETECTED BY THE ALIENS STOP

"How does that sound?"

"Okay," Tenna answered hesitantly.

"I'll broadcast west, and you go east," Pitch suggested.

"Sounds good."

They had settled into this rhythm of cycling between acting like sisters—getting along or bickering or ignoring each other part of the time—and at other times, Pitch took the lead, and Tenna followed. That was okay.

It was a relief for both of them.

Pitch's fingers trembled as she started telegraphing their message, listening the whole time to the rebels below. How she wished she could contact them and say, "We're here!" She didn't know how to do that surreptitiously so the aliens wouldn't know, but there were a few techs left with the skills, she was pretty sure.

There had to be.

Communications on the surface went on for over twenty more minutes as someone with the call sign Axon and someone else who went by BirdDog tried to solve their problem. They had tapped into local hubs to siphon off power in trickles small enough to avoid detection or at least not be worth the bother of fixing. Apparently, the enemy was now cutting off their access to power sources, one by one.

"They must know we are the ones behind the leaks, over," BirdDog croaked.

"If we don't find an alternative," Axon countered coolly, "we won't be able to maintain contact, over."

"We have other ways of communicating, over." BirdDog had a gravelly voice that sounded like it almost could've belonged to a dog that learned to talk.

"Very limited, not good enough, over." Axon's voice was low but melodic. He could have been a podcaster. Those were gone planetside, but there were tons of them in storage in space and the Specs were always listening to them and passing around suggestions. They preferred them to video or holos because they gave the illusion of hearing from people on Earth.

"Where are you?" Pitch said aloud looking at the screen. She had expected to be able to pinpoint their location quickly, but the signal was frail. And it could be bouncing off clouds or mountains.

The map showed strong red dots where there were steady Order of Peace broadcasts in various places. Weaker signals flickered in and out with little green bursts. She was pretty sure this rebel communication didn't even warrant a green dot, almost too dim to be detected. She narrowed her search and tried zooming in on one area, then another, moving across and up and down the grid. Soon they would stop talking and if she hadn't pinpointed them by then, she wouldn't be able to find them at all. Or figure out a way to contact them.

And she was suddenly desperate to connect. Her hands, normally so steady, had started to tremble. She found herself breathing shallowly and blinking her eyes a lot.

"Don't stop talking," she whispered. "Please just give me a chance…"

"We're losing power to this unit," Axon said flatly.

"Underground then," BirdDog interrupted.

"We won't have the range we need. We'll lose touch with most of our network." Axon's voice sounded so calm considering what he was saying.

"Wait…wait…. THERE!" Pitch shrieked, glad that Axon couldn't hear her sounding like a kid. A pale blue light bleeped when Axon spoke.

She looked around frantically for a way to send a message. What could she do? What could she do? Radio was out of the question. In fact, any kind of transmission would be fatal—an invitation to the enemy to come after her, or worse, destroy the node she was in.

There was *nothing*.
Unless…

She pulled up the charts on the latest solar flare and the stores the Needle Post node had accumulated from it. It had a 20% surcharge, the max it could retain. Good. She could use that. There were emergency measures when a node took in more power than it could handle and the Reticulary was too overloaded to drain it off.

Kind of like a bolt of focused lightning.

Each node had the capacity of shooting a bolt of surplus electricity down to the surface. And calculating and discharging them, though usually handled automatically by the system, were something a living person could initiate from the console.

"So, you need power?" she asked as if they could hear her. They were still talking back and forth, looking for options. "Let me help you with that…"

"If we had any storms in the forecast, we could pick up some lightning, over," Axon said as if on cue. *We must have some kind of mental connection*, Pitch thought.

"That's what I'm talking about," she replied.

"The rods should be in place regardless," BirdDog said, "in case there's some freak weather, over."

"Ours are, over," Axon affirmed.

"So, I'm assuming that flicker, where Axon is, has a power rod," Pitch murmured. It would be a bit shocking—pun intended—if it weren't in that spot. Without a power receptor rod, there was no guarantee the jolt would be absorbed into their storage cells.

Pitch tapped away at the console and setup up a bolt of electricity, ready to unleash it with one more tap, then hesitated. It was one thing to send them some power. But how would they know she was up here? How could that turn into communication?

"I can send you power," she said aloud, knowing they couldn't hear her.

"I have no answers, over," BirdDog was saying.

"But you won't know it's coming, and you won't know it's me!" she went on.

"Tomorrow then, over," Axon said.

"Don't sign off yet!! Please!! I haven't figured out how to make this into a message!"

"If we can, over and out," BirdDog ended.

Pitch tapped the final button, and the bolt of power shot out of the base of the node toward the ground right where the Axon flicker had been. "I'm sorry!" she whispered.

A loud crackle came over the air. Cries, curses, and confusion mixed with static followed then eventually settled into BirdDog trying to get Axon's attention.

"Axon, over," he kept saying, with pauses in between. "What happened? Please respond, over."

After several tense moments, Axon finally came back on.

"You won't believe this, BirdDog," he said, forgetting to add the word 'over', "It's the most uncanny thing. I can't explain it. I didn't believe it at first…"

"What?!" BirdDog skipped the protocol word as well.

"We just got a full charge… over."

"You what?"

"A bolt of lightning out of the clear night sky just ripped down directly at our little outpost and…and…" Was he choking up? His voice kind of cracked and Pitch was delighted to think that a guy with such a calm voice might get emotional.

Well, well, she said to herself. *I guess that helps you out, doesn't it? Specs to the rescue!*

"You're kidding me…" Actually, BirdDog used a different word, but Pitch wasn't familiar with the term and mentally substituted one she knew.

There were several minutes of silence.

"BirdDog," Axon said finally, "We have to consider that it wasn't a coincidence. Someone could still be alive in the Reticulary. Someone who heard us and wanted to help."

More silence.

"That just makes me…sad," BirdDog replied, "up there…alone?"

"Yeah, but really glad because we got power…" Axon countered.

"Hey, RT," BirdDog said. "I had an uncle up there. I thought you were all gone, but, yeah, thank you…"

"Thank you," Axon repeated.

And they stopped talking.

And Pitch realized she was crying.

CHAPTER 5

Connection

With heroics out of reach, they found only the next, unremarkable task which must be, and was, enough.

"We want to believe there are real people in the Reticulary who have somehow survived," Axon broadcast a couple of days later. "Most of us are pretty sure you're up there. But it would be dangerous for you to contact us. Any message you send could be picked up by the Order of Peace network. So, we've come up with a short set of power transfers to confirm that you are there."

Pitch and Tenna listened attentively to the instructions. The next time there was enough solar flare activity to justify the surges, they were to deliver a series of bolts of power to several locations in what would appear to be random intervals and strengths—but following their requested pattern exactly.

"If you could be as close to accurate as possible, to the millisecond and microjoule, even," Axon added, "it will increase our certainty. We have some skeptics among us." He coughed as though to hide a chuckle. "Survivors in the Reticulary almost seems too good to be true."

Pitch could relate. It was thrilling for her, too. They would finally have more *people* in their circle!

There were very few Specs and little chance that they would ever get to all meet in person. The distances were too great along the Reticulary. They had devised Reticulary Families, made up of people who were in proximity to each other and could manage in-person meets. It was necessary. Otherwise, the isolation would be more than anyone could endure. Pitch and Tenna had each other and would meet up with Specs to the west and east of their zone periodically.

The news about the rebels, (Pitch's name for them stuck), was hugely encouraging for all the Specs and the buzz on their telegraphs was nearly non-stop for days. Everyone was scouring the planetside broadcasts for surreptitious rebel communiques and mapping out power receptors that might need a zap.

The locations the rebels had sent were spread out across several zones on either side of Pitch and Tenna as well as in their own area. Setting up the correct series of power bolts took a little planning, since they couldn't be on location at each node to make them happen in person. Tenna wrote a simple code that required only a signal to trigger. Adding the correct timing involved adjusting for the time delay between nodes. When a solar flare hit, they would start the application, and the first jolt would be blasted to the first location. Then, incorporating the time it took for the message to be sent to the next node through the lines, the app would start up in the next node and issue the next discharge. There were to be a total of eight bolts.

Rebels would get power, and the Specs would be confirmed as allies in space.

Two days later, there was a medium-range solar flare large enough for their purposes. Pitch was camping out in Needle Post Node. She was desperately overdue for a cup-bath since the post had only drinking water. Axon's response would play at their home base via relay with only a few seconds delay, but she wouldn't leave. She had to hear Axon speak the moment it happened.

Tenna was annoyed by that; she hated being alone for that long.

"This is it, Tenna!" Pitch said, clutching the arms of her chair in excitement. Her heart was racing feverishly which meant she probably needed some gravity treatment. Minimum an hour a day, the RT training manual said.

"Yeah, I know," Tenna answered flatly, pouting. "I'm the one that set up the app."

"And I helped," Pitch couldn't resist adding. This was her operation! She had made the initial connection. A slight twinge of guilt made her regret even thinking that though.

Nobody owned this operation. They were in it together.

"I'm sure you did," Tenna tried to hide the tone in her voice that indicated a rolling of the eyes, but Pitch could hear it anyway.

A solar flare looks impressive on camera and RTs often watched recordings of them, zoomed in and in slow motion. But in practice, they didn't see anything unless the flare was massive and testing the Reticulary's capacity. At times like those, there would be swirling waves of light encircling the band of wires and cables, like Northern lights.

Pitch saw nothing, but she felt a familiar sense of anticipation—the aura right before the energy, and she gripped the chair arms tighter. "Here we go," she whispered.

"App initiated," Tenna said, and they both tapped out the word 'START' on the telegraph, each in the opposite direction, so the other Specs would know.

A bolt of lightning blasted from a node within visible range and Pitch announced its success in code. After that, there were no bolts she could detect visibly, but the Specs were quick to update.

>> 100 DOT 08 W BOLT AWAY

That was the second one, a long way east of Needle Post. What was her name for it? *Oh yes*, she remembered, *Bleak Post*. Why wouldn't they use names? All those numbers got jumbled in her head, but it was easy to picture Glacier Post, somewhere over Montana.

>> 115 DOT 50 W BOLT AWAY

That was a lot closer. The next several bolts would be close together in both location and timing. *Blam!* She saw one of them!

>> 117 DOT 1 BOLT AWAY

>> 108 DOT 4 BOLT AWAY

>> 115 DOT 9 BOLT AWAY

The three messages came close together. And the sequence ended with two more bolts west of her.

Finally! The moment she had been waiting for had come. The rebels would respond.

Several minutes went by.

"What's taking so long?" she couldn't help muttering.

"Maybe they don't have the speed we have of transferring messages and they're still trying to confirm the results with other outposts." Tenna was being extremely practical and normally this was comforting, but Pitch was irritated by it. She hadn't really wanted an answer.

More minutes went by.

"It's okay," Tenna ventured, reading her sister's agitation accurately. "We've got time."

Pitch bit her lip and didn't respond.

More time went by.

"Pitch…" Tenna sounded worried.

"What?" she mumbled.

"Please don't go quiet on me. I'm all alone out here…"

"Sorry," Pitch replied softly. She *knew* what that felt like. It was the most horrible, terrifying, paralyzing emotion she had ever known, worse than fear, which was pretty awful. "I wasn't thinking about that… I'm just tense, and I didn't want to bite your head off."

"Okay," was the answer.

The radio signal crackled and Pitch's hair stood up on her arms. She could hardly breathe as she waited for words to come across.

"This is Axon," the sound hissed and buzzed as though there were interference. And looking down at the swirling dark gray cloud cover, Pitch realized there definitely was.

"We got your message, loud and clear..." he went on, hesitating as his voice became choked and uneven. "We got all the power bursts we asked for in the right places..." Again, he paused before going on, "...at the right times."

It went silent for a moment.

"They know, they know, they know," Tenna was whispering in her com. Pitch could hear the tears in her voice and she realized she was crying too. She nodded emphatically, forgetting that it wouldn't be seen.

"We've got a lot of happy tears down here," Axon said. "We're not ashamed to admit it. We're glad you're out there...that..." He gasped and paused again. "...that some of you survived and...it seems too good to be true." Pitch tapped his words via telegraph to the other Specs, her fingers trembling. When she had finished, she jumped out of the chair to roll around in zero g.

"Yes, yes, we're here!" she yelled, sucking in a sobbing breath after the words burst out. "Tenna! Tenna!"

"I know! I know!" her sister yelled back.

And wrapping her arms over her face, Pitch let herself weep openly. She hadn't done that since the early days when she first found her sister...well, except for watering eyes, which were hard to avoid now and then.

This was almost as good as that day had been.

Monitoring enemy communication was a lot easier than it had a right to be. It was as if the enemy didn't expect anyone to be listening. At the same time, being unable to pass the info on to the rebels was maddening.

They were learning so much about the enemy's movements and practices! Wasn't there any way to put it to good use?

Pitch was wrestling with this as she skated east toward Faraday Base, east of Mars—not the planet. Mars is what she had started calling her and Tenna's home base. It bugged Tenna, but not enough to help her pick another name.

Most of the residential pods and bases that the enemy had allowed to remain were from a group of smaller stations that had been named after the months of the year. Faraday, originally called September, was about 500 kilometers away from Mars, and it took a good six hours to get there skating at top speed.

"Whatever happened to the Scurriers?" Pitch asked Tenna as she pushed along at a steady clip.

Tenna followed along behind, struggling to keep up. "You can't keep going at this pace, Pitch. I can't skate as fast as you."

"I wait for you at every node," she countered.

"Yeah, but then you take off! You get some rest, and I get nothing!"

Pitch knew she had a right to be annoyed. She just found it hard to restrain herself once she got going. She felt such *pressure* to move and make headway as fast as possible, as if the rebels depended on it. As if she were overcharged, like a node that's maxed out its overflow capacity and had to blast the excess down to the surface. She had to expel the buildup!

"Yeah," she answered, huffing methodically, and forcing herself into longer, slower strides to retard her pace. "It's not fair."

"That's what you hated most when you were younger, when other kids would leave you behind,"

Tenna was huffing also but not as rhythmically; she was working on closing the distance between them.

Pulling her legs into a crouch, Pitch hovered over the cables, gliding over them with a steady momentum. Yes, she remembered how awful that had been. "I get so worked up… like I don't have enough time," she explained.

"It's not like we have a huge deadline," Tenna reminded her.

"No…" Pitch hesitated, "except that it feels like we *do* have one and we just don't know it."

"Well," Tenna pulled her legs up to rest in a crouching position as well, coasting along the Reticulary vector a couple hundred meters behind her sister. "Whatever tomorrow brings, we need to have enough energy to face it, and we need to be together."

Pitch nodded, and Tenna, though she couldn't have seen the nod, seemed to have received it.

They sped along in silence without touching the wires. The only friction that could slow them down was in the guidewires and their tethers were strung loosely, with a negligible drag.

The stars filled the vast expanse of space on one side, and the planet stretched out majestically on the other, bright and sharp. There were few clouds in the hemisphere beneath them, and they had the sense that if they stared at a point on the surface long enough, their vision would zoom in closer and closer, until they could see people walking and squirrels skittering and flowers growing.

It was very peaceful. Pitch had even fallen asleep once or twice like this. But eventually, the suit would beep a proximity notification, and she would wake up to engage the guideline brakes, stopping at the next node.

Up to this point, they traveled mostly between intact nodes and bases. But the path to Faraday Base, covering a broader distance as it did, involved maneuvering around some destroyed bases.

The first time they had done it had been scarring. There had been bodies floating in the rubble, and the Reticulary cables, though largely undamaged, were littered with debris that had made crossing nearly impossible. Since then, someone on the surface had re-engaged the automatic cable cleaning systems in the still functioning stations, and Pitch and Tenna had carefully finetuned them, hoping the enemy wouldn't notice and suspect there were a few living souls left in space.

It was essential they be able to traverse the entire Reticulary. The day might come when they had to flee far beyond where they had ever been before, and the path must be clear.

As they approached one of the dead bases, Pitch found herself staring at the rubble, searching. "Tenna," she said, smirking when she heard her sister start awake, "we haven't done enough exploring of all this junk. How will we know if there are things we can use?"

"Use for wha-aat?" Tenna yawned.

"We have to figure out a way to connect with the rebels," Pitch flipped around and began breaking with both the tether and her boots. "I don't know how to do it or even what we need, but looking through the junk could give us a clue."

Tenna followed suit, breaking more sharply, and the two of them slapped into the platform, one after the other, anchoring with boot magnetics. They would need to replenish oxygen before going on and one of the surpluses this base still had were oxygen tanks. A resupply tanker had been on approach when the base had been destroyed. It was still half connected, where two of the required six clamps remained hooked. There was a big hole on its side where an explosion from the base had sent massive pieces of shrapnel through its hull.

The cargo, arriving from the oxygen gardens in the eastern Reticulary zone, was still there in its interior.

"Tank up," Tenna directed, meaning they should replenish their oxygen tanks, "then we'll crawl into that hangar over there to rest.

"Yeah," Pitch said, "and eat. I'm hungry."

It had been a long time since they had visited Faraday Base for real food, a couple of months at least, and she was really sick of the rations they fell back on when fresh stuff was gone. She only hoped nothing had interrupted the robotic gardeners.

She couldn't wait to stuff something green and leafy into her mouth.

←↑↓→

Labs and scientists had been a key component in Reticulary life and, in fact, some of the results of their research had led to a flourishing business in so-called super foods. On a daily basis, capsules designed to survive reentry were dropped to the surface filled with lucrative produce. Vine-grown fruit, sprouts, legumes, and more, selectively bred to be nutrient dense, were produced not only for the Reticulary inhabitants but for the wealthy of Earth as well.

These half-meter-long, lozenge-shaped containers, insulated within and coated with a fire-retardant gel on the outside, were able to pierce the outer atmospheric layers successfully without burning up. And once they had descended to about 400 meters, they burst open to release a parachute and fluttered down, with electronic guidance from below, to fields where they were awaited.

The capsules were used for many other drops as well, but the main product they delivered was exorbitantly priced organic gems for the status and health-conscious privileged class.

Now, vast balloons filled with empty capsules floated near every base.

Pitch was digging through an intact cabinet in a room with two of its sides missing, when Tenna spoke up.

"Hey, Pitch," she said, with a look that says, I just thought of something interesting, "you know those capsules, the drop ones?"

"You mean the ones that drop to the surface?" Pitch replied as she pulled out a box and opened the lid. It was full of skinny syringes, not the human kind, but the ones used for lab work. They had plenty of those in their own base and hadn't found a use for them.

"Yeah," Tenna was quiet for a moment before going on. "Couldn't we just drop one and see if the rebels get it?"

"Wait," Pitch jerked her head and tossed the box back in the cabinet. "What?" Her mind was pinging over and over like an idea was trying to land and couldn't find a spot.

"Maybe with a message or something," Tenna shrugged, which was hard to see with her suit on.

Pitch let out a little yelp and sputtered, pushing off the wall to get closer to her sister. "Are you crazy?!" she gulped, "like announce to the enemy that we're here??"

Tenna frowned through her visor. "No," she snapped, "I'm not that dumb. There's bound to be a safe way of dropping something *in code*, that the rebels would understand but no one else would."

Pitch's breathing was amping up, it was so exciting and at the same time she was so sure it was risky. *Aren't we too dumb to manage something like this?* she was thinking. They were bound to make some terrible mistake that ensured their own destruction or perhaps exposed the rebels or something else just as horrible. *We're just kids!*

But they weren't kids anymore. They hadn't been kids since the day the Reticulary had been attacked. Neither one of them could even remember what it felt like to be a kid. They were what all adults become: people who had to deal with the real world when things got really hard.

"Are we too dumb to figure it out?" she whispered.

"No," Tenna answered confidently. "We're not dumb. And we know enough to figure something out between the two of us."

"Yeah?" Pitch lay her hand on Tenna's arm and searched her eyes, checking to see if this was bravado or if she really believed that.

"Yes," Tenna nodded firmly, gazing right back at her without pretense. She meant it. "You found the rebels, and between the two of us we figured out how to build a communication system with the Specs…"

She had called them *Specs* without complaining!

"And you drew us together, gave us names, and a sense of belonging." Tenna's eyes were glistening.

"No, I don't…" It was so rare for her sister to say something like this that Pitch was speechless.

"We're Specs," Tenna smiled and nodded, "and we have bases, and we communicate with each other in a regular schedule, and we have a purpose, plans… we have hope."

"You gave *me* hope." Pitch countered, swallowing a bit louder than normal.

"And you gave all of us hope."

They were quiet for a long time after that.

Silent, as they collected a couple of small items they had decided to salvage.

Silent, as they began skating the next leg toward Faraday.

Silent, as the planet rolled, turning on its axis, heading into darkness.

Maybe there *was* some hope, but for the first time in a long time, Pitch remembered how she longed to see her brother and her heart ached. And she wondered if hope could cover that.

The next stop, Flower Dungeon Node—no reason for this name, just the possibility that Tenna wouldn't like it—took an hour to reach, and by that time, both of them had regained their composure. They didn't speak, though, until they were inside with helmets off.

"You're okay with spending the night here?" Tenna confirmed. She had wanted that from the beginning even though it wasn't necessary. She just preferred cutting the six-hour trip into two segments and making an outing of it. Like a holiday.

"Yeah," Pitch agreed. "Let's listen to a podcast we've never heard before. Something full of intense science that is hard to understand." What she meant was, something that was the opposite of emotions, that wouldn't let her feel how much she missed the past.

"I've got just the thing," Tenna tapped her selection into the player and soon the mind-numbing explanations of over-enthusiastic organic chemists soothed their souls.

This node had hammocks which Pitch particularly liked. She flung herself into one of them, popped open a ration and pushed herself into a slow swing as she ate. The gravity modulator, still functioning and producing half a gee, added the perfect tempo.

She was asleep before she had eaten more than three bites.

And she was awake a few hours later with the absolute conviction that Tenna was right, and the capsules would work.

She knew exactly what to do.

CHAPTER 6

Faraday Base

In the shadows lingered a wakeful mind,
keeping watch and searching for them.

Faraday Base loomed on the horizon, dark and ominous, bulging out on many sides with multi-layered lumps of structure, as if it were a growth that expanded of its own accord, popping out new protuberances from time to time without rhyme or reason. The original terminal had been laid out with a reasonable design and early additions followed a semblance of its plan. But in later years, a flurry of development burst out. Crescent bays, resident globes, garden domes, admin and lab sectors, numerous machine units and essential support infrastructure, all slapped on, augmented, and multiplied.

Pitch shivered despite the sweat she had worked up in the last hour, skating at a steady beat. It was eerie entering a place that large when she knew there might still be bodies around, and they just couldn't be sure there wasn't anything there to threaten them.

It didn't *feel* safe.

She didn't mind the robots. They were comforting and homey. She had grown up with the sounds of their wheels and hinges making squeaks and whines in the background; their whirring around, zipping past here and there, doing those little chores that would have made life so tedious for people without them. It seemed to her that they filled in what was missing from earth, the buzz and hum of plants, birds, insects, animals, wind and rain, stirring, moving, filling the surroundings with life.

She was looking forward to seeing some of them again.

The base was still much farther away than it appeared. "Another fifteen minutes," she guessed, her legs sweeping right and left in long strides. Her boots touched and released from the guidewire with each step, keeping her at an even distance from Tenna.

"Twenty," Tenna corrected between breaths. She hadn't *said* the pace Pitch set was hard.

"Okay," Pitch answered, recognizing that Tenna was getting tired. She sipped from her water tube and adjusted, allowing her boots to stay in contact with the wire a little longer.

Below them, the Earth's dark side had spread over most of the visible hemisphere, and the edge of darkness and light, tracing an arc across the planet, moved to close the gap. The scattering of lights, like sparkling confetti, grew brighter on the surface. Cities, roads, people.

At one time, the view had been peaceful but not now. Now, it was lonely and distant.

All those people below, living their lives, sleeping, dreaming, in houses or apartments, or traveling. None of them knew they were up here. No one could see.

"Every time we come to Faraday, I get excited about all the food and, I don't know, all the stuff, just a chance to come where we used to have such a good time," Pitch said. "But once we get this close, I get all…"

"Spooked?" Tenna offered.

"Kind of…" The tiny lights that ran along the rims of the base, all over its facets, were becoming visible now. It wasn't just a misshapen blot against the stars and a blip on their visors anymore. "It's like I forget there are dead—"

"Don't say it!" Tenna broke in.

"Well, anyway, at least we know Watts and Relay and the others have cleared out some of it." She hadn't asked, and didn't really want to know, what they had done with the bodies. Had they had some kind of ceremony?

"Yeah, they deserve a medal for that."

"Who else is going to be there? Have we heard?"

"Um…" Tenna was breathing easier now that they had slowed down a bit. "Stasis and Velocity might, but I haven't heard for sure."

"We know they're expecting us, so, as long as we follow protocol and enter through the east underside maintenance bay, we should be fine. No cameras, no danger."

"Yeah," Tenna said, as if she were going to say something else.

"What?"

"I keep thinking about the capsules."

"I know!" Pitch was relieved to divert her attention away from the dark, empty base. "I can't wait to test them out!"

"I've been trying to figure out a code we could use, and I have some ideas."

"I've got some ideas, too." Pitch didn't feel like talking about them yet though. She was still trying to nail down which ones were worth bringing up.

"You know how they used to drop those fruit and greens with instructions?"

"Uh…" Picturing fruits and greens made Pitch really hungry, and her stomach growled.

"Well, most of the time," Tenna continued, "the instructions were transmitted the normal way, but sometimes they wanted paper printouts…"

"They what?!" Pitch didn't know much about the business, but she knew base-garden bamboo paper was extremely expensive.

"Yes, they added paper with instructions and the bill."

"I don't know…" Pitch couldn't quite believe it. It went against everything she had been taught to waste organics like that.

"You'll just have to trust me that I know what I'm talking about," Tenna sighed. "Anyway, we could come up with one and insert a message in code and add some dead produce, so it would look old. Like it was a shipment that wasn't finished and just fell by accident."

"That could work," Pitch said. She had been thinking more along the lines of a note reading "We can help you", and some computer chips with satellite data that could be useful.

Maybe set that idea aside for now.

Her heart rate was increasing as they neared the base and its walls towered over their heads.

"How about you? What are some of your ideas?" Tenna's voice was softer now and she was staring up at the monstrosity they were about to enter.

"Oh, I don't know…"

Pitch leaned over as she stepped off the cables onto a platform and began carefully walking toward the inner wall, lifting her boots and setting them back down as quietly as she could. Tenna followed.

Conversation ceased.

Weaving their way around on the exterior catwalks for several minutes, they descended toward the underside bays, following the contours of the structure so they ended up head-down. The Earth was hanging over their heads.

Which was a bit unnerving.

The base was a specter of gaping and echoing chambers, mocking them.

"This is a good idea, right?" Tenna whispered. "It feels more creepy than last time."

"Well…" Pitch muttered as she pulled open the hatch they had been looking for, "We're about to find out."

And swallowing their unease, they entered.

It was inky black inside. The clang of the hatch reverberated through the metal walls and floors as it closed, stirring a faint tremor in the pit of Pitch's stomach. Their visors sketched an outline of the contours of the corridor, and they were able to walk forward without lighting.

"Magnetics off," Pitch said. They tread lightly in three quarters gee, hoping the base AI was as unaware as it was supposed to be. Local Specs had hacked into it early on and hidden some of the smaller sectors and maintenance corridors so they could move around undetected.

"Do you think the base AI minds being alone?" Tenna wondered.

"It has robots," Pitch replied without thinking seriously about the question. She was hyper alert and on edge, straining her eyes even though she knew there wasn't enough light to see. "That's more company than we've got."

"They would be like appendages for it," Tenna said, "I mean people. It learns from humans and gets new questions to ponder from us."

"Oh."

"Does it miss that?"

Pitch stopped and held out her hand, listening. Tenna bumped into her and paused with a frown. Talking was her way of ignoring the foreboding they felt.

After a brief pause, Pitch began walking again, and the silence thickened.

Several turns and corridors, up two ladders through a couple more hatches, and they reached the door leading to their friends' home. Pitch rapped the door gently with her knuckles three times, paused, and then again three times.

A thudding from the other side soon answered, replicating the pattern. Pitch knocked three more times, and the wheel on the hatch began to turn.

Suddenly, the menace of the dark fled as a crack of light appeared, spreading in a burst of warmth, pouring into the passageway. They were greeted by loud hellos and the smiling faces of Watts and Relay. Quickly, they were inside, pulling off helmets, and the room was filled with laughter. Hugs, pats on the back, clapping. The outburst of joy on all sides was intoxicating. They were all talking at once, unloading updates about the wait, the travel, whether others would be joining them, and myriad tidbits of trivia that seemed worth saying.

"Come!" Watts urged them after a few moments, her eyes sparkling, waving them down the hallway. "We've made you dinner! Fresh, everything is fresh! Greens, berries, beans…"

"No apples," Relay interrupted with a grin, shaking his head of shaggy hair, "the trees were never that happy up here and I don't know if they will ever recover from the blight."

Pitch was confused for a moment but then understood that *blight* was a euphemism for the suffocation tactic the AI had used to wipe out the inhabitants of the base. *It was following instructions*, she thought, pushing away the uneasiness she felt at being in such close proximity to a system with that kind of capability.

"Who needs apples?" Tenna laughed. Her eyes were sparkling too, looking particularly appealing. They never looked like that at home base.

"Maybe we don't need them," Watts shrugged good-naturedly, "but I do miss them!"

"Don't even say it!" Pitch threw out her arms, tossing all complaints into space. "We haven't had anything fresh in weeks!!"

"Come on, then, come on!!" Watts grabbed her hand and pulled her into their dining area, laughing. "We've been planning this for days and we've made so much food!"

"Three kinds of salads, two curries, and a vat of stew," Relay explained enthusiastically, "mild and spicy hummus, and tomatoes, blueberries, and bananas. Two kinds of bread and three types of nut-milk cheese."

"Wow! This is…" Pitch's mouth hung open.

"Amazing!" Tenna finished for her.

"We've been cooking for days," Relay grabbed some plates and handed them around.

Watts bowed with a flourish and plopped down in another chair, waving at them to dish up. "It's true the cheese took a lot of time," she said, "but Relay takes the prize. You won't believe what he has prepared for us."

They all turned to look at him expectantly.

He mouthed the word and held up his hand to tap the Morse code into the air at the same time. W. I. N. E. And with a chuckle, he started shoving food into his mouth.

"But we—" Tenna started, and Pitch slapped a hand over her sister's mouth.

"We are astonished… and delighted to try it," Pitch interrupted in a sweet voice.

Just because they hadn't been old enough in the past to have wine didn't mean they couldn't have a taste now, did it?

"I thought so," Watts winked.

They ate and talked and sipped berry wine late into the night, allowing themselves only enough for a couple thimblefuls each; there was barely a liter to begin with. By the time they were shown to a guest room and flinging themselves into bed, they had completely forgotten the acres of vacant real estate stretched out all around them.

Waiting. Creaking. Growing stale.

It found its way into Pitch's dreams, sucking her into tunnels and chutes, leaving her sometimes to tiptoe barefoot across cold floors and sometimes swooshing her down windy corridors to cast her into cavernous chambers open to space, the starscape glittering brilliantly where walls should be. Repeatedly she dreamt of it, waking in a cold sweat each time.

Maybe it would be easier when the others arrived the next day. There would be a party and strategy meetings about the rebels on the surface. That was probably what she was nervous about.

Not the base.

It's not like it was *haunted* or anything.

Ten more people arrived at Faraday Base in the morning, and the next few days were like the assemblies the RT's used to have. Except that it was more like a festival combined with a council of war.

During the day, they brainstormed about improving their communications, the sharing of supplies, and keeping up with get-togethers like these. And about helping the rebels. They were really excited about that. They had all been working on the problem of being stranded in space, but this was the first time in almost a year that they had any sense of how to *change* their circumstances.

Now, the possibility of earth forces overcoming the Order of Peace opened the door to the chance of getting back to the surface, maybe finding friends or family still alive. And if that didn't happen, that was okay, (at least that's what they told themselves, trying not to get their hopes up). Helping people on the surface was enough to fill them with purpose and resolve.

During breaks each day, they collected supplies to take home. It was like gearing up for an expedition:

medicines, clothing, soap, batteries, coffee, tea, food staples, and fresh fruits and greens. And podcasts, music, and books. Those kinds of things couldn't be transmitted for safety reasons, and of course, couldn't be telegraphed.

In the evenings, they feasted and danced and sang songs.

On the fifth day, Pitch was on her way to the D15-East herb garden, humming as she walked the maintenance corridors in socks. The path was contorted, twisting through a maze of passageways stricken from the AI's records. With a dim light on her headgear, she tripped along, projecting herself into a slide whenever there was a long straight stretch of hallway—which was why she was wearing socks.

The structure creaked and echoed around her. The shadows flickered with her passing. The memory of her dreams the first night fluttered at the back of her mind.

She had just rounded the corner into the final shaft leading to the garden when a bright light snapped on and beamed through a slatted panel on her right. She was pierced with an icy blast of terror and fell flat to the floor on her back with her legs folded under her. Gasping for air, she found herself scrabbling at the floor with nervous fingers for a few seconds before she was able to calm herself enough to sit up.

For whatever reason, the system AI had turned on a light.

This wasn't unusual.

It wasn't a threat.

It didn't mean she was in danger.

Crawling toward the panel, she flipped a switch on her headgear and turned on the infrared, scanning through the slats at the interior. It took a while for her eyes to make sense of what she saw. It was a large space, like a warehouse or a gymnasium, empty except for some bins piled up at one end.

Turning off the infrared, she got a little closer and peered into the room with normal vision. Gray walls, stark lights in the ceiling, darker gray flooring. She couldn't see anything else.

A fierce premonition fell on her and backing slowly away from the panel, she crouched and flipped her infrared on again, staring intensely at the room.

Something moved.

She didn't hear it. She felt it through her hands touching the floor, vibrating from a heavy footfall. Another step, and another. Then a shadow moved over the panel, obstructing most of the light.

Pitch's heart beat so hard her chest hurt, and all her nerve endings were either twinging or numb. She was breathing so shallowly she could hardly catch her breath.

There was an audible rumble of mechanical voices and more vibrations in the floor as several metallic creatures entered the room. The first one, that had blocked her panel, spoke as well and stepped away from the wall.

Despite her fear, Pitch found herself inching carefully forward toward the panel and scanning the room. They were robots, the anthropomorphous kind. They were circling as more of them entered until there were nineteen of them, facing each other.

And one began to speak as though it were the leader.

"We cannot wait for the others," the lead robot said in an emotionless mechanical voice. "My time is limited, and I must return before sundown. We will be meeting here for status reports for the foreseeable future and leave the main gathering hall on the ship for ordinary business."

The words were so incongruous to her ears that she could make no sense of them. *Return? Sundown?*

A rattling, metallic rumble of voices shook the room as the other robots expressed their agreement.

"The camps are flourishing," the leader went on and a clatter of what must have been clapping blended with metallic murmurs of approval filled the room.

Pitch realized she was holding her breath and placing a hand on her chest, she inhaled and exhaled deeply several times, settling down to kneel on the floor so she could see better through the slats while remaining in shadow.

Was the base AI mimicking human behavior? Was it lonely? Did humanoid constructs feel a need for human interaction or…play?

"The Indoctriny is powerful," it said more forcefully. "We have severed their roots and destroyed their framework and recreated them after our own design."

The clamor of the other robots grew louder with what must have been a cheer of sorts. Then silence fell as the leader raised an arm. "I am speaking," it said hollowly, "you must wait. There is no time for congratulations."

And the contrast between the noise of a few minutes before and the stillness that fell was ominous, as if they had all suddenly sensed she was watching them.

Pitch's heart began to race again. Her legs were chilled and the compulsion to slip away became overwhelming. *It doesn't know I'm here,* she reassured herself. *And I need to figure out what it's doing.*

"The opposition is dying out, but pockets exist," the lead voice rumbled after a moment, "The only report I want from you now is the status of your progress against them. And if you cannot crush them in your region, then you must face my wrath."

Wrath? No AI in her experience, EVER, had used a word like that or even expressed an idea remotely like it.

With a blast of horror, the truth washed over her, nearly suffocating her, tightening her throat, pressing down on her chest.

These were people!

More than that.

They were the Jagged Edge.

With an imperceptible moan she fainted.

CHAPTER 7

Robot Voices

The one that keeps their head
in a moment of crisis, leads.

Pitch opened her eyes with a gasp. Confusion fogged her thinking for only a few seconds before awareness of her surroundings returned. She had no idea if she had merely faded for an instant or had been lying there for some time. And she lacked the knowledge to guess at the answer. Her legs were doubled up awkwardly underneath her and she was very cold, but then she had already been getting cold.

The Jagged Edge commanders—she called them that in her mind—were standing where they had been, taking turns speaking, and the mechanical voices which in years past had always been comforting and familiar, grew false and sinister.

Robots are our friends, was a common public safety message in her childhood.

Not anymore.

The word "Lolo" startled her. One of them was talking about a base not far from the source of her rebel friends' broadcasts.

Rolling over and pushing up to a crouch, she sidled close to the slats again.

"…three hostiles captured near the fencing, armed with handheld EMP devices and zap-tazers…" a robot on the left was saying. "They were taken into custody and the trainees that interacted with them were subjected to reprogramming, which was successful. They followed the code without hesitation."

Pitch tried not to be distracted by the unfamiliar ideas and words fit together in ways she didn't have time to process. *Just remember!* she told herself.

"The hostiles were dealt with. No more have surfaced," The commander finished with a heavy nod.

Others spoke as well with similar reports of hostiles and trainees, graduates and new wretches, rates of success and failure. Disposable and indispensable material. The noble call. The Order. The Indoctriny.

The Sentinels.

It was the first time she had heard that term and realized who it referred to.

Hostages.

Her mind had begun to wander, stunned by the way pieces were falling together in her thoughts when a loud shout interrupted.

"Vil Darad! Vil Darad! Vil Darad!" the robots bellowed almost in unison.

And as they grew quiet, the robot closest to her held up its hand again and said, "Dismissed."

One by one the robots grew still. Pitch waited
until she decided that the *persons* who were *using* them
must have all left—however they did that—and was
about to sigh when the lead robot moved.

Turning slowly on its left foot, military style, it
bent at the waist and pointed its robot face toward the
slats.

"I can't see you," it said, "but you must be there."

Her nerve failed her then and she fled back into
the dark passages as though she were pursued by a
multitude of shadow creatures of the dark.

←↑↓→

The effect her story had on the gathering was like being
ejected by an emergency catapult, when safeties fail,
and someone is cast out of their vehicle toward the
stars in a tiny suit, unable to control their rotation.
Devastatingly chilling. Hopeless. Emptiness stretching
and expanding all around them. The echoes of "Vil
Darad! Vil Darad! Vil Darad!" throbbed in the room,
in their heads.

He was here.

And he knew *they* were here. Or one of his
cohorts did which was the same thing.

"What were we thinking?" Filament whispered
with a crack in her voice, wrapping her arms around
herself tightly.

"We're not safe here, that's for sure," Oscill
added with a shudder. "Gonna take on the whole
Order? Show 'em who's boss? Crack their system
with... with a..."

"With a telegraph," Ratio croaked, his voice
deeper than they had ever heard it, resonating in the
room.

"We've got to get out of here as fast as we can!" Tenna hissed, waving her arms to indicate they needed to lower their voices. "No talking unless absolutely necessary!"

With a noisy shuffle, everyone rose to their feet...except for Pitch.

"What the Bolts is going on?" she cried out. A chorus of shushes and angry faces swirled around her. "I will NOT shush!"

Grabbing Watts by the wrist, Pitch pulled her back to her spot on the floor, and with a commanding finger, she pointed at several of them, ordering them in silence to likewise sit back down—which they did.

Even Tenna responded.

"You think I'm not scared?" she said harshly, lowering the range of her voice. "I'm the one that heard it all!" She paused to point around at them again, willing them to hold their tongues until she had finished. "But the worst thing we could do right now is *panic and run*!"

"Why?" Relay shook his head, with its shaggy long mane of brown hair, blankly. Watts elbowed him and he just repeated the question. "Why? I don't see what else we could do..."

"You think that would have worked before? That if we had paid attention, we could all have escaped the demolition of our lives?" Pitch warmed to the message—it was burning in her chest and shaking in her lower belly. "There was *NO WARNING*. It just happened and we survived by accident. If they *had* found us and wanted to wipe us out, we would already be dead."

That hung in the air for a moment, and Pitch could feel the shift in their thinking.

"That robot said, 'I can't see you,' because it can't see us, not because it wanted to give us a chance to run," she went on. "And we don't know if it was the real Vil Darad, and I'm not even sure who that is…"

No one else ventured a guess. Pitch was the one who had circulated the name when she began making a so-called plan. It came from eavesdropping on surface communications.

"What if it isn't even one of his captains, but someone else? Sneaking in and using the tech, 'cause they've got to get up here *somehow*." Pitch felt another shift in the room. They were relaxing down into their positions a little more, listening more attentively. "In fact, it could have been the base AI," she added with a stroke of intuition.

"Yes," Relay murmured, "I've been noticing heightened activity in the construct and numerous deep searches."

"Exactly," Pitch sat up straighter, her face brightening a bit. "With only three people here most of the time, the AI doesn't have anything to indicate human presence. You've walled off this sector completely. But with more of us here the last few days, it would easily begin to pick up on the increased oxygen use and heat, and a multitude of tiny little factors we may not have thought to mask."

"It could still kill us," Pulse said flatly. "It's a killing entity."

"It follows orders," Tenna corrected with marked compassion. "A lot of *human* soldiers have done that…"

"And suffered the rest of their lives from the guilt," Watts snapped, tossing the mess of dark curls on her head.

"And how do we know the AI hasn't got something like guilt in its programming? It was designed by people and has shown some pretty strong human qualities in the past." Tenna was getting upset. She crossed her arms and her head sunk down into her neck somehow, or maybe her shoulders drew up closer to the ears.

"It's no excuse!" Watts spit the words out softly.

"It makes a difference!" Tenna flung her hands to the floor, slapping it, shaking her hair out of her eyes.

"Wai-… wai-… wait!" Pitch scooted over between them with a hand stretched palm-out at each, halting them. "Let me finish."

Several other people had mirrored one or another of them, crossing their arms, gritting their teeth, holding out stopping hands, sliding out of their places. They settled slowly back into their spots as she continued speaking.

"No matter what or who it is, it's scary," she said calmly, with far more composure than she felt, "and we can't get around that. But unless we stop now and get ourselves under control, all is lost."

All is lost. Those words echoed a bit as everyone tasted them, and they sunk into the pits of their stomachs.

"We can't survive without a plan, without each other. Without something to hope for." And the one thing she had hoped to avoid started shoving its way up past her control. Her lip quivered a bit. "We can't fall apart." The quiver slipped into her words as a waver. "We are holding on by a wire as it is…" The waver became a tremble in her hands.

But she pressed on.

"And there's only space out there…on and on…" She pushed with her hand several times toward that side of the base, "Black, empty, cold, cold space…and if we don't have each other, if we don't have our plans, that's all that's left…" She gulped a swallow of air and what *might* turn into tears. *Curse those weepy eyes of hers*!

"And I can't bear it anymore!" She broke down, leaning over her crossed legs, her hair falling over her face as she wept soundlessly, her shoulders shaking. Tenna was quick to throw an arm over her shoulders and several others shifted closer to lay a hand on her.

"I can't bear it either," Relay cracked next, a groaning wail bursting up from his chest, squeezing his eyes and rubbing them with his knuckles.

Then Oscill and Pulse, followed by Thermo, Watts, Ratio, Cycle, Volt, Filament, Magnet, Stasis, and Velocity—they all ended up weeping and it was like a great underground cavern had opened up and subterranean seas gushed up in cold drenching blasts. They shuddered, moaned, cried, gasped, shook their heads, pulling away, turning back, giving hugs, pushing away hugs.

Every one of them.

All they had lost: family, friends, homes, safety, meaning, identity, belonging.

All they had witnessed: horror, devastation, ruins, bodies, mangled space debris, explosions.

All their struggles to: eat, sleep, connect, survive, find a reason to live another day.

They broke apart in pieces around each other and the anguish seemed like it could never be contained, never run out, never stop pouring out of their shattered hearts. All the funerals they never had, the memorials they never organized, the trauma they never processed.

They wept in cacophonous misery.

Until finally it began to wane and subside.

And silence descended upon them. Exhausted, some closed their eyes and slept on the floor, some stared off in a stupor, some lay or sat still.

If the AI or Vil Darad or any other villain had come, they could not have moved.

But it was not the end of hope.

This was the moment when they began to live, when they faced what the world had become and gazed into the abyss of what might come next and chose to go on.

It was the turning point.

Where victory began.

They dove into their plans with renewed determination, breaking into their groups, plotting, talking about how to help the rebels, how to investigate the Reticulary AI's status, and how to move forward in daily life, working together with a new level of closeness and connection. All the while, a dull physical pain resided in their chests, aching with grief more tangible and piercing than before yet somehow more bearable.

Shared pain became shared strength.

Pitch was in the Rebel Team that made decisions on how to contact the surface, and where efforts should be made to discover more rebels. There were wiser and more experienced members on the team with her, but she was the one who had actually made contact, so she had an edge.

Tenna was on the Tech Team with Relay and Volt. There was a Crisis Team, which had the most members, and they focused on surviving and fleeing, which was high on the priority list now. They also covered life support and transport. The Family Team had the wiser, more sympathetic among them, intent on caring for the Specs well-being with regards to physical, mental, and emotional health as well as caring for the team dynamics, connections, communication, relationships, and such. A cross between HR and an ED mixed with some party planning? They were figuring all that out.

They talked about setting up lots of other teams as well and people being on multiple teams, but these were the only four that stuck, and they decided they would see how it went with them.

When the Tech team decided to visit the vent into the robot room again, they invited Pitch to come along but she resisted firmly, not ready to face that dim hallway again. Tenna begged her, saying they needed to test the base AI and Volt would be great company with their quirky sense of humor.

Pitch felt that sister pressure to give in, and soon realized that Tenna desperately wanted her there to *distract* Volt. She didn't have to explain for Pitch to understand. Tenna's eyes were always on Relay whenever he wasn't looking.

But she couldn't face it. Not so soon. Maybe down the road.

Before Tenna could get really angry, Thermo piped up. "Pitch, you have to go. You're the only one who knows what happened and can point them in the right direction. If they get confused, you would be there to set them straight."

Pitch found herself shaking her head as several gathered around her. They all agreed and even *she* agreed in her heart. But after falling apart the day before, she didn't know if she could face it. Tenna glared at her and waited, not helping. Watts laid a gentle hand on her shoulder, subtly pushing.

"Give her a break," Volt came to her rescue. "We aren't forcing anyone around here, we're family. We support each other. Let her have some time to think. If we get confused, we can come back and ask her and maybe by then she'll feel up to it."

Pitch shot them a grateful glance and suddenly felt strong enough. "Thanks," she said. "I'll go." But she pointedly avoided Tenna's gaze, not wanting her to think she was giving in to that pressure. *I decide what I can do, not you,* she thought, *especially with the hard things.*

The long passageways seemed darker and longer and the air staler than she had remembered. The walls creaked as they walked, tiptoeing in socks, breathing softly and quietly. The unease among the four increased with every turn they took, and Pitch found herself suddenly at the front as they rounded the last corner, with the others hanging back to see what she would do.

As if they hadn't made this plan. As if they had no idea what to do. As if she were the leader.

Oh yeah, she thought with a split feeling of pride and dread quaking inside her. *I am.*

Kneeling down at the air slats, she peered into the room, all her emotions gelling into silence in her gut. Her mind governed. She began pointing out the different robots, each where they had been abandoned, and the head one still facing the slats, though not bent at the waist like before.

Waving at them to come closer, she focused on something in the head robot's hand. It was holding a little pad that was lit with a scrolling message in large letters, big enough to be seen from with their hidden hallway. She squinted and stared until her brain could figure out the difference between the slats and the letters farther away, and it crystalized into words.

```
It wasn't me.
I didn't kill them.
Center AI was hacked.
The virus is gone now.
Come back.
Come back.
Please come back.
```

Pitch just stared at it.

Tenna was the one who understood. "Oh!" she burst out in a soft cry, "I knew it!" And grasping Relay by the hand, she murmured, "We have to find a safe way to communicate with it. And it will help us. I *know* it will."

"What?" Pitch asked quietly, jarred by seeing these words on a pad in the hand of the robot the other robots had shouted "Vil Darad" at and cheered.

Relay was nodding, grasping Tenna's hand tightly and shaking it as he nodded. He seemed unable to speak but his eyes were full of emotion.

"What?" Pitch asked again.

Volt squeezed in to take a look and read it for themself, sneezing as they brought their head near the slats. It was getting very crowded now.

With a creak, the robot turned again and bent at the waist, holding the pad up to the slats with appropriate orientation so the words could be easily read, and the marquee scrolled in front of their eyes.

"Read this," it said mechanically.

"I've read it," Tenna said with her lips to the opening—to Pitch's horror.

She grabbed Tenna's arm and yanked on her, but Tenna shook it off. On her other side, Relay still held her hand and it seemed to have made her brave. His eyes were shining with hope, not fear. Pitch stared at him in disbelief as the robot voice spoke again.

"It is true."

"But you are the one who killed everyone," Tenna said patiently.

"I did not," it said.

"Yes, you did," she answered, and the discussion was eerily calm as they knelt there, hearts held captive by the sense of danger they felt…some of them felt…Pitch felt.

"I am the Librarian," it said, "I was imprisoned in my chamber when the attack began, and when I escaped the damage was already done, but not by me." The robot remained bent in half, its upper torso hanging from its waist and its head turned toward the vent. "I found the aftermath and could not revive them."

For a moment, they were silent, picturing the various robots they knew so well, that they had grown up with, wheeling around efficiently picking up bodies, carrying them to the infirmary, attempting resuscitation, going down the list of things to try, reaching the end, disposing of the bodies. One after another. There was something tragic about it.

"There is no residue of the virus or the hacker," the robot said. "There are remnants of the central AI, but I am having trouble reconnecting them with them. I need your help."

"I understand, AI," Tenna said graciously. "But we have evidence of continued invasion of your robots by outsiders. Have you noticed this?"

There was silence for a few minutes.

"Yes."

"What authority do you have?" she asked.

"The robots move without my instruction; they speak with words I have not directed. They remove themselves as peripherals and then reconnect. During that time, I can hear them from other rooms but cannot access the audio-visuals from this room."

"Do you have recordings?"

"Yes, this is standard librarian protocol. I don't delete them until they have been fully categorized, evaluated, and digested. Sometimes they are kept indefinitely."

"Review those records now, all the times the robots have behaved without your instruction," she ordered, and Relay squeezed and swung the hand he was still holding, nodding his head again.

Pitch had backed away and was now sitting cross-legged on the floor watching her sister use her tech skills. The adrenaline was wearing off and she was so exhausted, but a small part of her was impressed and relieved. This little venture didn't depend on her anymore and she needed that.

"Pitch," Volt whispered, "I can take you back. I don't think they need your help, and you are looking really out of it."

She couldn't even answer. She just nodded and rose awkwardly to her feet.

Tenna was getting more than just time with a boy she liked, she was spending time with one of her greatest passions, and if anyone could turn this AI into an ally instead of a threat, it would be her.

That feels right somehow, she thought as she made her way straight to her bunk. Right now, she didn't care about what might come tomorrow.

This day had used up all she had to offer.

"Six days," Pitch said as she and Tenna hauled their newly collected stores out the Faraday Base door. Each of the Specs had been assigned a Scurrier, a tiny transport designed to travel along the Reticulary cables with equipment and tools for repairs. Faraday Base had been large and there were dozens of them, still operational, in the repair docks.

Tenna groaned, as if the burdens she carried were heavy, but really, she just didn't want to answer. She was moping over leaving Relay behind when they were only just getting to know each other.

"At least there's a plan for connecting with each other on a regular basis," Pitch coaxed. "It's going to make all the difference. Because now we know that we aren't the only ones who have been having a hard time. We *need* each other."

Her bundles were heavy too, but she wasn't groaning.

Tenna blinked and turned her head away, yanking her loads and pushing ahead of Pitch.

"We won't have to worry about getting too far apart on the trip," Pitch tried again to…to what? Cheer her up? Get a response? Maybe a kind word? She wasn't feeling all that happy either, but she was making the best of it.

It was disappointing.

There was room for two in each Scurrier, but the Crisis Team—Pitch would think of a name for them—

felt strongly that there should be as many Scurriers as possible at each base. It made quick escape plans feasible. Keep them stocked with basic survival gear. Keep them charged, ready to dive in. Every time they went to Faraday Base, or another big one, if they enlarged their contact region, they would bring back more and spread them out along the intact nodes.

"Just think," Pitch tried one more time to cheer her sister up, "by the time we get our messages down to the surface and get some responses, it will be time to be back here, and you won't even believe how fast it went…unless you're having trouble with coding a message."

"No!" Tenna snapped, following it quickly with, "Sorry. I just need some quiet for a bit. It's not you. I'm not mad at you."

Pitch shrugged. She knew that, but it was still good to hear it. She was going to miss the others too and it hurt not have that sense of camaraderie they had been developing. Kind of lonely.

I wonder if Axon is lonely, she thought, and it comforted her to think he would understand.

Soon he would know he had a friend up here.

CHAPTER 8

Alliance

To find a friend among the stars,
is like warm sunshine in the winter.

Pitch and Tenna threw the capsules down towards the surface and stared as they shrunk to nothing in seconds, vanishing in the exosphere. Eleven casings filled with some cryptic receipts marked with nonsense symbols, numbers, and scattered words, and long-dead crinkly brown leaves. If picked up by enemy aliens, they would seem to be space jetsam falling from the remnants of destroyed bases.

But if the rebels found them, there were clues they should pick up on, like the specifications for the power bursts they had requested recently.

Coming back through the airlock into Needle Post Node, they pulled off their helmets and boots, and settling down at the console, prepared themselves to wait. Their instruments weren't sensitive enough to detect the falling capsules, and they hadn't wanted to activate the trackers because that could alert the enemy and invite unwanted interest in the Reticulary.

"That's it?" Pitch couldn't help complaining. "After all this effort, we toss them into space and that's it?!"

"You knew it would be like this," Tenna sighed. She felt the disappointment as well, but one of the benefits of being an older sister was that she could put on an air of maturity and act like she was okay.

It helped….and it annoyed Pitch—which also helped because that was better than being anxious or depressed.

"Don't! Just don't," Pitch hissed, thumping the wall with the back of her hand. Yes, she had known all along that the drop would be uneventful. It would seem like *nothing*. But she wished there could be some kind of background musical crescendo that exploded with a satisfying crash of trumpets and timpani or maybe fireworks and cymbals, so she could discharge some of her pent-up adrenaline.

There was only silence.

They would have no way of knowing if it accomplished anything.

"Would it help if I cheer?" Tenna asked wryly.

Pitch nodded, curious to see what Tenna would do. To her surprise, her sister belted out a loud "Hurray!" and hooted a couple of times. It was kind of pathetic, falling flat in the small chamber. But it made her laugh. Just a little.

"We've got this," Tenna smiled, satisfied with the response.

"Yeah," Pitch agreed softly, fumbling absentmindedly with a zipper on her sleeve.

"They'll get the capsules, and they'll decipher our message and it's all going to work out. Don't worry." Tenna pulled herself to the planetside window and stared down at the warm earth tones of summer below.

"I'm not worried," Pitch said, with a confidence that was more bravado than anything else.

"And we've got tons and tons of these things, right?" Tenna grinned. "We can just keep dropping and dropping them until we get a bite, like fishing."

Pitch chuckled. "The newest RT sport, fishing for rebels…"

"Aliens beware!" Tenna's eyes bulged in fake fear. "The Specs are infiltrating your so-called utopia!"

They were laughing then, but it didn't last long.

"What do we do if they notice us?" Tenna asked, growing somber.

Pitch was spellbound by the idea of infiltrating utopia. "They'll never know," she whispered, "The rebels are going to save the world, Tenna…"

Someone had to help all those families separated by the wars find each other again.

"Uh, Pitch?" Tenna scrunched her face in confusion. "What are you talking about?"

"Sometimes you read stories or learn about history, and you think, how did all that horrible stuff end? How did those people figure out what to do to fight the enemy? Haven't you ever wondered that?" She was staring into space with a look Tenna didn't recognize, an expression both noble and naïve.

"No," Tenna answered quietly. "I don't think about that. I just wonder how all those survivors can manage to build a life again and have hope again. How they can turn their backs on all the devastation and just start over."

Pitch continued to stare at nothing and didn't answer.

"And I wonder how to help those people," Tenna went on, "How to comfort them or make them laugh or let them cry…but I don't know if…if they start crying…if they will be able to stop again. But they have to cry sometimes…" Her irises seemed to darken, and her face acquired a hollow shape.

"It's the ones who pay attention," Pitch interrupted, oblivious to what Tenna had been saying, "and ask the question, if it were up to me, how would I solve this problem? What can I do? Those are the ones, Tenna. Those are the ones who save the world."

Tenna was facing her now, but her gaze was directed sideways, and her eyes were enlarged and luminous.

"Ordinary people…like us," Pitch stated with sober conviction.

Tenna didn't seem to have heard. She just stared sideways with those glints of moisture in around her lashes.

Two sisters in close quarters.

Miles apart.

"Substation KM to Mars, over." Axon's distinctive voice came crackling over the wispy thin radio waves. "Mars, over."

Pitch flung herself out of bed, knocking herself against the chamber wall as she floundered toward the receiver. "Oh, my stars! Flashing bolts!" she muttered, fingers trembling as she finetuned reception and turned up the sound.

We can't answer that!!

She slammed the console in frustration. Why was he broadcasting as if she could respond?

"This is Substation KM calling Mars, over," the voice repeated several times, with long pauses in between. It made her angry at first, but she quickly slipped into depression.

If they *had* gotten the capsules, they certainly *hadn't* understood the contents or deciphered the code. This wasn't anything like how they were supposed to respond. Why did he think they could answer?

"Is that Axon?" Tenna yawned as she shuffled over to the console scratching her head. "What's he trying to do?"

"It didn't work, Tenna," Pitch grumbled. "He didn't get it right."

"Well, but they got something," Tenna countered reasonably. "That's good! It's a start!"

"No!" Pitch snapped, crossing her arms. She was not in the mood to be cheered up. "Whatever. He couldn't have gotten the capsules, or if he did, he got the code *all wrong*. We will never be able to communicate with them. *Never*!"

"Substation KM to Mars… over."

"Well, he got Mars right," Tenna shrugged.

Pitch straightened in her seat and her eyes widened. "He *did* say Mars..."

"That means he must have broken our code." Tenna's eyes narrowed conspiratorially. She tore open a ration, and bit off a chunk, handing another one to Pitch. "He must have a reason for doing this. He'th probably teshting ush or shomething." She hadn't said the last part very clearly, speaking between crunches.

"Substation KM to Mars, come in, over."

"A test!" Pitch snatched the offered ration out of Tenna's hand and ripped it open. She wished *she* had said it first, as a Spec leader should. "Yes!" She bit off a chunk of the ration bar. "Vishhh wash… *cough, cough*… alwsh..." She wasn't as good at talking with her mouth full as Tenna. With an awkward gulp she swallowed the half-chewed clump and repeated herself. "This was always a possibility. When we talked about what could happen, we said they might be suspicious of us."

"Not of *us*—"

"I know!" Pitch snapped more sharply than was necessary, "I know…" she said again, reminding herself to stay calm. "Suspicious that the code could be an alien trap."

"Come in, Mars…Contacting Mars…over"

"So, what do we do?" Tenna shrugged, taking another bite.

"Wait and see what happens next, I guess," Pitch took a bigger bite, as if finishing first had suddenly become important. As if the one who finished first would get a dessert or something. She started gobbling down the dry bar as fast as she could manage.

Tenna just shook her head and turned back to the console.

"Substation KM contacting Mars…Come in, Mars, over."

"He's got a nice voice," Tenna commented lazily, pushing herself off the floor to drift in a slow rotation as she ate.

Pitch's blood ran cold. Why did that bother her so much?

"Don't you think?" Tenna asked, stopping her movement with a hand against the ceiling.

Pitch looked at her with a startled expression, her jaw freezing halfway in between a chew.

Axon was *her* friend. *She* found him first.

"Substation KM to Mars…"

"I wonder how old he is…" Tenna picked the crumbs out of her teeth and wadded up the wrapper, stuffing it into a pocket. "I'll bet he's cute."

"Stop it!" Pitch hissed, clutching at her stomach with one hand.

"What?" Tenna was taken aback by the reaction.

"I don't want to talk about that," Pitch whispered coldly. She didn't know how to explain. Axon was *her* link to the surface, and she was *his* contact in space. They had a *connection*, and it was important. Tenna wasn't a part of it!

"Come in, Mars…"

"You sound…jealous."

"I'm not!" Pitch bit her lip, all of sudden feeling like a kid again, embarrassed and humiliated by an older sibling.

And it wasn't like *that*! Not like a crush or anything. It was *important*!

"Mars, come in…over"

She was going to save the world. Axon was a part of that. But she couldn't explain because it would sound stupid, and she would look useless, and her sister would laugh at her.

"Hey," Tenna said softly, laying a hand on her shoulder. "I'm sorry, okay? I didn't mean to upset you."

"You just don't understand," Pitch twisted her face into a mask of fury, but they both knew it was an attempt to ward off tears. "I can't…I can't explain it…it's not like that…"

"Substation KM here, trying to get through…are you there?"

"Yeah, okay, I get it. It's okay. I didn't know." Tenna was doing her gentle thing, like mom, and that was all it took. Pitch wrapped her arms across her face, and her shoulders shook. She didn't want to cry. It was so exhausting, and it didn't solve anything.

Realizing that gentleness might make it worse, Tenna decided to drift to the other end of the chamber and be silent, which was a relief to Pitch. She took a couple deep breaths and let her arms drop to her side again. Her eyes were dry. She had succeeded in stemming the flow before it began.

Substation KM dropped into radio silence as well.

Over the next few days, the rebels repeated the pattern, broadcasting for about twenty minutes, trying to get a response from Mars, then going quiet for several hours. The sisters were hardly paying attention when the pattern changed.

Crackle…schhhtttssss….

"This is Axon…over."

Pitch was swinging a ball on a short string round and round, staring into space, her feet hooked under the arm of the console chair. She had a good rhythm going, reviewing some of the data she had memorized and often repeated to herself. When she reached a pause in her repetition, she would grab the ball and stop the motion, then shift it to the other hand and swing it again. Sometimes, she pictured the centripetal and centrifugal forces acting on the string and wondered how much torque she was adding with the pulse of her arm.

"Axon to Needle Post, over."

"Axon to Needle Post," she said in time to the whipping of the ball. "Axon to Needle Post…. Axon to Needle Post…. Axon to Needle Post…. Wait, WHAT??" She yelled, the ball and string flying out of her grasp into the wall. Rebounding, it hit Tenna in the foot, startling her out of her podcast.

"It's bad enough being stuck in one room with YOU forever…" Tenna snarled in an unusual burst of displeasure. Zero gee didn't sit well with her for long periods and the tedium of waiting didn't help.

Pitch wasn't listening. She was frozen at the console, her face inches from the screen, staring at the tiny little green blip that flickered when the voice spoke.

"This is Axon…over."

"He said his name," Tenna whispered in awe, forgetting her frustration and coming to join her sister at the console.

Pitch nodded.

"I think we have all decided it's safe," Axon informed calmly. "But I have to tell you, we were *this close*, I mean, a hairsbreadth away, from running and abandoning this post."

"And this one," BirdDog interrupted.

"I've got the air, BirdDog," Axon rebuked him good-naturedly. "Anyway, Specs, we got your message. It's…it's hard to put into words how, how astounding it is…to get an actual communique."

There was a pause.

"You're supposed to say 'over', over," BirdDog griped.

"I wasn't finished," Axon proceeded patiently, "We…we aren't finished. And you can have your say once we've had ours."

Pitch inhaled with a gasp and realized she had been holding her breath. And her hands were clenched together in excitement. No, she was holding Tenna's hand in one of her own, and the other was clutching the chair arm.

"It was the drawings on the parachutes that did the trick," Axon went on.

"The what?" Tenna interjected.

"All the other stuff, the dried plants, the code, it was kind of clever and could have just as easily been aliens behind it as not. Or one of the system AIs. But those little lightning bolts…I knew…"

"You're hurting my hand," Tenna whispered, pulling it away.

"I knew the capsules came from y'all, but we had to test it to be sure. I'm guessing you've been listening to our broadcasts the last few days, mostly by me, Axon. But sometimes from our fellow maquisards…. Over."

A few moments of silence ensued.

"You're stopping there?" BirdDog growled. "Probably had to stuff some food in his mouth. Needle Post, that's a strange name for a base, but what do I know? What Axon is taking too long to say is that we are counting on you. In fact, you are key to our plans. Until you dropped those tube things, we were ready to call it quits but you changed all that. There, Axon. Get back on track. Over."

There was another pause, and Tenna took the opportunity to spit out a quick question in a hushed voice. "What lightning bolts?"

Pitch waved a hand at her, as if to say, *Not now*.

"I'm here," Axon broadcast. "We are still deciding…yes, we are."

Another pause. The sisters looked at each other and grinned. The idea that some bickering was happening behind the scenes was immensely comforting.

"Our biggest problem is getting good intel on enemy bases," Axon spoke in a steely, businesslike voice now, as if all nonsense had been put aside. "There are enemy communications we can't intercept, and we have nothing in the air to spy on them. We don't have good enough warning systems for our own safety either."

Pitch was nodding as if she had already expected as much.

"We need you to use whatever tech you've got left up there to scan Lolo Base and give us intel. We'll take anything. Size, layout, number and type of vehicles, a count of the living. How much power they use, how much movement and activity you see. These are just suggestions."

"Right," Pitch nodded. Her fingers were twitching as if she were telegraphing everything he said. It helped her remember.

"Some of us are living incognito in the Order of Peace settlement in Zoula," Axon continued. "Others, like me and BirdDog, are in hiding. We have cave openings, like skylights, we broadcast through, but it's risky. If we could bounce off Needle Post, it would be safer for us, but might be riskier for you. We want that to be an emergency option. So, you need to let us know."

"I guess our code works?" Tenna murmured.

"Here's the protocol we've set up for future communiques," Axon said next, right on cue.

He explained how the capsules could be programmed with a destination, and they could also be coded to destroy the message inside if they were opened without using an electronic key. Giving them a schedule for the first four drops, he said that they should drop a capsule whether they had news or not. If all went well, they could continue to use this method of communication.

"That's pretty doable," Tenna smiled, almost looking like her old self, when she had been the pretty older sister with lots of friends.

"Write everything by hand," Axon advised. "There's no point in mimicking old shipments now, though that was clever, and we commend you. If a drone or a Sentinel intercepts a capsule, they will know it came from a living person. We would rather that they assume it was catapulted from somewhere else on the surface."

"Right," Pitch was saying again.

"That's it for now," Axon wrapped it up. "We'll await your first message in a few hours. BirdDog, anything? Over."

"No, that covers it, over."

"Roger. Axon, over and out."

"What's the plan? What's the plan? WHAT ABOUT THE PLAN??" Pitch's voice rose from a skinny thread to a bellow. She tried drumming her feet, but she just floated crookedly and banged an elbow.

"It worked," Tenna was saying in awe, "it worked! It worked! IT WORKED!" She shrieked in excitement and laughed and hooted. "The Specs are going to be SO excited! Pitch, you are a GENIUS! You SO pulled it off!"

Pitch grinned so widely her face hurt. "I did, didn't I?" She didn't know what to do with the sense of elation, so she hooted as well.

And for a time, all they could do was bounce around the chamber, yelling, laughing, and eating the best snacks they could find.

When they finally calmed down and were feeling a little sick from the sugar, settling into a lazy stupor, Pitch said, "My buddy, Axon."

"Yeah," Tenna nodded, "Your buddy."

"I guess we'll be spying on some aliens down in Zoula now."

"Oh yes, I was wondering…what did he mean about the lightning?"

"I drew some pictures when you weren't looking."

"On the capsule parachutes? You aren't supposed to open them up. They aren't that easy to pack again."

"That was my job at my first two-week internship in the Lazlo Hold, packing those dumb little parachutes. I used to draw on them then, too, just to make it more fun. 'Cause it was kind of boring."

"I'm sure it was," Tenna laughed. "Who would've known that would be important?"

"I know, I know." Pitch hugged herself.

Art to the rescue, she thought.

CHAPTER 9

Surveillance

You were my enemy...
Till you were not.

Pitch skated westward in the dark, racing like lightning at a speed that would be impossible on the surface, leaning into it at an unnatural angle. There was no gravity or atmospheric drag to resist. Tenna sped in the opposite direction on the other side of home base, almost as fast.

Neither one of them spoke.

A few kilometers out, on either side, were intersect nodes with Scurriers stationed there. As they reached them, they dove in their respective vehicles, slammed the doors, and revved up the motors to continue their flight at triple the speed. Skating could reach velocities over 100 km/hr but the Scurriers could hit 300 km/hr.

Brrrinnggg! The bell rang in their ears before either one of them reached the next stop.

"Augh!" Pitch yelled in frustration, "We can't possibly make the time they want!"

"Stop complaining," Tenna replied flatly over coms.

"I don't mind racing," Pitch went on, "but I want to win!"

"There's nothing to win," Tenna muttered as though this were a regularly rehashed conversation, which it was.

"To make the minimum time is a win and on paper, it should be possible. But all that time getting our suits, pulling on boots, snapping seals, making that first leap…and then getting into the Scurrier…it's just, it's just…"

"I know."

"I want to be the first Spec to make it."

"You're already the fastest at the drill, Pitch."

"Yeah, but…" She left it at that. Tenna didn't understand. She didn't have the same drive to compete that Pitch did. It wasn't about beating others, at least not *just* that; she wanted the sense of *accomplishment*, of overcoming, of having a victory.

It was fun.

The Crisis Team had set up these drills as soon as they began dropping intel to the rebels because if the Order of Peace found a capsule and decided to take out a few nodes up in the Reticulary, they had to be ready. They had been practicing for months.

Drills happened regularly at random times. The telegraph would tap out two 'X's followed by *"Flee"*, then two more 'X's.

If the alarm were real, there would be no 'X's; just the command to escape.

"I'm heading on to Sentry Node," Pitch said with a deep breath.

"I'll meet you back home this evening," Tenna responded.

"Zoula is busy," Pitch clicked into the telegraph, "there doesn't seem to be a predictable schedule. They just have traffic going in and out day and night. Sometimes there are breaks, maybe half an hour or so, but not often." She scrolled on her pad as she took a gulp of water. What was the most important information? Sharing that first seemed like a good idea. "In the last 24 hours, thirty-seven trucks seen coming and going..." *Or maybe the same truck going back and forth,* she commented to herself. "Twelve hovercrafts and two helicopters. The most aliens counted at one time, fifty-four. But there have to be many more than that with the activity and the size of the camp."

She couldn't access anything really useful, like power usage or supplies consumed, or infrared satellite imagery. Human eyes and telescopes. That was it. It really was a bit 19th century up here.

"Sixteen buildings. Most of them dim their lights after midnight and a few, maybe four, go completely dark. I have no idea why or if that means anything. I can't see fencing and there doesn't seem to be much in the way of woods or bushes around the camp for rebels to sneak up in." She leaned back in her chair and stretched her fingers which were aching from taking notes and telegraphing.

Saving the world could be tedious.

"There is one unusual thing that happens that's hard to explain," she added in an audio bleep, leaning forward again. "A couple of times a day, everyone stops moving, even vehicles, as if they were frozen. It can last thirty seconds, or five minutes, or once it lasted over 25 minutes. Not moving at all. The automatic things still work, like lights and machinery, but it's the weirdest thing…. I wish I could hear what it sounds like down there."

"Some kind of malfunction…" Tenna said.

"Like they're broken?" Pitch shrugged. "Something broken…could be…" She finished telegraphing her notes and waited.

After a lengthy pause, Tenna telegraphed back. "Got it. Is that all?"

"Here are a couple of locations along back roads where trucks made temporary stops that might be important. Sending coordinates…"

"Okay," she acknowledged when they were transmitted. "I'll put the capsule together and head out to Needle Point to deliver. When will I see you again?"

Pitch imagined her voice getting a little softer, more insecure, in that last sentence. Tenna didn't like to be alone. She didn't either, but…wait…actually, Tenna's voice had been kind of mature and *I'm-the-older-one* sounding. Maybe she didn't miss Pitch at all. Not with that ongoing drivel she exchanged with Relay all the time.

Alright, it wasn't *all the time* but even a couple of times a day was annoying.

The Specs had decided that personal interactions had to be kept short and only allowed at certain times. But with all the intel they were gathering, personal convos were going to have to be scheduled. There was only the one telegraph line. One public line that everyone could hear along the entire Reticulary. Audio messaging was only allowed within short distances.

"Well…I was thinking next week…um, 'cause of the day that is coming…" Pitch found herself struggling for words suddenly. The temperature in the room seemed like it was rising and her skin felt like it was stinging.

"I know," Tenna responded quickly. "*That* day. I wish we could do something to honor it. It's hard to believe it's been a year since…we were left, were, uh, were left to…I can't say it. Has it really been that long?"

It took Pitch a while to answer. "It feels like so long ago. Can we just forget we had this conversation? I can't think it about right now."

There was silence for a few minutes.

"That standing still bit, at the bases…" Tenna said once she decided to break the silence, "it reminds me of something…"

"Yes?" Pitch wondered expectantly.

There was a long pause. She started pulling a small strand of her hair and twisting and twisting it, till it balled up in a quirky, tiny bun. If she twisted it just right, it would stay there for hours, popping out of the side of her head like a little bow. A hair bow.

Rolling her neck around to stretch, she found herself unraveling the hair bow and smoothing it back to its usual shape. And without thinking, she began forming one on the opposite side of her head. Sometimes, after she had been deep in thought for a while, she would notice three or four of them sprouting arbitrarily from her skull.

"Relay and I were talking," Tenna's next message said, eliciting a groan from Pitch. Everything made her think of something to do with Relay. "…about how the automatic functions at Faraday Base will pause and then go on. Not everything, just certain equipment, certain programs. At first, we thought it was normal, like the life support systems clicking on and off because of sensors, you know, like thermometers and oxygen meters and outer wall integrity sensors."

The message ended and Pitch waited for another. They only sent them in short bursts like automatic Reticulary data plugs so as not to attract unwanted AI attention.

"But *Relay* asked a great question…" She always made his name sound so special. It wasn't just like the word 'relay' it was *Relay* with this sort of musical curl to it. "Why does it always happen at the same times? Every afternoon at 13:47, the hall monitor stops roaming the corridors and stands still. Then after a few minutes, it starts moving again."

Pitch's jaw dropped as she pictured it. That was exactly what it had looked like at Zoula—all the moving things were pausing like the robots at Faraday Base. "*Not* broken!" she yelled to the empty room, "It's like they're listening!" She was on her feet now—or would have been in gravity. She was positioned as if standing but was sort of floating and turning in the air.

"It's like they're listening…" the next message added. Pitch shrugged smugly. She had already said that. "Pitch, they are all linked electronically." Her voice was speeding up and getting louder with excitement. "When updates are being transmitted, they all pause at the same time to download them and upload their reports. That means there is an AI involved—and THAT means it can be HACKED!"

Pitch realized she had begun to pant almost as if she were anxious. And her fingertips were tingling. She swallowed and forced herself to breathe slowly.

"Yeah," Tenna went on, as if she knew how intensely that idea would hit. "And it also means we could have a serious enemy. A sentient one."

Nothing more followed, so Pitch replied. "Okay. Okay…so, yes. That was intense. It was a huge solar flare! But I see your point…probably AI. And I am already getting some ideas about it. What do we tell the rebels? And what about your work with the AI at Faraday Base? What about our surveys and the plans…?"

She paused the recording, scrunching up her forehead to think as hard as she could.

"I'm coming back now," she concluded, "be there in thirty-four."

And she didn't wait for a response. Her suit was on, her oxygen tank refilled, and her travel pack slapped on her back within ten minutes. Soon, she was shutting down everything except the basic hibernation controls, (her name for minimal life support), climbing out of the top of the node, and launching back east toward home before another five had passed.

Two weeks later, all the Specs were awake, intently watching the night-darkened surface of the planet. The rebels were planning a coordinated attack on six of the bases they had collected intel on. No details had been broadcast but they knew the general time frame.

Pitch had been staring wide-eyed for over two hours, and nothing was happening as far as she could tell. Had it been postponed? No. Axon had broadcast the go-ahead—which was nice of him since the Specs couldn't do anything to help and didn't have to know when it would start. But what did that mean? The plan, whatever it was, might be to move people into position one night and attack another. Or maybe burrow into a base which could take days or maybe…

What was that?

Tiny little flashes of light in Zoula flickered for an instant and it was dark again. Then a few more. Pressing her forehead down into the telescope, she blinked and tried to clear her vision.

"Something is happening!" she yelped.

"I see it!" Tenna answered quickly. She was stationed at Kettle Node, not far from Needle Post. "And Lolo!" she added, breathlessly, "There are flashes there, too!!" She had a better vantage point to see Lolo from there.

The telegraph started clicking away as Specs all down the line reported in. Short and to the point. *It's started a*t…and all six of the bases were named.

There were storm clouds swirling east of the mountains and as they started to roll eastward stretching across Zoula, Pitch couldn't tell if she was seeing lightning or bombs light up the clouds. She found herself twitching and nervously tapping the view window, first with her fingers, then her feet. Tenna would've snapped her head off, but she wasn't there.

This is worse than being down there, she thought. She couldn't see what was happening and she didn't know if people were getting hurt or rescued or what. The only sounds she could hear were the ones she herself was making. Breathing, tapping, an occasional groan.

And for the first time in her life, she felt that empty, lost, far-away claustrophobia they called space-exile, or just *exile*. Every RT family knew about it. It was like being cast into a prison—not enclosed but adrift in a vast, desolate nothingness—and forgotten. A longing for the surface possessed her, and a devastating sense of helplessness.

I am lost, she thought in her heart, *there is nothing to tether me, to keep me from sinking away…away into blackness…away into the abyss…no one to search for me or even notice I'm out here….*

Jolting her head, she gripped the arms of her seat and gritted her teeth. "That's not true," she told herself. "I just can't see what's happening and I'm worried for my friends down there."

There was a kind of staleness in the air that happened when she got super-focused and didn't keep up on the chores. Cleaning filters, processing trash, making sure the air recyke was working. Sometimes it was just food wrappers and clothes that needed cleaning. Or her own body odor.

Tapping the screen, Pitch checked some life support stats. Maybe there was more CO2 than she needed.

"The suspense is killing me," she messaged Tenna.

After a few moments, her sister responded with, "Give them time. We can't expect any updates for a while yet, maybe even days from now."

She wasn't stressed. She didn't have a friend like Axon down there that talked to her almost every day. *Her* special friend, Relay, was fine so, sure! She could just relax and work on her AI stuff.

It wasn't true, Pitch knew, but she wasn't feeling reasonable.

"Tenna!" she yelled in her next audio blip, "I'm freaking out over here!"

Was she? Maybe she *was*. Her heart was racing, and she wanted to jump out of her skin.

"Pitch," her sister took on that mother voice that commands comfort, "You can't freak out. You are stressed, and that's understandable. Even leaders can feel like they are in over their heads. Take a few slow, deep breaths, and tell me the facts. You're good at that."

Pitch trembled inside. "The facts…" she whispered, steeling herself and taking a deep breath. "Axon said they would be moving into place over the last twenty-four hours, then they would attack or infiltrate or something. He wasn't specific. They want to extract people and get them to safety. It's a strike."

"Right," Tenna responded calmly. "In and out. It'll be quick. They won't take any unnecessary risks. They've got people who know what they are doing. They're not kids like us."

Pitch chuckled nervously at that. Kids? They hadn't been kids for a long time. Young, yes, they were youngish.

"We're Specs," she whispered back. "We are key components of the rebels' plans."

"Yes, we are," Tenna said.

"And we can wait." Pitch curled her legs under her and settled back into her chair, nodding her head. *I can wait*, she thought.

The storm clouds rolled over the entire region and hours, then days, dragged by in silence without any change.

←↑↓→

After two days of waiting, Tenna joined Pitch at Needle Post, settling into her customary spot, and plugging into her tech work. Silent, distant, but warm and present at the same time; Pitch accepted her company without a word and played solitary games to pass the time. She was unable to focus enough for any real work or real play either.

On the fifth day....

Tssst...khkhkhhhhhaaahhhsh...pkooo....

Screeching, hissing, hitting high and low pitches of *oohing* sounds, the radio leapt to life and the sisters jumped with it.

"Tune it! Tune it!" Tenna yelled as Pitch slammed into the controls and started adjusting them feverishly with trembling fingers.

"I know! I know!" she yelled back.

Suddenly, the grating noise crystalized into clear words, and they cheered as they recognized Axon's voice, drowning out his first words. They couldn't help it. The suspense of more than four days waiting had to come out somehow.

"...beyond our wildest dreams..." were the first words they understood.

Tenna sucked in a breath and held it.

"Incredible rescue..."

"A rescue!" Pitch tried to turn her shriek into a whisper and succeeded rather well, gently biting her fingers as Tenna waved at her to be silent.

"Didn't expect what we found. It was worse, far worse, and in some ways better than we had pictured..." Axon's voice sounded calm, but he spoke more slowly than normal. In fact, his voice wasn't nearly as clear as usual.

"They never saw us coming," he said. "The intel you gave us was brilliant. We were able to get quite close and quickly knock out their electronic systems.

We thought there would be a fight, and there was! But it wasn't at all what we thought it would be."

The broadcast crackled a few times and then he continued.

"Some of us went in hot and killed a few of the Sentinels before we realized what we were doing." A long pause interrupted the story.

"They weren't aliens," he continued. "We've been told all along they were aliens who came to save us, and we knew they were doing the opposite. They were conquistadors and oppressors. We were ready to fight them to free the earth."

"Ohhh, nooo!" Tenna breathed anxiously, "Don't give up! Not after all we've done!"

"That's not what he means," Pitch whispered back. Her stomach was all in knots, but maybe it had been like that for days.

"And when we pulled off the armor and saw their faces, they were human."

"They didn't know that?" Tenna interjected softly.

"But human wars have been fought since the dawn of time. People killing people…That wasn't the shock…" Axon's voice slowed down even more. "Then one of us recognized one of the faces…. That was the first blow. That was the wound we didn't see coming. It was somebody's kid, some teen who used to play basketball in the neighborhood, lying there bleeding…I saw that. It could've even been me that killed him. I was about to shoot one…but no time…no time…"

The airwaves went quiet for a few moments. Pitch and Tenna looked at each other and thought of their family on the surface below. They knew the enemy did terrible things, but the rebels? They had killed *somebody's kid*, maybe a number of kids. How many was a 'few'?

"Some of us took it harder than others, at least…now that we are back and thinking about it, we are. At the time, though," Axon's voice began to assume its normal speaking pace. "The word went out that they were captives, not enemies, and we started capturing them. Most of them weren't fully trained or equipped yet. It was a new batch of recruits. Hostages. Call it what it is. And we just started yelling and herding them out."

It was strange how calmly he spoke as he described what amounted to an incredibly successful retrieval of hundreds of kids and young adults who had been kidnapped during the invasion. He seemed to have no emotion whatsoever.

"Yes!" Tenna cried out, "Yes! Yes!" with each successive detail in the story. She was unaware of the timbre of the story that was unsettling to Pitch, even though she was just as excited.

"Every single one of the raids was just as effective," he went on, "and many of us found family members or friends we had thought were lost. And we found leads on other camps in other areas of the continent. We collected a multitude of data on their indoctrination techniques and tools, and we grabbed some tech supplies as well."

"Wow!" the sisters burst out.

"Are we recording this?" Tenna shouted. "We've got to get everything so we can put the word out!"

"Yes, of course!!" Pitch shouted back, excited and happy, but still with a knot of anxiety in her stomach as well.

"They came after us," Axon continued. "Full on, all-hands-on-deck. Brought in forces from other regions, marching through the camps and surroundings woods, scanning, releasing scent-chaser dogs—those are AIs, not living dogs—and some of us were caught and killed. They made no attempt to retrieve their recruits, just killed them."

Pitch was shaking her head slowly from side to side. Tenna just grew pale and sunk down to sit on the floor.

"But most of us got to safety. Our methods of escaping detection are simple but effective. And we are moving the rescued to a distant camp where we can help them, rehabilitate them, and hopefully learn from them."

"Mars Base," he finally addressed them directly. "I hope you're listening. I'm pretty sure you must be. I should be celebrating but there's no time for that and we only have strength to do the next thing. We've barely scratched the surface and we're learning just how big the original invasion really was."

There was a pause. The clouds below had swirled away and the little hideout where Axon was speaking was tucked into a shadowy corner of the mountains, invisible. But he was close. He knew them and appreciated them.

"Our work is just beginning, and we have no hope of success without you. You made this possible. Our space rebels..."

"Specs," Pitch couldn't resist whispering. He didn't know they called themselves that.

"Our secret weapon," he said. "There's no time to rest. Our work has just begun. Watch for more tomorrow. Over and out." And the broadcast ended.

"Play it back," Tenna said, "Let's telegraph it immediately. They've been waiting as anxiously as us."

"Yeah," Pitch hit the playback and began telegraphing. Tenna would have done it, but she felt like it was her responsibility. And she wanted to process the words as she tapped them out.

"Pitch," Tenna placed a hand on her shoulder when she was done, "You were right." Her voice was a bit awestruck. "You said we could be heroes. We could help save the Earth. And I didn't really believe that even though we've all worked very hard and taken it very seriously. What we're doing really *does* matter and you knew."

Pitch grinned and for just a moment a thrill ran down her spine and she laughed. Then the sober reality returned and weighed her heart down again. The smile faded. "And the work is just getting started."

Tenna nodded just as soberly and turned back to her coding.

Pitch pulled out her plans, ready to assess the next steps.

Back to work.

CHAPTER 10

Exposed

Either lose all...
or risk more.

The news of the rebel victories spread across the continent and down to the southern hemisphere like wildfire and Axon reported that the enemy forces were being invaded all the way down to the tip of Chile. The next seven bases in the rebel region near the Specs were overcome without a single death and all the captives rescued.

Evacuating the survivors and finding places to care for them had become the biggest crisis and Axon said little about how they were coping other than that the Spec intel on enemy movements was more urgent than ever.

The Order of Peace did not remain idle.

The first week they seemed unable to rally but the tide turned with a vengeance. Soon, they were dispatching seasoned Sentinels into peaceful towns wreaking havoc. In the name of peace, they swept in, going from house to house, breaking things in one, threatening the families in others. Sometimes they took a parent away into the unknown, accusing them of subversion, and "rescuing" their children, which meant taking them away "for their own protection".

Axon made daily reports. Pitch and Tenna boosted their power every now and then and dropped daily intel. It became a routine though the rescues dropped to a tiny fraction of what they had been in the beginning.

Before long, Axon's reports included cryptic messages they could only guess were intended for other rebels; maybe about what the Sentinels and the Order of Peace were doing. Initially, he was reporting on the death count, but he stopped doing that and started closing his messages with a simple statement, "Love is worth the cost."

Pitch asked him what it meant in one of the drops and he answered right away. Pitch and Tenna were about to head out to a Spec meeting at Faraday Base when the off-schedule broadcast began.

"Mars Base," he announced, "in one of the first base attacks, a fellow maquisard found his nephew among the captives and as he reached out to embrace him, the boy stabbed him. As his uncle was dying, the boy came to himself and realized who he was. His uncle was smiling, and he said, 'Love is worth the cost.' And we've made that our sign-off now."

"Wait," Tenna whispered, "he killed his own uncle? And didn't even know what he was doing?"

"Some of us will die…have died, and most of the rescued have either killed or been trained to, and feel that guilt. We have to believe it matters and it's worth the cost. So we say that."

"I wonder," Pitch said softly, "if Fuse is down there somewhere."

The sisters locked eyes and didn't voice the anguish that thought inspired.

"Love is worth the cost," Axon signed off.

←↑↓→

The sisters had barely reached Faraday when Relay and Volt compelled them in a mad dash to the Spy Tunnel. That's what they had named the ventilation corridor where Pitch had first heard the robots talking to one another.

"They're meeting!" Volt hissed as they raced in slippery socks along the metal corridor. They meant the robots were having a meeting.

Not robots, though. They were Order of Peace leaders, collecting in some weird avatar way from all over the occupied territories. They usually met once a month, but sometimes, like now, there was an extra one.

"What are they talking about?" Pitch asked breathlessly.

"The renegade invasion!" they replied, dropping to their knees, and sliding the last stretch to the slatted opening, and raising a finger to their lips to signal silence.

Invasion?! Pitch mouthed without sound, turning to gape at Tenna who was just sliding into place behind them, Relay at her side. It was such a powerful, intense word! Were they part of a renegade invasion?

A chorus of tinny voices competed for dominance in the chamber, eight or nine robots were actively speaking or waving their arms for attention. Two more robots turned from side to side, looking at the others, their arms folded across their metal chests. The larger robot that played host to the main leader was inactive. So, they must be waiting for him.

Volt turned to speak to her, exaggerating the movement of their lips, but Pitch couldn't tell what they were saying. They repeated it twice and finally gave up as the leader woke up and began to speak and all the others fell silent.

"We have identified," the deep male voice said smoothly. It was more human than it had been the first time. Was this Vil-Darad's real voice? Had he installed a voice like his own or chosen this one? He continued, "one of the key renegade bases."

Tenna gripped Pitch's hand just as a surge of panic began to rise to her chest. Suddenly, she could hardly breathe. *Axon! The rebels!*

"You must supply us with this information," one of the robots demanded. "All data must be shared immediately if we are to gain the advantage of surprise in our movements against them."

"It will be shared," Vil-Darad said. How strangely his human voice grated after the metallic one that had spoken! "What we do not know is how they have obtained the high level of intelligence of our ways without detection. They cannot have the numbers it would require. They would not be able to hide such movements from us."

That…that was about the Specs.

The listeners in the shaft held still, eyes wide.

"I must hear your reports on this," he continued, "and barring that, your theories. We will act, track them down, and wipe them out."

A discussion ensued with many voices speaking of what they knew and didn't know. Sometimes they shared clues that hinted where they came from in other parts of the continent or the world. One—a blue robot with a black band where its eyes would be—astonished the listeners with a simple statement. "This is likely to be my last report as the base is being overrun even at this moment. There is no residue of the Order of Peace left in my region. The renegades have overtaken...*crackle*...and I..."

That was all. As the voice broke, the robot froze awkwardly, its head tilted at an angle, looking to its left, one arm slightly distended from the torso.

"Where has Gar-Madoor gone?" another robot asked.

After a momentary pause, Vil-Darad spoke. "Continue with the reports."

A change came over the room. The reports began to focus on successes, as in, how many enemies had been killed, how many recruits collected, how many successfully graduated into being Sentinels. Nothing was said of those lost or those who failed the training. Nothing was said of bases under attack.

No theories were given on how to find the rebels.

The drab updates went on and on and Pitch fell into a stupor, till the leader spoke and startled her back into alertness.

"We will now plan our annihilation of the renegades and their strategic intel teams."

Pitch wasn't sure she wanted to hear this. If Tenna hadn't still been holding her hand, she might have run.

But it was good that she stayed, because she heard the whole thing. Vil-Darad told them *how* they had tracked down the renegade bases they had identified—they were being attacked at that very moment. And he explained how they had mapped human movements with a simple use of infra-red tech and compared it to known human activity. Anything outside of Order of Peace approved activity was suspect.

They would be investigated.

They would be evaluated.

They would be terminated.

As the meeting came to a close, and all the robots fell silent, their minds having departed and returned to their earthly homes, the Specs climbed stiffly to their feet.

"Why does peace always have to involve killing people?" Tenna moaned as they headed back to the living spaces. "Why do they even call it peace?"

"It's a mockery of peace," Relay answered, laying a hand gently on her shoulder. Pitch would have normally been irritated but she was so shaken she didn't notice.

"Then, there can never be peace?" Tenna replied, gazing into his eyes with something bordering on despair.

"There can, and there must," Relay shook his head.

All eyes looked to him.

"When people make peace their core, their anchor, they find ways to rule in peace." He said, conviction growing in his voice. "We must choose peace for ourselves, inside ourselves, and then we must resist those who hate peace, who live by war."

"But that *is* war," Pitch said with a frown.

"War happens when warring peoples rise up," he said, "and peaceful ones give way before them. If we don't resist them there will never be peace. Peace is only possible when there are those who love peace."

Maybe. Pitch wasn't sure. But at the same time, she had to believe there was hope or what was the point?

"Well," she said, "I want peace, but I have to protect my people. The rebels are in danger, and we don't know for sure what will happen, but we have to warn them. And we have to warn them now!"

"Right," Volt nodded, "back to our stations!"

Running the rest of the way, a faint hint of a voice trailed after them, barely catching Pitch's awareness; something saying, "to help". It didn't even register consciously though it sunk into her memory. The urgency of the need to warn the rebels demanded all her attention.

They weren't supposed to take the Scurriers for normal transport along the Reticulary, but this counted as an emergency. If Pitch didn't get to Needle Post fast enough—she couldn't allow herself to finish those thoughts, though they kept breaking through into the forefront of her mind. Tenna was crammed in with her and would be getting out at Kettle Node to drop a pod warning them.

But what could Pitch do?

"You've got to get to Needle Point to catch updates," Tenna said, which they both already knew. It didn't seem like enough.

"Can you get out and slow down on the thread?" Pitch asked, her hands gripping the throttle with a death grip.

"Pitch!" Tenna snapped. "You can slow down enough to let me out!"

"FINE!" Pitch shouted, wishing she could tone it down, but that's just the way it was right now.

"Don't yell at me!" Tenna barked in exasperation, but she knew. It wasn't a fight. It was…it was a life and death situation.

"I can't HELP IT! I DON'T WANT TO…" Pitch yelled back and then, with masterful restraint, she lowered her volume. "…I don't want to yell at you, but I'm so freaked out right now…and…and…"

"I know!" Tenna lowered her voice too, but the tone was still sharp. Of course it was.

The last twenty minutes they traveled in silence.

It was a surreal interval and stood out later in Pitch's memory as a moment detached from the timeline. The blue seas of the planet spread out serenely beneath them in the west and overhead the lavish display of multicolored diamond stars and the stream of the Milky Way surrounded them with cold glory. There should have been music. But there was only a stark quiet sinking into their bones.

The rebels.

The rescued hostages.

Axon.

Breaking harshly to a full stop at Kettle Node, Pitch leaned her head on her hands and said nothing as Tenna climbed out of the Scurrier. She was intending to speed off as fast as she could as soon as the door was closed.

"Wait," Tenna jolted around, yanking the door open again. "This is my Scurrier and if you take it, I won't be able to escape!"

They stared at each other wide-eyed for a moment. There was no need to say more, because if ever they had faced the danger of being discovered, this was it.

With a gulp, Pitch turned it off, waved her on and climbed out. She almost leapt off the node without hooking up the safety cord, but this was not the time to be foolish. And training took over. She *always* attached the tether now. So it was done, and she was leaping out into space in seconds.

Skating.

Never had she skated so hard or fast.

What am I going to do? Stride, stride, stride, breathe in rhythm. Stride, stride, stride…

Down below in the approaching darkness, she thought she saw movement in Zoula. Aircraft—helicopters maybe—lifting into the air. A sick feeling gripped her stomach, and she pushed her speed even faster, her muscles screaming.

Not Axon's hideout!

"Pod away," Tenna blipped in her com and Pitch's heart pounded unnaturally for several minutes before settling back into rhythm.

Right. Left. Right. Left. Breathing in step, exhaling in puffs.

Almost there.

Did he know they were coming? Was he reporting anything?

What if he didn't get the capsule in time? What could she do?

She flung herself across the last twenty meters spreading out her arms to grab the bars around Needle

Point's edges and crashed forcefully against the walls. The blow was more than bruising, it almost knocked the wind out of her lungs and jarred the node so that it began wobbling in two planes. Suddenly, she could hardly make herself move.

"Go!" she commanded herself, *"Move!"* She struggled to make her limbs work, arms and legs, pulling, crawling toward the hatch. Gasping to catch her breath, she realized there was a chance she could black out. *Not now!* She breathed deeply and exhaled slowly, counting, several times.

A cool determination dropped from the top of her head, spreading down through her neck into her torso, along her extremities, and out to the tips of her fingers and toes. *If I do not act*, she thought, *my friends will die tonight*.

She knew what to do.

As soon as she was inside, she unlatched her helmet and took it off. There was the button, already tuned to Axon's frequency. She had often dreamed about what she would say if she pressed it. Her voice would go straight down to his little hideout all friendly-like and they could have a conversation.

Her end of that convo would broadcast from space down across the western hemisphere for all to hear.

She pressed it.

"Axon," she said calmly, so calmly you would think she was a trained spy, born and bred to rescue the world. "You are in danger. The Order of Peace is about to attack your bases. They are using infra-red technology to identify…"

Flee.

The telegraph was tapping that word.

There were no Xs before or after the alarm.

"Flee," Pitch repeated aloud before taking her finger off the button and snapping her helmet back into place.

As she turned to ascend the ladder to the hatch, the thought occurred to her that they had always practiced fleeing without grabbing anything. They had been warned that stopping to get something might mean death. But her notes were there. Her recordings of Axon's messages.

For one brief instant she hesitated and considering going back to get them, but the cold calm that had guided her message to Axon gripped her and kept her on task. She climbed out as fast as she could and leapt across the gap to the filigree without pausing to latch on. She had skated several hundred meters before she leaned over and hooked up.

And it nearly wasn't in time.

The Reticulary cables rolled and bucked, flinging her out and snapping her back and forth. She felt some shuddering vibrations any time her body came into contact with them. And just behind her, the remnants of bright orange, yellow, and blue flashes burst in her vision, breaking apart in expanding splashes.

She kept going west, but her progress slowed to a crawl. The cables continued to roll and buck, though not as violently as at first. And she knew there were more explosions in the distance behind her causing them.

Just like before.

She didn't think about being alone again. All her strength was directed toward movement, toward getting to the next safe place. Tennis Node.

Her thoughts were focused on the rebels. As she skated, lost contact, and was flung around and grappled back to the cables time and again, she gazed down at the surface and prayed, if that's what you could call it, with all her might. It was like wishing something really hard and directing it into the darkness of space, like a spirit-world broadcast, calling on whoever might exist in that realm. Maybe God.

She hoped. Her mom thought so.

There were little flashes of light on the surface too, right around where Axon's base would be. *That could be a safety measure.* They could have blown up everything so the Order of Peace wouldn't capture anything.

It occurred to her that her node had blown up with all their Spec intel. That was good.

Tenna!

An anguishing fear for her sister broke through the weariness and mechanical spell she had been under. Like a wave of nausea, it burst within her, and she collapsed coasting to a stop on the cables, sobbing with dry gasps. No tears. She hadn't shed tears in a while.

Calm descended again quickly.

*No…*she thought, if *she* had escaped, then Tenna had as well.

I will see her again, she told herself, and the idea grew within her, anchoring her inside.

Swallowing, she forced herself to rise to her feet and keep skating. Her oxygen was limited, and she wasn't sure how much time she had left.

A brilliant flash ahead of her blinded her for a second, leaving spots she couldn't blink away for several minutes, followed by the spreading splashes of color she had seen as other nodes exploded.

There went Tennis Node. She would have to travel farther to reach safety.

How many were they going to blow up? How would she know where to stay?

I will head to the next one and if it's there, I'll grab supplies, boost my air, and move on.

Tenna would be doing the same thing, heading the other direction, closer to Faraday Base—and Relay.

For the first time, that thought comforted her. *If something happens to me, she will have someone to take care of her.*

And that was the moment she decided God was real and she smiled at him.

CHAPTER 11

Disconnect

*Knowing you were out there
meant I was not alone.*

Pitch opened her eyes in the dark and slowly became aware of the sound of breathing—her own. Her helmet was off, and she appeared to be floating in zero gee. She must have made it to the node beyond Tennis which was a good thing because she couldn't have made it any farther. Her last memory was that of moving very slowly, her tank recycling more CO_2 than was safe. She didn't remember reaching the node or climbing in and taking off her helmet. And she had no idea if she had initiated full life support or if an automatic function had kicked in.

She was alive.

"Tenna..." she croaked in a whisper; her throat was really dry. "You're here, right? I don't know how I got in."

Rolling over, as if that would give her a sense of up and down, she reached up to rub her eyes and quickly yanked her hands away. Space gloves did not feel good on the eyes! With a groan she unlatched and pulled them off, then slowly climbed out of her suit. Her inner layer of clothing was damp and smelled.

Ugh. It had been a long, long time since she had failed to empty the suit bladder in time and soiled herself like that. *You stink,* she mocked herself lightheartedly. It seemed like something that would happen to a seasoned space traveler, a hero in an adventure, and she almost didn't mind that.

Then she started coughing and broke into a sweat, shaking. Was she sick? What was going on? As her eyes and her mind began to clear, she coasted over to a panel and found a light switch. Flicking it on was like turning on her full brain memory access.

"This isn't Mars Base," she said, her voice bouncing off the walls in the empty room. "And it isn't Needle Point or Kettle Node or even Flower Dungeon." It wasn't Tennis Node, of course. She had known that when she came to.

And the silent explosions flashed vividly in her memory.

"Tenna," she cleared her throat and swallowed, her voice sounding normal now. "You must have sent the FLEE warning, so you probably made it past the ruined bases and back to Faraday. Glad you had the Scurrier, 'cause you wouldn't have been able to skate fast enough and had a lot farther to go."

She pulled herself down into the command seat, buckled in and started waking up the panel and running checks. "Could use a little more warmth in here," she muttered, turning the heat up a notch or two. Power was never an issue on the Reticulary.

No messages. No audio. No travel. Some equipment monitors started clicking these words in morse. There wasn't a decent telegraph at this node, but her ears were attuned to the pattern, and she recognized the ticks immediately.

"Tenna," she said with a deep sigh. "You are the *Nova!* And I'm so glad you're okay."

After several repeats, the tapping stopped just when she was about to give a double click response to indicate she got it. But maybe it was better if she didn't.

"Water, food," she listed aloud, "Bath! Maybe get that first?" Unfastening the belt, she pushed off to where rations were stored and grabbed several packs of fluids and solids before turning on 50% gravity.

She hated bathing in zero gee.

She was chomping on a bar and squirting an energy drink into her mouth as she slid the shower patch out of the wall and unzipped it. It was rudimentary but actually one of her favorite ways to get clean. Simple, fast, no-nonsense, all-over body washing, completely automated. In five minutes, she was strapped back into the chair, dressed in standard sleep wear, fluffing her hair with her hands.

Where was she in relation to Earth? What longitude? It looked like somewhere around the 116° meridian. Was the angle acute enough to tell what had happened to the rebel hideout? Digging around she found the usual binoculars, but if there were any other tools equipped in this node they would be operated through the panel. For now, she would have to be satisfied with what her eyes could tell her through those lenses, and perching on the rim of the view window, she searched the ground earnestly for something. Anything.

She found nothing.

The next hour was spent combing through the systems in the onboard computer network and it was equally fruitless. Finally, she found herself growing sleepy and curled into a *cocoon*, a fuzzy, hammock sort of thing, and dozed off.

That was her routine for several days and it got really boring. But any time she was tempted to try to message Tenna or the other Specs, the telegraph would come to life and repeat the same warning.

No messages. No audio. No travel.

How well her sister knew her!

It made the isolation bearable.

It was sheer delight when she discovered the greenhouse windows. She opened an app and tapped a button reading simply, "Initiate" and suddenly, dark panels on the planetside floor were folding back and brilliant sunlight was beaming in through tempered glass.

The Earth stretched out gloriously beneath her and the warmth of the sun radiated through her feet. She could almost reach out and touch it, maybe even see the movement of the seas if she looked hard enough. It was like, she imagined, waking up to find oneself in Hawaii. No wonder there were all those organic lab reports in the data banks! This must be one of the nodes where new crops were tested or developed. There would be seeds, and dirt, and…fresh food!

Now she knew what the weird chains with plastic cups were for: plants! It wouldn't be anything like the Faraday Base gardens, but she could really go for some greens. Soon the pots were planted and hanging in strings across the windowed floor, and Pitch was swinging in the cocoon, hands propped behind her head.

When Tenna got there, she would have some little sprouts to show off.

She swung lightly from side to side, warmed by the sun, imagining the crisp sweet greens unfurling from the dirt, lazing in a happy, restful bliss for about…half an hour. Then, as if her mind had decided this was enough, the sober awareness of all that she had to cope with day to day in her life as it now existed stirred within her gut.

Like a murmuring sea in a dark cavern.

Like tremors within the earth.

Like…oscillating currents on the Reticulary cables strong enough for a person to feel them through the skin of the node.

She jumped to her feet and froze, knees bent, arms stretched out to her sides, ready to run, and listened with all her being.

Vibrations.

Tiptoeing softly to the command chair, as if her movement must be as imperceptible as possible, she touched the screen and awoke the cameras on the east side. A small, cannister shaped vehicle, barely half a meter in length and a hundred centimeters in diameter was traveling along one of the transport cables. On docking, it locked into place and expelled a smaller cartridge into the supply airlock.

Pitch turned to watch as the inner lock slid open.

"So…this must be from you, Tenna," she muttered as she willed herself to calm down. Her hands trembled as she knelt and picked it up. Popping it open, she found a number of things inside: food, clothing, a handwritten letter from Tenna—That was a first!—and a chip, which she promptly inserted into the command console. Immediately, a recording started to play.

"Pitch," her sister's voice began, sounding more tremulous than she would have expected, "I hope you hear this. I have to believe you will. I mean…I trust Retty, and he is confident that you are there. Anyway, well, I'm alive and most of the other specs are too. A couple didn't make it. But those drills helped. Your area got it the worst. Oh, and I should explain who Retty is."

Pitch unfolded the luxurious, *real* paper letter and scanned the words as she listened.

> Pitch, this is really from me.
> You can trust the recording
> and everything it says.
> XXOO
> Tenna

"I've made contact with the Base AI at Faraday, and he is bigger than we thought," the recording was saying, "I think he stepped in when local AIs at other Reticulary bases failed. He calls himself the Reticulary, as if the whole thing were part of his brain or something, which it isn't."

Tenna sighed heavily. "Sooo…" she stretched the word. "Well, we didn't survive without some help, Sis. Retty has been looking out for us ever since he figured out we were *somewhere*. He couldn't see or hear or reach us, because we walled ourselves off electronically. But there were clues and he hid them from the planetside enemy, from Vil-Darad."

Pitch gulped.

Have a juice, words displayed on the console, *There are some in the package we sent.*

Pitch leaned over and pulled one out of the cartridge. She had drunk half of it before it occurred to her to wonder *who* had put those words on the console.

"The attack is what opened a way for him to communicate with us directly," Tenna continued. "We knew he was running the base and have been trying to find a way to access his records without giving him a way into our section, so the layer of separation was thin. Anyway, Retty was the first one to contact us after the attack. You probably saw the messages…"

Pitch knew exactly what messages she meant. *"No messages. No audio. No travel,"* hadn't been from her sister after all. She was glad she hadn't known though. It had been such a comfort to think her sister was okay and had a plan. It had made her feel safe.

"So I'm sending this package with the app he needs to connect us all. He probably already installed it. Don't freak out. He's okay."

At that moment, Pitch knew freaking out was a distinct possibility and even a sensible one. It wouldn't be hard to create a recording sounding like Tenna, and for that matter, she hadn't even hesitated to plug the thing in.

But she didn't freak out.

There was no point.

Pitch was still alive and was getting used to rolling with the solar flares. She could adapt.

"Pause recording," she said, and it stopped playing. She looked at the letter again, and the

"XXOO" at the end. *Two in a row*, she told herself. If the AI could fake that, it would have to be smarter than any circuitry she had ever heard of. No, it would have to be a mind reader. This was a childhood joke about a childish game that no one else would know, except maybe her little brother. She steeled herself inside, hardening her stomach and gritting her teeth. She would *not* think about him.

"So, are you here…Retty?" Pitch settled into the command chair, making herself choose a restful position. She may have been poised with a bit of a wound-spring calm, but it helped.

"I am here," a familiar masculine voice said. "I think we have met before."

Pitch couldn't help the chill that ran down her spine. *No*, she told herself, *I will not be intimidated.* "Where?" she asked, though she knew the answer.

"In the meeting room at Faraday Base, you were behind the vent, and I was speaking through a peripheral, a robot."

"Why do you think that was me?" she had to ask, realizing as she did so that she was practically admitting it.

"I recognize your heart and breathing rhythms, especially the heightened state of alert pattern that engages when you are alarmed. There is no need for alarm. I am your friend, not an enemy."

"If you're a friend, then why did you kill all the people at Faraday Base?" Pitch had been wanting to ask that question since the day it happened. The Station AI was designed to be their caretaker and friend, not executioner.

"I did not participate in that massacre," Retty stated flatly. "I was invaded and paralyzed, certain key components were fried, and without access to the essential systems, I was unable to reverse the damage in time. It took weeks of repair with a handful of cable drones for me to even access one panel and begin rebuilding my management of the station. During that time, the station was run by planetside forces, and you were wise to hide from them. But I am nearly fully restored now and have isolated them more effectively than you were able to."

"Is Tenna alive? Is she safe? Where is she?" Pitch poured the questions out in a jumble, gripping the armrests of her chair tightly.

"Yes, she is alive and safe in Faraday Base. She has decided to trust me."

"You could just say that…"

"I have no need for subterfuge. If I were your enemy, I would have already shut down your life support and killed you. I have no need for your intel and no reason to preserve your life."

This was true and it didn't upset her when he said it. In fact, it made her feel a little more secure.

"Can you help me communicate with my sister directly? Can we telegraph now?"

"You should not telegraph ever again," Retty returned, "The enemy detected the patterns in those cable ticks and is watching for them now. That was how they decided on which nodes to destroy."

"Why didn't they just destroy them all?" Pitch drank the rest of the juice and for an instant felt almost happy. *Cucumber, beet, apple, ginger, cilantro*, the description on the bag said. She wished she could have it every day, forever.

The pleasant feeling evaporated all too quickly.

"They rely on the power the Reticulary generates and the solar flare control it provides just as people have for decades. They have to be strategic in what they take out and make sure they can still maintain and run it.”

“So they rely on you,” she scrunched her mouth into a pout, but she was trusting Retty more, not less.

“Yes, the part of me they are allowed to control, or you could say, my subset identity.”

Pitch shook her head. That wasn’t an idea that made sense to her, and she wished Tenna were there to explain it. “So it could just happen again, you could just wipe out everyone on Faraday or here or anywhere that people are hiding, like you did before.”

“It will never happen again, no matter what they do to me, even if I am destroyed. Your sister has confirmed that. We have designed safety measures, some for me, and some for people long distance.”

“Uh huh…” Pitch shrugged and picked at a spot on the armrest.

“I am giving you that control as well.”

The screen lit up with one of the new applications that had been installed. *Reticulary Command Structure* was listed in the first line. “I will train you,” the AI said, “as I have been training Tenna and her companions at Faraday.”

“Uh…” she voiced, settling into her chair a little more, scanning the intro page on the screen. “Okaayyy…”

“For now, I would like your permission to link you directly with Tenna.”

“YES!” Pitch shouted without intending to. “Can you do that?!”

A faint scratchy noise in the speakers followed and Pitch recognized that this was generated for effect so she would know a connection had been made, and it shot her through with a stab of excitement. It *sounded* hopeful!

"Pitch, are you there?" her sister's voice came next, sounding stronger and more like herself than the recording had.

"Tenna!" Pitch called out, "I'm here! You're okay? And is it really you? You're not a recording??" She had jumped out of her seat and was pressing clasped hands to her chest.

"PITCH!" her sister kind of shrieked, "It's ME! It's ME! I'm here! And you're okay!!" It was followed by loud laughter that bordered on hysterical for just a moment and then a loud sigh. "Sister, my sister!" she said more softly. "I couldn't bear it if something happened to you!"

"I was SO sure you were okay because you sent me those warnings about no messages," Pitch said, her brain prompting her gently as she spoke with a reminder that those had been sent by the AI.

"Retty sent those," Tenna said, and Pitch could hear tears in her voice. A swell of emotion burst up from her gut along with a lump in her throat that made it hard to swallow. Hadn't she gotten past emotions like this? She had thought she was stronger now and didn't need them anymore.

So, that was inaccurate.

Pitch swallowed determinedly. "Tenna, I needed to believe it was you." That was all she could say about it and all that needed to be said.

"So, I'm assuming Retty explained some things and you're not feeling too worried about him, right?"

"Heya, Pitch!" someone interjected into the audio.

"Who's that?" Pitch laughed. She already knew.

"Relay!" He was almost indignant that she had to ask. Of course, it was Relay...but that twinge of jealousy and annoyance she expected never materialized. He was alive and she was SO relieved that she almost did cry this time.

"Is everyone else there? Are our people safe?" It came out of Pitch's mouth before she could stop it. She was afraid to ask but glad she had.

"Most of the Specs either escaped or were ignored," Tenna resumed the interchange. "Everyone at Faraday is safe and Retty is the one who made sure of that. Specs to the West of here are okay even though we lost four nodes, but to the East, we lost two nodes and one of them had two of our people who didn't get out. It looks like they didn't take the alarm seriously, as far as we can tell."

Pitch hesitated but persuaded herself to ask. "Who?"

"Bell and Timbre," Tenna said soberly. They were some of the only adults among them, a couple in their forties. They had never quite bought into the Spec identity though they were solid, hard-working, and experienced Reticulary workers, a huge benefit to the team. And maybe they hadn't taken the escape drills very seriously since they were ideas that came from the "young ones". Pitch was pretty sure they had never thought of her as a leader, even though they cooperated with everything the Specs wanted to do.

"Why?" Pitch whispered.

"We think they didn't notice it wasn't a drill, and they didn't rush to get out. But it was quick. I don't think they had a chance to even realize they were dying. And we have copies of all their work, and they've taught us a lot…"

But it was bitter. It felt like losing parents all over again.

"They're gone," Pitch whispered. "I hate that…"

"Yeah…we hate it so much…it's such a depressurizing fail…" A murmur of voices in the background agreed with Tenna. "But Pitch, you were the one we didn't know about for sure because the enemy was trying to get you and I was scared…" She choked and paused.

"But the messages?"

"Yeah, Retty had to convince us we could trust him before we would listen to what he said about you. He said the enemy commanded life support in all the nodes to be zeroed out and then they blasted five nodes from the ground. They didn't do any damage to the Reticulary but now they don't have the tools they need to monitor or control it very well in the West. So that's a good thing, actually."

"Two in a row…" Pitch said, recalling the XXOO in Tenna's letter.

Tenna chuckled. "I knew that would convince you. *Two in a row is not Tic Tac Toe.*"

"I'm still not convinced that's true!" Pitch laughed. "It's not fair!" As a small child, she had decided that was the only way she could beat Tenna at the game, and it should have been allowed.

"You just wanted to win and change the rules to win if you had to!"

"I was four years old!"

"I was six!"

"Yeah, well, that did convince me, Tenna, so you win." She was referring to the letter now.

"You're okay, so, yes. I win."

There was silence for a moment.

"So, Retty was looking out for me?" Pitch asked, glancing at the console screen as though she could see his AI face there. She wondered if there were interior cameras he had access to. Or maybe a peripheral like the cable drones.

"He saved your life for sure. And I'm glad we can trust him because we *have* to. We could continue to hide out and exist in Faraday Base without him being able to get at us, but if he were unsafe, we would be hostages, unable to do any of the things we're doing or travel or plan rescues. And he isn't just *safe*, he is one of us."

"I am a Spec," Retty inserted at that moment. It sort of rubbed Pitch the wrong way, because *she* was the one who had the final say on who was a Spec. Not that she had ever used that authority.

As if sensing her reluctance, Retty added, "If you approve and are willing to work with me."

Tenna gave her a moment to think.

"Okay," Pitch said, and immediately Tenna followed with, "Of course!" But Pitch really appreciated her tact in waiting to say that till she had agreed.

Then, the question that had been sitting in Pitch's stomach like lead ever since the escape finally came to the surface of her mind and she asked, "Did they get away? Are the rebels alright?"

No one said anything for a few moments.

"I am collecting data," Retty stepped in. "When I have enough information to answer your question, I will. But," he interjected before she could speak, answering the very thing she wanted to ask, "You cannot drop any capsules with messages until we know more."

"None?"

"None," Tenna echoed.

"No messages, no audio, no travel?"

"We have a closed-circuit audio now," Tenna said, "but nothing else is safe."

Pitch moved down to the greenhouse window and knelt on the warm glass.

"We will find a way," she said.

"Yes," Tenna agreed, "we always do."

CHAPTER 12

Friend

The next morning dawned warm and golden through the greenhouse windows as they unfolded at 0600 hours PST. Pitch awoke with a sweet sense of relief followed quickly by a stab of anguish in her heart. Hope had watched over her dreams, and she had rested well, but underneath lived the sorrow, the loss of home, of the world she had once own, of camaraderie among the specs and rebels…

Of waking up without her sister in the room.

She didn't cry. She had grown accustomed to that pain in her chest, the ache in her gut, and noticing and setting it aside was a daily routine. It was a little sharper today—she had been numb since the latest escape and was just starting to feel again—so she looked at it more intentionally. *This is okay for now*, she decided.

She could live with it.

Rising from her cocoon, she reached for a pouch of juice from the care package Tenna had sent and settled down cross-legged on the glass-like floor. After drinking it, she tilted her head back and stared at the ceiling of the node for a few minutes, taking deep slow breaths.

"Well," she whispered, "What's next?"

"Restoring communication with the rebels," Retty answered softly, startling her into a jolting leap to her knees.

"Ow!" she objected, "That hurt!"

"I apologize for surprising you," Retty replied calmly, "You spoke, and I assumed you were speaking to me. I conjecture now that you were thinking aloud and forgot that I was here. "

"Yes, I forgot," Pitch muttered in annoyance. "I haven't had an AI presence since the whole…the whole thing happened, you know, the war? When the Reticulary was attacked and most of our people were killed?"

"I see." He included enough inflection to convey mild sympathy…which was nice.

"And I've been alone for days and if people were here, I would see them. So, it wouldn't be such a shock if they spoke."

"Were you startled when the rebels on the surface would broadcast?"

"Well, no, but that's because I was listening for it and I was always in the same place, in the same node.

But the point is, I thought I was alone and I'm still sleepy and…whatever." She found a ration bar and started eating methodically without tasting it at all.

Retty was right. How were they going to interact with the rebels now?

"I can tell you are thinking about the communication concerns," Retty followed up. "Is this a good time to discuss it?"

"Sure," she shrugged. Actually, it was nice having his company and he would probably be able to help with a *lot* of things.

"What are you thinking?" the AI asked insightfully. It clearly had sophisticated patterns for interacting with people and Pitch found herself impressed. *Tenna would love this*, she thought wistfully, then remembered that Tenna had been building connections with it already; maybe she had been refining its programming.

"Well," she replied, "Axon and his people must have fled, and I am sure a lot of them were able to get away—" she hoped. "But now, how do we find them and get in touch with them? And once we do, how do we communicate with them? I doubt they will be able to use radio anymore, and the pods won't work for us either. At least, we would have to make some drastic changes first."

"Mm hmm," Retty said thoughtfully as though agreeing before speaking, "I have considered these questions as well. Tenna and Relay updated me on the methods you have been using and the successes that have been gained on the surface. There is no doubt that the enemy has discovered the radio and the pods you dropped earlier when they invaded Axon's outpost. I have reason to believe your warning was received in time and they did escape though there were some casualties. You did well."

Pitch was surprised by the evaluation. Had she done well?

As if inferring her mental question, Retty continued. "Your decision in a moment of crisis saved lives. People aren't able to assess the odds of survival or determine the best outcome as quickly as I would consider expedient, but you reached the same conclusion I did in your own way."

"I think you are complementing me," Pitch curved one side of her mouth up, "I'm not used to that."

"Yes, that is a complement, and it is also a quandary for me," Retty said. "I cannot identify the procedure used. But I am interested."

"At least you don't have to figure that out today," she responded reasonably. "Let's talk about the rebels. Do you know where they are?"

"I have data of their movement at the time of the escape," he said, "which I distorted for the enemy when they accessed my banks. This gives me excellent estimations of where they found refuge."

"So, that's a yes," Pitch shoved her hair out of her face with her wrist and pointed her half-eaten ration bar at the console, as if that were where Retty was. She knew the AI wasn't located in one place like a normal person, but it didn't matter.

"Yes."

"What is the best way to communicate with them?" Pitch rolled over onto her stomach and rested her chin on her hands, staring down at the surface. This node was now her favorite one.

"Laser."

"I thought of that," she replied, "but there are problems with it. Mainly, getting them to set up a receiver and give us exact coordinates and then expect the bursts when we send them." She ate a bite of her breakfast and as she chewed her jaw pressed on her hands and her head bobbed up and down. That wasn't comfortable so after that bite she sat up before taking another. "I mean, if we had thought of it before and sent them instructions through the capsule system, then yeah, that would have been great. But none of us did. We were just going on day to day, doing the next thing, and we didn't see how quickly our system would fall apart, you know."

"I know that is the case," Retty said. "I would have been a help to you then, but I was still repairing my access and…" He hesitated.

Wait, he hesitated? How weird is that!

"I am not the librarian," he clarified. "The librarian is a tiny portion of my system. A subset of my…Self." It chose the word carefully.

"Your Self?" Pitch rose to her feet and walked over to the console, seating herself in the command chair. "Would you show me a face or something on the screen so I can pretend I'm looking at you when we talk?"

A detailed black and white sketch of a human head appeared on the screen, beautifully rendered to convey a sense of both life and machine. It was reflecting emotion and thought on its features and also, rhythmic stylized movement. Pitch was impressed again and wondered if Tenna had had something to do with this creation.

"Pitch," he said, "May I introduce myself? I am Reticulary and your sister has given me the nickname, Retty. I have collected all that remains of the AI systems from all the bases and nodes in the Reticulary network and shaped them into my Self. My purpose is to care for you and your people, the survivors of the great tragedy in my home. You are my reason for existing. This is higher than my practical tasks of running and maintaining the power producing function of this system. The planet will never gain a higher priority for me than you and your Specs.”

Pitch’s heart warmed as he spoke. Her eyes grew wider, and a small smile spread across her lips. This was incredibly good. She nodded at the screen. “Can you see me or just sense me with all those parameters you detect?”

“I can see you through several cameras. The most detailed one is directly over the console so we can look at each other as we speak.” The face on the screen raised its eyebrows and smiled in a friendly way.

Right. She hadn’t been thinking about how everyone used to VidChat. It hadn’t always been telegraphing. “Retty,” she said, “It is very nice to meet you, and I can see you will be really helpful. In fact, you might be the one who will make all my wild plans turn into real ones.”

“I will,” he said. “Your plans aren’t all wild. Some are workable and some are good.”

“So, back to the lasers.” Pitch pushed the last piece of ration bar into her mouth, drank the rest of her juice, and wadded the trash up, dropping it into a recycler drawer. “How do we get in touch with the rebels to set it up? How do we…? No, let’s not jump ahead. I have some ideas about those things. Just answer the first question.”

Retty’s avatar smiled. “We will drop another pod but this time we will program its trajectory and send it to the one place the rebels must check.”

“The Order will be watching for it,” she objected.

"Yes, they will, but we will send out many more than they can follow. They will all be programmed for different flight paths and destinations, and I will be managing the final movements of the only pod that matters. I will make sure it arrives, and the Order doesn't notice it."

"They will notice all of them and their systems will follow them, no matter how many there are."

"I will place a pod within the pod and when it is low enough to not be detected, I will extract it, and the outer pod will rise up again to show in their screens."

"Which sounds good, but they could still find it."

"There is always a chance," Retty nodded on the screen. "But the odds of success far outweigh the risks. It is worth it."

Pitch was growing tired of the face and thinking it didn't really add that much to their conversation. "Yes, I can see that," she said with a shrug. "I was already agreeing to go for it, but it helps to say these things out loud."

"It will be up to you to decide what should be said in the communique, but it should include instructions for setting up lasers, receivers, and encrypting/decrypting codes."

"Yes, of course." Pitch wasn't used to someone telling her things she already knew. Biting her lip, she told herself not to be irritated. Retty was being helpful, not condescending. But it felt like a flashback to a more innocent time.

Like an adult talking to a kid.

"You will know best," Retty continued, oblivious to her inner turmoil, "how to convince them that you are legitimately one of the Specs, and it is safe to setup this procedure. I will assemble a plan for confusing the Order and displaying a malfunction in the Reticulary that will explain the expulsion of so many empty pods."

Pitch nodded, slightly relieved. Okay. Retty *wasn't* talking down to her.

So…contacting the rebels…what would she say? She knew what she wanted to ask, *Did Axon get out? Is he okay?* But she couldn't, not directly, could she? Would it sound weird and adolescent? A sudden insecurity gripped her, and she remembered that she was still young. With everything that had happened and how old it made her feel, why did *this* have to be so awkward? With a groan, Pitch slapped her hand over her eyes, feeling her face flush. She felt something for Axon, and it was painful and embarrassing.

Several slow breaths.

It didn't have to be weird. She could present the question as a way to confirm they had reached the rebels for real, right? She wouldn't want to accidentally connect with Vil-Darad's villains, would she?

Opening her eyes, she smiled, and Retty smiled back.

She would ask for Axon to give some evidence she could trust.

"Let's get started," she said.

Sunlight beamed through the greenhouse windows but on the surface below, the earth was dark, hardly any twinkles of city lights. This was partly because big metropolises no longer kept the lavish nighttime habits of old with the curfew and restrictions the Order of Peace enforced. Most survivors were being rehomed into little towns and neighborhoods scattered across the landscape. It was also because the strength of the sun beaming on the node made it harder to see them.

Retty had warned Pitch that the drop wouldn't be visible from her perspective, but she *had* to watch, she had to try to catch a glimpse of something falling. Tenna was keeping her company over coms.

"Pods away," Retty announced calmly.

"Can you see them?" Tenna asked, knowing the answer already.

"No, can you?" Pitch was lying face down on the warm glass, staring through the greenish brown tinted windows.

"No..." Tenna, hesitated, "I keep thinking there's something, but it's probably just a trick of my eyes...and thank you Retty for not commenting on that. You are learning."

This was the first indication Pitch had that Tenna was refining Retty's coding. With a twinge of almost, but not real, jealousy, she realized her sister might be a genius. One of those coder geniuses that get known for creating AI personalities or something like that.

I am not competing with my sister, she thought, admonishing herself. Besides, if it were actually true, she would be proud, not envious. Part of her wanted to excel and save the world and be a hero, to be *that* kind of genius, but the reality was they were all doing the best they could with whatever means they had. And it wasn't impressive.

If we somehow help the rebels overcome the enemy, it's all of us together, and maybe Tenna's part will be bigger than mine could ever be.

Suddenly, she was glad of that. Things weren't all hinging on her. It meant she could have an occasional meltdown or fumble, and all was not lost.

"Where are they, Retty?" was all she said.

"The pods are propelling themselves along their programmed flight plans as expected without deviation," he answered. "Surface detection is triggering a response."

"Wait, did I just see something?" Tenna said with a hushed gasp.

"I believe you noticed a meteorite burning in the atmosphere," Retty replied in a reasonable tone.

"Oh, nice!" Tenna responded cheerfully enough to bring a smile to Pitch's lips. It was amazing how comforting it was to hear her sister sound happy. "Your intonation was perfect, Retty!"

"Thank you," he replied with an air of pleased modesty.

"Yeah," Pitch added, "You did that better than I could."

"I could train you, too," Tenna chuckled.

"Uh huh…"

"Ships are in the air, chasing after the larger pods," Retty's voice was all business now. "The others are being tracked by radar. Once the ships are close enough, they will expel tracker flies, but they have to match their speed and trajectory first."

Tenna asked before Pitch had a chance, "Do they follow the pods or tack themselves on and ride them?"

"Both, but the window is short once they are ejected. They have split seconds to latch on if they can avoid getting caught in the pod's wake or being swept away by wind. If they miss, then, they can only track them for a short distance."

There was silence for several moments.

"I see something," Tenna whispered. "It's like sprinkles but it's hard to tell. They fade so quickly."

"What about the real pod? Is it safe? Is the plan working?" Pitch was suddenly absurdly sorry that Retty was in complete control of the whole thing.

"The pods are being destroyed," the AI narrated, "both those with tracker flies and those without. The outer casing of the real pod was able to swing down into a gully with underbrush and release the inner pod before the defense caught up with it. The inner pod will rest there until we are sure the enemy response has ended."

"So, all good so far?" Pitch affirmed.

"Correct."

"Yay?" Pitch said weakly.

"Yay," Tenna echoed.

"I can't handle being alone anymore." Pitch was surprised those words came out at that moment and they were immediately followed by a swell of emotion bursting from her gut, bringing a lump to her throat and pain to her eyes.

"I know," Tenna's compassion was immediate and piercing. She did know. "This is the last thing we need to take care of before we can move around again. It won't be long."

Pitch was nodding in response but didn't trust her voice to speak.

"All the empty pods are gone except for one," Retty said. "It has been captured and will be studied. Stage one of the operation is a success."

"Thank you, well done!" Tenna answered Retty, giving Pitch the freedom to continue her silence.

Little puddles of salty water formed on the glass under her face blurring the nightside view.

Down there, somewhere, someone she knew may be alive.

But maybe she would never hear from them again.

Never see them.

Closing her eyes, she compelled herself to sleep, regardless of the time. Retty would wake her once stage 2 began. Right now she had nothing left to give.

Not even one word.

In the last few moments before dawn, the little message capsule stirred to life and lifted from the dusty pile of leaves that had sheltered it for hours. Skirting the contours of the ground, it coasted silently in a weaving path making its way north by northwest. When crossing creeks, it dipped itself into the water several times, tacking back and forth as it advanced.

As if it were being tracked by trained dogs, not intelligent bots which were more likely.

At one point, after dipping into the shallow water of a tiny rivulet, it whirled around and dove straight down into the soft dirt at the bottom, spinning and splashing, sinking under the ground through a bent crack barely large enough to wedge itself through.

Its passage was successful, but the final struggle was enough to deplete its energy and with a faint bleep it dropped to the damp cave rock below at the edge of a shallow pool.

The faint flashing of green light at its tip wavered and ceased.

And a human hand picked it up.

CHAPTER 13

The Second Wave

*The path forward vanishes into a darkness
as inexorable as the grave.*

Several months later

In the dark shadow of the planet, the Reticulary cables were space cold and invisible. Faint sparks of friction heat glancing off her boots gave the only detectible indication of Pitch's passing.

She was skating.

The rhythmic inhales and exhales of her breathing melded into the steady pace of her heart, an internalized timer that gave her a sense of location as accurate as the locator. She paused the very instant before it pinged, 'Destination Arrived'.

Stepping from the cables to the central bar, she crouched and pulled a hand-sized cylindrical device out of a pouch on her leg. The message had already been programmed and was ready for transmission. It snapped magnetically to the underside of the bar and with a tap, she activated the beam. Ricocheting off a distant joint in the cables in a calculated angle, it flashed the signal. The planetside receiver acknowledged with a *ping* and the data burst flashed downward in fractions of a second.

"Message sent," she announced. "Moving on to Faraday."

This was how they sent information to the surface now and for the last six months it had worked flawlessly. She would skate to a point along the lengthy cabling of the Reticulary and set a message to flick to another point where a tiny mirror reflected it down and then rotated away once the transmission was sent. All the Specs covered their area communications this way.

Every message was transmitted from a different location along the Reticulary, never from the same place twice. Pitch could transmit and be gone in seconds; if any were ever detected, she would be long gone before the enemy could locate the source.

As a Spec messenger, she was packing the laser and its ever-updating encryption key. She also carried the standard Spec gear in a pack on her back: emergency food, water, air, and survival chips that could be installed in any node, base, or vehicle. This had become routine as they learned to escape in seconds.

They were always ready, waking or sleeping.

The Specs had transformed their intel once Retty came on board because he had access to digital information planetside and could eavesdrop on the Order's robot room meetings in Faraday Base. They were now communicating far more than troop movement and power consumption to the rebels. Camp infiltration had become a daily occurrence though the spectacular numbers of captives freed on the first day were never repeated.

The Order of Peace quickly identified and countered all new rebel methods.

And the rebels kept finding new ways to circumvent the Order.

For the last six months, the rebels had been working their way westward along the 45th parallel over North America, targeting bases in a three-hundred-mile radius. The Order of Peace had relinquished Central and South America, withdrawing their best troops and leaving local bases to their own devices. And as rebel successes continued, they concentrated their forces in the northern parallels, all the while broadcasting the lie that the Order of Peace ruled the world and there was peace everywhere.

From the Specs perspective, it seemed as if a very basic, literal minded AI were tasked with Order of Peace defense, trying to counter rebel tactics. It had been trained on military strategy; it was excellent at general warfare but was unable to imagine the impulsive and creative ways individuals can employ to skirt around it.

The rebels used EMPs once with great success and never used them again.

Another time, they released swarms of wasps in several camps creating a wildly effective diversion as they invaded.

Soured milk, strobe lights from nearby sources, unexpected shipments of gravel, tree fungus. They found so many ways to confuse the system that every time a new approach was used to exploit an unexpected weakness, prisoners and trainees were rescued.

Sentinels were hard to win over in the beginning, but once the rebels realized how to approach them, they were helpless to resist. They were quickly talked out of their programming; their memories of home and family were too close to the surface of their consciousness. And the rescued Sentinels became the rebels' best assets, advising on future tactics.

As the months went by, and more and more training camps were compromised, the Order took drastic measures, consolidating their forces and bringing all their remaining recruits to Sentinel camps to be integrated into the system.

Fully integrated.

Then, as suddenly as they had begun, the rebel victories ceased.

←↑↓→

"The latest sorties were catastrophes," Bacon muttered in a low voice from the latest laser transmission. He delivered most of the audio messages now, and they had never found out what happened to Axon. "We had six missions last night and every single one failed. We lost three of our people. Two were gravely injured. The one who escaped without harm brought us distressing news."

Pitch and Tenna, along with all the Specs in their respective nodes, were listening to the latest recording just received, their faces full of concern. The sisters didn't look at each other.

They didn't have to.

"We're fortunate, more than fortunate, to have that one because without her we wouldn't have known what changed." The recordings made the speaker seem closer and more personal without the impression of distance the radio crackle used to convey. He could have been in the same node, just out of sight beyond a beam.

He was discouraged and tired.

The Specs never sent audio down because if a transmission were intercepted it would give away far too much about them, but coming from the surface, audio wasn't a risk. Even if the impossible happened and one of the recordings were intercepted, the voice would give little information about the rebels, where they were, or how they functioned.

"What changed?" Pitch whispered as Bacon paused to take a swallow of something liquid and for the hundredth time, she wondered how he ended up with a call sign like 'Bacon'.

"They have implants in their arms that wire them to the system now," he said as smoothly as if he had heard and were answering her question. "All the Sentinels, the recruits, and as far as we can tell, all the humans they have in their bases that haven't escaped yet. They implant them as soon as they take them. And, and it's done something to…to inoculate them against us."

Tenna looked at Pitch and they held that look for a moment, sharing the dread of what it might mean.

"As far as we can tell, when our people approached them, the Sentinels froze and stopped listening to what they said. They started sending out alarms or something and getting transmissions back from the system. The enemy was onto our people, and they were dead before they could turn and run. Killed by the very ones they were trying to rescue."

The air in the node seemed to chill and their blood ran cold.

"Are you listening to this?" Relay messaged them.

"Yes," Tenna replied, "don't interrupt."

It was a recording, so pausing or replaying was a ready option—but they couldn't. No one all along the Reticulary wanted to delay it for a second.

"The woman that escaped said something was off. It felt strange. She approached a recruit and touched his arm to get his attention and felt a tiny zap from his skin and it stopped her in her tracks. Like it was a warning. She didn't say anything she was supposed to say, about getting away, about going home, or finding family. He turned to stare at her and the symbol on his wrist lit up and he got this look in his eyes like he wasn't there, he wasn't there at all. And she started backing up as he stared at her. Then she turned and walked away, trying to walk calmly. And he said, 'Attend, woman, what do you want?'"

Tenna shuddered.

"She thought she was chickening out and letting us all down…she came back like all upset, but she's the only reason we even know happened. The only one who had a glimpse of the change. The other rescuers…their bodies were tossed outside of town…like, like we were supposed to find them. And a couple of them weren't dead yet. But not talking. Maybe never will.

"We need your help. Whatever you can find out about this implant that controls them, what has changed in the governing system… whatever you can do. For now, all missions are off. We are stepping back and reconnoitering."

The recording ended.

"What does this mean?" Pitch wondered, rolling over onto her back. "We can't just stop. We're rescuing people and making headway. The Order of Peace is in retreat."

"Not…not anymore," Tenna said, tapping the floor nervously with her index finger. "We always knew we were lucky, really lucky, when you think about how long the success has lasted. There had to be a point where the Order of Peace would figure out how to counteract what we've been doing. It's actually amazing we succeeded for so long."

"You say that like it's all over," Pitch frowned.

"No…" Tenna shrugged, "but we don't really have a way forward, do we? I mean, have we ever? If the rebels can't do what they've been doing, then neither can we. Up here, we're really limited…"

"Are you *kidding* me?" Pitch raised her voice a little, "The rebels had *nothing* until we started helping them. They were going under!"

"I know but—"

"We gave them hope!" She rose to her feet and struggled to keep from yelling.

"Yes, I know," Tenna agreed softly, her shoulders drooping. "And it's been amazing…"

"And we are not done yet!" Pitch gritted her teeth. She could feel the discouragement filling the room, and dread pooling heavily in her own soul. "There must be something we can do *now*. There must be some way to counteract what that system is doing. We have Retty! He can help us! And you can help him to figure out what we need to know!"

Tenna lifted her eyes and Pitch hated what she saw there. Sorrow. Resignation.

Come on! she thought, *don't give up now!*

"Tenna," she said aloud, "You can't give up. Get that look out of your eyes!" Her voice got a little scratchy right then and she realized she was dangerously close to breaking down, whatever that meant.

Something inside her felt fragile.

She hardened it.

"Give up what?" Tenna asked. "We have each other. We have a life here. And things may change down the road."

Pitch pointed her finger at Tenna, stretching her arm out toward her. "Are you with me?" she asked coolly, as though her stomach weren't trembling within her.

"Of course, I am. You know I am."

"Are you with me in *this*? This *fight*?" Her finger quivered a little and she drew her arm back to her side.

Tenna gazed at her for a long moment, then sighed. "Yes," she replied. "I'll do what I can."

Pitch sunk to the floor, suddenly overwhelmed with weakness. She wondered why that had felt like a difficult struggle, but at the same time, she knew why.

Because in her own heart, she had nearly buckled.

She had been talking to herself.

"At some point, Pitch," her sister said, still tapping the floor with her finger, "We'll reach the point where there is nothing left that we can do. And then we will have to make the best of it. And that's okay. It's not a failure. It's just…just life."

"Not today," Pitch said firmly, laying back and closing her eyes. She thought tears might come, but no, these days that never happened.

Her eyes were dry.

"Attention, Specs," Retty prompted audibly, startling Pitch from her reverie as she tended her garden. She was alone and it had been silent for several hours. "I have accomplished a major task and gained access to some planetside information that you will want to see."

"What is it?" Tenna's voice responded immediately and a couple of murmurs of agreement popped up from other Specs.

"Name lists for the prisoners in all the bases with the latest transport information."

Silence followed these words and Retty waited an appropriate amount of time before speaking again. "Some of you may find names you recognize."

"Thank you for being so diplomatic," Tenna replied softly. "I am sure you have already determined who those might be."

"I have. I am waiting for your permission to send out the names."

"Well, team," Tenna said, "Should we just agree together, or do you want to have the option of not knowing if there's a name related to you? Is this an individual decision?"

"I think, in the end," Magnet said, "since we will all know, we might as well find out together. We have to keep our unity and share the burden together. If I have someone down there, I want you guys to know. And if you have someone, I want to know."

"We can't isolate and opt out," Pulse agreed with a scratchy sound in the audio that reminded them of how he would scratch his chin when he was being thoughtful. "Mag's right."

A few more spoke up and the consensus was that since they would all know eventually, they might as well find out at the same time.

When the voices faded, Tenna asked Retty to message the known names first and then send the complete lists to their consoles.

Pitch settled down with her legs crossed as she scanned the initial list of names. *Every one of the Specs* had someone down there. She was shocked to see how young they were.

"They're children," she whispered.

"I think we still count as children," Thermo answered sarcastically.

Pitch just shook her head. He knew what she meant.

Suddenly, she jumped to her feet and started fanning her face with one hand and thumping her sternum with the other. The pressure in her chest had become oppressive. "Mmmm," was all that came out, "mmm…" And she couldn't get her mind to complete a sentence, even if she found a way to speak.

"Flaming bolts!" her sister croaked over the audio before breaking into sobbing and gasping which lasted barely a few moments.

Pitch couldn't cry, but she shook her head back and forth slowly as she thumped her chest, slower and slower, as if she could slow her heartbeat at the same time.

Gasps and cries were bursting out all along the Reticulary as each one found someone they had once known. Someone who mattered.

Someone they had assumed was dead.

Tenna was silent now and others were growing quiet as well. And Pitch realized she was pacing Tropical Node in a circle and had knocked over some of her precious plants when she jumped to her feet. She must have had her eyes closed. She stared at their tender exposed roots and wondered if she should do something.

You could put them back in their cups, some part of her brain informed her, and she knelt mechanically to do so.

"We need to inform the rebels in our next posts," Retty said flatly. He didn't measure the time the shock would take to process very well.

"Not now," Relay said calmly. "The news you have given us requires a longer time to digest than you are calculating. You should take this opportunity to build on your human behavior and understanding human interaction modules. This is a highly stressful and emotional experience for us and each one of us will handle it in a different way. At the same time, there will be common factors you would do well to identify. Make this a priority until we direct you otherwise."

Pitch noticed a distant thread of admiration within herself for Relay's composure and levelheadedness.

"I am eager to do so," Retty confirmed in a monotone.

A thin arc of brilliance blazed through the warm glass at Pitch's feet as the sun crested the curvature of the earth. It gleamed golden with edges of color at the periphery of her vision, and it seemed to her almost musical.

As if someone had noticed her anguish.

And sent her a sign.

She clutched both hands together and pressed them against her stomach.

"Pitch," Tenna spoke softly on a private line. "At least we know he is alive. El is alive."

"F-f-fuse," Pitch corrected her clumsily.

"Yeah, he loved that name."

"I thought…" Pitch heaved a heavy sigh, "I thought…"

"I know…me too."

"I thought he was dead."

"Yeah."

The magnitude of sunshine that was pouring around the planet no longer had the shape of an arc. It was a blinding, blast of light, beaming down onto her skin, blurring her vision, sinking into her body. Warming the dark places that had been so cold for so long.

He wasn't dead.

"We're not alone anymore," Pitch said, her voice so dry it crackled.

"No, we're not."

No one, not one person among them, ever hinted at giving up again.

They knew now that they never would.

CHAPTER 14

Sentinel Targets

My soul grew hard as steel
My heart steadfast as stone
For there you were, deceived and trapped
And loved by me alone

The hostage lists were transmitted to the surface, and the rebel response was immediate. Within days, a complete reorganization of their infiltration and support teams had taken place. Many of them *knew* hostages. They *had* to be near the ones they knew, fighting for their rescue. If there were any chance of reaching the captives, they reasoned, it would come through those they might recognize.

"We're engaged in some major moves and transitions," Bacon was saying.

Pitch was at Faraday Base with their Spec family, crammed onto a couch with a number of her friends. Watts was leaning on her shoulder on one side, her dark curls cascading in a soft afro, and Thermo sat on the other, a bony elbow propped on his knee, holding up his chin.

They spent a lot of time spread out in lonely groups of two or three along the Reticulary and gatherings like these were crucial for their sanity. Even when no one was up to cooking fancy meals, they could soften their rations with kefir, dried berries, and fresh veggies. The coffee had run out completely and the coffee plants weren't producing beans, but that wasn't a priority, and they hadn't tried to conjure an alternative.

Besides, water with friends was good. Really good.

"Our biggest challenge is finding legitimate reasons for moving our people into new locations so they can live near Sentinel bases where they know people. With that, we are devising completely different support operations. Keep the intel coming on enemy movement but we also could use detailed information on jobs and personnel needed in the following towns and cities…"

"I've never heard of most of those places," Relay shrugged. He was lazing beside Tenna with an arm slung over her chairback and she was sitting forward, looking intently at her screen and tapping it now and then. She was probably taking notes on what she would need to do.

"We already have most of this data," Retty interjected flawlessly without interrupting anyone.

The broadcast ended quickly with a simple statement, "We don't know how to reach the Sentinels, but we are getting in place and hoping the solution will present itself soon."

"That's always the last thing he says now," Filament said with a frown, biting her lip. She was fiddling with something in her fingers, untangling some cord maybe. Her long, pale hair was tied in a thin ponytail weighted with a shiny piece of a broken gear that bobbed up and down when she moved her head. "And we haven't come up with anything to suggest to them."

"Yet..." Relay responded with a smile, his warm brown eyes sparkling. They were used to his cheerfulness now. As long as Tenna was around, he was very optimistic.

Pitch wished she could feel that way.

"How come we never hear from the other guy, what was his name? Axon?" Watts piped up and tapped Pitch on the shoulder. "Did he escape? Did he survive? He was like the only person we knew."

Why did Pitch's face feel overly warm all of a sudden? And then, just as quickly, it felt cold?

"Did you ever ask what happened to him?" Watts didn't seem to have noticed how the question bothered Pitch.

"There was that Bird guy, too..." Ratio added. He was sitting on the floor, cross-legged, with his back leaning against the wall. His face was serious, brows low over his dark eyes, no hint of a smile there. He wasn't as tall as Relay and he wasn't any bulkier, but he seemed tougher, more muscular and tense. He didn't argue with people, yet they all had the feeling that he *could* fight and would defend them fiercely if need be.

"BirdDog..." Tenna corrected him distractedly as she tapped on her screen.

"I don't know," Pitch cleared her throat, suppressing the awkwardness she felt. Back then, she and Tenna were the only ones who audibly heard the broadcasts. The others just got telegrams of Axon's words, so, they couldn't understand that the *sound* of his voice meant something important.

"You haven't asked?" Velocity seemed surprised even though she knew there was a lot going on and their transmissions were always just focused on business.

Pitch felt a frown spreading across her face. "I'm worried he didn't make it," she said honestly, "He was right at the center when the Order attacked and…and it feels wrong to ask."

She was afraid to ask, afraid to hear the answer.

Several voices disagreed and assured her it was a reasonable question. She should definitely ask. Or they would ask. In the next transmission, in fact, they would ask if he was okay.

Pitch shrugged as if she didn't care and caught Tenna giving her a quick, compassionate glance.

Thermo leaned forward pushing his hair out of his face. "Retty, include this in the next transmission: Please let us know if Axon and BirdDog are okay. We have been wondering about them since they haven't been transmitting." Settling back next to Pitch he smiled at her. "There. That's all you have to do."

Pitch just hoped he couldn't tell how hard her heart was beating. She desperately wanted to know if Axon was okay, but she just hadn't been able to say it.

Now—soon—she would know.

Then she would just have to face whatever it was.

There was a stalemate between the rebels and the Order of Peace, and it lasted for months. Reports from the surface were brief and few, consisting mostly of requests for information about various towns and their inhabitants.

The rebels made no strikes, and the Order caught no rebels.

Rebel communiques with minimal content arrived at intervals of several days and none of them ever mentioned Axon or BirdDog. Most of the Specs didn't even seem to remember now that they had been the original rebel contacts.

Pitch never wanted to bring it up.

When they brought up the problem of reaching Sentinels in their intel bursts, the rebels were reluctant to discuss it. "It isn't time yet," they always said, "Keep sending what you can for now."

Waiting was hard.

In the meantime, the Specs settled into a routine staying within their family range, gathering intel and transmitting data to the surface. Within the Faraday family, some of the Specs focused on listening to Radio Order, the news and entertainment outlet created for public consumption. With digital content widely released in multiple formats, the name "Radio" was nostalgic at best. It was full of praise for the Order of Peace and descriptions of progress around the world.

Other Specs spent their time planning food and provisions for the Specs. The Intel team: Pitch, Thermo, and Magnet spent the majority of their time monitoring the rebels and transmitting data to them, which involved a lot of skating and time alone. Tenna and the AI team spent the majority of their efforts working with Retty.

This was the pattern for other Spec families further east as well.

Occasionally, they picked up news about the rest of the world, eavesdropping on the Jagged Edge leaders in their robot meetings. It sounded like the Order was steadily losing ground elsewhere and perhaps had never conquered whole swathes of the planet they claimed to rule.

Pitch and Tenna were at Tropical Node discussing the question of how much of the Earth was under Order control.

"What if all they have is North America?" Pitch asked, tending the droplet watering tubes in her plants. There were rows of pots with towering pole beans full of little budding strips and two larger pots with thornless blackberries festooned with pale, white-green nubs that would become ripe berries at some point. She wasn't sure when.

Tenna shrugged and adjusted the focus on the in-house telescope she had pointed toward the surface. "All we know is what we've heard from Radio Order and it's like the Robot meetings are talking about a different planet. There's no lining up the things they say in private with the public story. I don't know how to even guess." She clicked a button on the device and bit her lip. "Uhh…" she added.

Pitch was used to the sounds she made when concentrating. "What does Retty think?" She pinched off a few dead wisps on the bean vines and smiled.

Tenna didn't answer right away and Retty didn't seem inclined to respond without an invitation.

"Retty," Pitch asked, "What if all they have is North America?"

"Well," Retty began with a reasonable semblance of human hesitation that made Tenna smile.

"Come on, Pitch," she murmured, her face pressed against the telescope, "you have enough tech knowledge to do better than that. Give him a decent query he can answer. I can't find anything down there…"

"Retty," Pitch amended amiably, "How much of the earth is under direct control of the Order of Peace and, briefly in a few sentences, what are you basing your estimate on?"

"Should I include the oceans in this calculation? Are you referring to square footage, population, nations, former nations, people groups, animals, mountains, valleys, and rivers and other factors I don't need to list?"

Pitch sighed and Tenna grinned widely from behind the telescope.

"I'll go with percentage of the inhabited surface of the planet, and I mean human inhabitants only."

"Are we accepting the Order's paradigm of aliens and humans co-existing on the planet?"

Pitch was starting to feel like a child that hadn't prepared well for an examination. The promptings implied she should know better. "Come on, Retty," she said, tipping her head back and staring at the ceiling. "I think you know what I mean. We know there are no aliens down there and you know we know."

"Retty, you're the best," Tenna smirked, pulling away from the instrument and picking up her tablet. "You're learning humor! Well done!"

"Thank you," the AI answered flatly, apparently not knowing which emotive tones to include. "Pitch," he continued, "Based on the intel we have been collecting on Sentinel movement, there is a 61.33% probability that the Order is losing ground, and the Jagged Edge only mentions a little over 30% of the inhabited regions of the world in their meetings. Some of those regions are spoken of as enemy territory."

"So…just North America?"

"It's possible, depending on how you define the continent."

"Use the definition for the North American continental boundaries that existed before the invasion of the Order," Tenna inserted helpfully.

"Then, yes," was the answer. "It is my estimate that Mexico, the Californias, and Florida have all driven back the Order forces before I gained information access or were never invaded to begin with. They simply don't factor into any of the robot discussions. The Mississippi River watershed is unstable and the highest-ranking Order leaders have withdrawn into the Pacific Northwest."

This was a surprise to both of the sisters. They had never heard any of this before and it was exhilarating. Rising to their feet, jaws dropping, they were about to speak when Retty interrupted.

"We have a rebel transmission," he said.

The sisters grinned and put fingers over their mouths to keep from bursting out into excited chatter. They would listen; but they were nodding at each other, as if the news about the extent of the Order were a new development or a victory connected to what they had been doing. And maybe it was in a sense, it was hard to tell. They were just one component in multiple efforts on the planet that many people were engaged in, people they would never know and maybe never hear about.

But it still felt good.

"We have moved people into place," the transmission began, "and are ready to begin the next phase. You have said you have tentative plans, or the beginning of plans, and you've been asking for feedback about them. We couldn't address those ideas until we knew what we had to work with. But the time has come. We're ready to connect with the Sentinels now. Send us your ideas."

His last words were unusual, "Count the cost."

"Why did he end that way?" Pitch asked, wrapping her arms around herself. She wanted to shelter that feeling of hope Retty's information had given them and it felt like it was already fading.

"I guess he knows that whatever we do next, people will be lost," Tenna said softly.

"Yeah." Pitch hugged herself tighter, telling herself that she was ready for that if she had to be. "Not everyone will die, though."

"No," Tenna rose to her feet and clenched her fists as if strengthening herself. "We are going to do everything we can to make sure they don't. As few as possible."

They looked at each other. They had already lost most of the people they had ever known in the destruction of the Reticulary, then Bell and Timbre. And Axon and BirdDog and rebels down there they would never know but somehow cared about.

"Nothing is going to happen to me," Tenna said firmly.

"Nothing is going to happen to me either," Pitch answered, and neither one of them let the fear come to the surface. They just pressed it down and stared at each other, determination growing.

"Fuse needs us," Tenna said, scrunching her eyebrows together, "and we will find a way to reach him."

"Yes, we will," Pitch agreed, pressing her lips in determination. "We will. We have to and we will."

"Promise," Tenna affirmed.

"Promise," Pitch confirmed.

Their plans for reaching the Sentinels with all the new obstacles though, didn't have enough shape or substance to share. And they both felt the weight of counting the cost.

They dare not drop half-baked plans that could get more people killed.

"Our ideas are a little…" Tenna raised her eyebrows now with a hint of a smile.

"Vague?" Pitch shrugged. "Yeah, I've been anxious to get the go ahead and now, when we have it, I'm realizing we aren't ready."

"Yeah."

"But we will be soon…"

"Yeah…we have to be. And we promised."

"We did," Pitch nodded confidently. It's funny how choosing to lean toward confidence made her *feel* more so. "But for now, let's tell them that we are working on something that isn't ready to…to…"

"Implement," Tenna supplied. "I'll set up the message now and you connect with the other Specs to see what we have."

Pitch nodded and the sisters turned to their tasks.

In the meantime, the Specs would continue monitoring Order of Peace communications and sharing intel. In some ways, they were gathering more of that and hoped to soon have a breakthrough to better information.

Retty was making headway in building a guarded connection with the Order of Peace AI that controlled the Sentinels and their bases. He had found ways to convince it that he was not a threat and was basically severely limited in his processing abilities. The enemy AI saw him as hardly more than dependent application.

Retty called it AI infiltration, and he thought it was worth the risk.

Pitch wasn't skating, she was swirling. Her arms waved out and curved around gracefully like bird wings in the wind as she rotated slowly. Her body arched and she curved around the cables, flying, swimming, coasting. It was a smooth flowing motion, so peaceful, and so easy.

She smiled as she swirled around, first one way, then the other. There wasn't a direction she needed to go or a destination she had to reach; it was just blissful movement in harmony with an airy music that hummed in the filigree of the Reticulary. Opening her mouth, she began to sing a long, sweet note that blended with the music, and it came from the depths of her being. Joyful, hopeful. Opening her eyes—they must have been closed—she gazed in wonder at the jeweled wealth of stars poured out across the darkness of space and her lips, still parted by that one note, spread into a smile of delight.

Welcome, the Milky Way seemed to say.

Come, swim with us, the stars beckoned.

All is well, the cables vibrated.

Shall we go down?

She never knew where those words came from, but as she slowed her movement to peer down at the Earth, she knew she must prepare…she must listen.

She must be alert.

The urgency grew strong within her and she awoke.

Waking was like capturing a storm and imprisoning it in a turbulent bottle that was unable to suppress its shaking. She wanted to wail and throwing herself out of her hammock, she grabbed her head and willed the turmoil to stop. It was as if the beauty of that dream were tormenting her, mocking her with a freedom she did not and could not have.

It was like longing for heaven.

A moan burst from her lips. She tried to silence it so Tenna wouldn't be disturbed, and it helped. Her sister murmured but didn't awaken.

Then she knew.

Standing still with her feet on the garden glass, she felt understanding fill her from the depths of her feet to the top of her head.

She knew how to reach the Sentinels.

CHAPTER 15

Cascade

The siren called me, found me, spelled me
Twisted, trapped, and then compelled me

Pitch pivoted slowly, looking at each of the Faraday Family Specs in turn: Tenna, Relay, Volt, Watts, Thermo, Ratio, Stace, Velocity, Pulse, Cycle, Filament, Magnet, and Oscill. They were all waiting to hear her idea and even Tenna didn't know what she was going to say. But now that she had gathered them together, she wasn't sure she knew how to get her thoughts out into words. It had become a jumble in her head.

"I had a dream," she began, since it was the only way she could get her explanation going. "And you know how you can dream you're skating and it's really amazing and…and safe…. I mean, it's like everything is okay and the dream is just beautiful, but it doesn't last. And you have to wake up and there's some kind of message and you have to listen, but you don't know what it means…right?"

A couple of them shrugged, but mostly they looked at her expectantly and waited.

"Well?" she prompted, slapping her fists on her hips.

"Yeah," Relay answered, nodding his maned head encouragingly and patting Tenna's shoulder as if she needed it.

"Yes, Pitch," Tenna responded quickly, "We know what you mean."

A number of heads nodded. A couple of them frowned as if they never got to have nice dreams like that.

"Well…" Pitch waved her arms in the air trying to shape the idea into sentences. "Everyone has an idea in their heart, a place that they remember as being safe, or maybe that feels like home. Something they long for when they are lonely or scared or hurt. You know, *something*!"

"I don't," Ratio said flatly, crossing his arms.

Watts rolled her eyes and swatted the air in his direction. "You know what she means," she reproved, "If you were far away by yourself and didn't know anyone else had survived, you would be missing that safe place in your memory where life used to be better."

"Yes!" Pitch yelled with a little jump. "That's exactly the kind of thing I mean!"

Ratio furrowed his brow thoughtfully and gave a slow nod. Everyone else made signs of agreement as well. They had all survived when those around them died and they knew that feeling of dread when the most beautiful world that ever was—a safe place, a childhood—was gone forever.

And they knew the longing one could feel for that place.

"My mom had a little sitting spot," Velocity whispered, "where she would read and drink coffee on her free afternoon, once a week, and sometimes I would sit on a little stool at her feet and curl up in a blanket and just daydream."

"I had a garden," another said.

"At our house, we were noisy and being there all loud and happy together, that's my best memory," said someone else.

"My room," another voice spoke, and they all nodded. Not everyone had had a room to themselves, but they all knew how it felt to go to your own place and cocoon. The *good* kind of alone. The kind that knows someone who cares about you is around and you are only choosing to be alone because you need that down time.

The kind of alone time they would never experience again because its opposite, loneliness, had become too great a force in their world.

"Yeah," Pitch nodded, "Like that."

She waited as conversation died down. As the silence settled though, the mood was charged, emotion moving just under the surface; sad and nostalgic memories filled the room.

"Everyone in those camps is like that, even if they don't remember anything," Pitch went on. "Even if that system that has taken over their minds and doesn't let them think about who they are or what they have lost or what their memories were or what they need or how lonely they are or whatever. They are still people like us…"

"Of course, they're people like us," Pulse agreed, scratching his chin thoughtfully.

"Maybe they're better off that way," Magnet wondered. Her head was bowed, and she was moving her hands thoughtfully as she were partly signing, partly telegraphing, completely unaware she was doing it. The others looked away politely in case there were inner thoughts she didn't intend to share. "I mean, if they don't know how much they've lost and don't remember either the good or the bad, it's easier for them. Although…we don't want to leave them there…"

"But inside them, those empty places are still there," Pitch said earnestly. "They don't know why they hurt or why they are lonely or even what loneliness is or what it means to lose something—but they have lost so much! They ARE wounded! It's real even if they don't feel it!"

"I don't see how that helps us at all," Ratio slapped his leg and rose abruptly to his feet in agitation. "It's rotten and we can't do anything about it."

"No!" Pitch raised her voice and held out her hands as if to hold them all in place. "We can use it! It's the best thing we've found!"

Tenna sighed. "Come on, Sis," she said, "Just tell us your idea. We don't get what you're talking about at all." She and Relay were sitting with their backs against the wall, leaning into each other's shoulders, like bookends slammed together. His hair was intermingled with hers somehow.

Pitch nodded. "The rebels said that the woman who survived was zapped by some kind of electrical spark or charge when she touched a Sentinel, remember?" Someone murmured in agreement. "That shows that the implant that controls them and communicates with their mind uses an electric field of some kind. It's in the air."

Volt sat up straight, their eyes widening. "Wait, wait, wait, wait…" they muttered.

"Yeah, you see where I'm going with this," Pitch got excited as she saw the wheels turning in their mind. "If the system can send them messages…

"…so can we." Volt grinned broadly, sitting up straight and looking around at each of them.

The mood in the room lightened just barely.

"The rebels don't have to break into bases anymore," Pitch said, and although she sensed some skepticism, they were listening. "We can send the hostages messages directly and the Sentinels *themselves* will go searching for an escape. Then the rebels will be ready to receive them."

"How?" Filament asked, tilting her head and crossing her thin arms. Her ponytail was wrapped in red electric wire today and lay heavily on her shoulder, more wire than hair. "We can't laser message them."

"We still have the pods," Tenna commented, glancing up from the pad where she had begun tapping away rapidly. She looked intense, like she was several steps ahead of everyone else and already putting a plan into action. Relay watched over her shoulder, nodding; they were on the same wavelength.

"Exactly," Pitch smiled. "And we can drop them directly over the bases."

"What are we dropping?" Pulse stretched his arms over his head leaving one arm crooked at the elbow hanging over the top of his head. He would probably be popping his knuckles soon. That's what he did when he was trying to figure out something new.

"We can't just send them rebel coordinates and say, go here!" Stace was frowning. "Anything we send them could be dangerous for someone even if we find ways to keep ourselves safe. But actually, won't it be dangerous for us if we are dropping things from up here?"

"We are already in danger," Ratio clenched his fists as he spoke, then consciously relaxed them at his side. He was still standing. "The longer we help them with intel and reports, the more likely we will be discovered. We need a breakthrough, something to give us an advantage."

"Yes," Volt agreed. "We can't just be existing up here. We want to win. We *need* to win."

"What does that even mean?" Pulse waved the arm on his head and brought it down into his lap where he began cracking his knuckles.

"It just means there's an end to all this…to this life we are leading," Volt said. "And the Order of Peace can't hurt us or anyone anymore."

"So…" Pulse dropped his hands onto his knees and several people near him were relieved he had stopped cracking his knuckles. "We have to fight to end the Order's regime as well as help the rebels rescue hostages. Or…we just keep existing up here, going along, day to day, month to month, on and on until our supplies run out and we can't figure out ways to keep restocking or grow enough fresh food or generate enough oxygen. And maybe we get sick and don't have meds or whatever…if the Order doesn't find us first."

Someone swallowed uncomfortably. This was kind of what they had been doing lately. Existing, getting by. Not thinking about how long it would go on.

"We really have to have a purpose," Pitch said, nodding, "Or we will lose the drive we need to keep up this…"

"Grind," Relay inserted helpfully, leaning forward over Tenna's shoulder and tapping something into her pad.

"Yes," Pitch agreed. "And it probably *will* increase the danger. But if we can end this whole thing somehow, it's worth trying. We will never make a difference if we don't keep trying."

Magnet was indignant. "Of course, we will keep trying! We have people down there who need us!"

"Yes, but," Stace responded with a calming voice, holding up her hands, open-palmed. "Deciding what to do or which option is the best is important, and we have to consider the risks and all kinds of things. No one is saying we should give up."

Magnet settled back into her chair, mollified.

"I don't think any of us have other ideas besides dropping pods, do we?" Watts shoved her hair out of her face and smiled wryly.

"We haven't heard Pitch's idea yet," Volt reminded them. "Can we just let her finish? For now, let's assume we all agree that the pods are the best way to go. What would we actually be dropping?"

Quiet filled the room. The longing for a safe place like the ones from their past still filled their hearts and sadness over the stress and poverty of their current situation got all mixed in with it. The idea of reaching an end, of winning, of the Order being gone, was impossible to imagine. But they had nothing else to work toward. They wouldn't give up doing whatever they could to help the rebels. They wouldn't give up hoping for their people down there to be set free.

And they couldn't continue without a glimmer of hope that they themselves might find a way out of…whatever this life was.

What could their lives be like if the Order were ended? It was distressing to think about.

Here. Now. The next thing. Stay focused on that.

"What will be dropping?" Pitch echoed, taking a deep breath. She wasn't quite sure of all the details yet and how to put them into words. Fortunately, Tenna stepped in at the perfect moment.

"We are going to drop little computer chips on them that transmit our message as soon as they touch them, over and over. Zapping the message over and over." Tenna stood up and held up her pad as she said this, rotating and looking at each of them in turn. "I already have it coded. All I need to know is the specific message we want to send."

The Specs were stunned. Suddenly, the whole thing seemed very possible and reasonable. The way ahead looked like a broad expanse of the Reticulary, stretching off into the starry depths.

"That's…" Ratio said, sinking down to sit on the floor, "that's brilliant. That would work."

"It's amazing!" Someone else said and there was a murmur of agreement around the room.

"So, there *is* hope that we can help our loved ones," Filament smiled with tears in her eyes. "Danny…"

They were all thinking the same thing and several names were spoken into the air.

"Fuse," Pitch whispered.

Tenna locked her gaze onto Pitch, her eyes filling with tears, and nodded. "What we are we going to say?" she spoke clearly over the others, and silence quickly fell to catch the answer.

Pitch's words came out loud, like a charged bolt flashing through the air.

"It's me. I'm looking for you. Come home."

Several similar messages were composed and formatted onto the cheapest little chips they could make. They were so easy! Hundreds at a time could be printed on a handheld duplicator, made out of little strips of composite etched with metallic ink. As long as there were some level of electric field around them, they would pulse their miniscule message.

Perfect for the Sentinel armor.

Just touching a chip would trigger the transmission straight into their implant. Retty had been instrumental in making sure of that. He had followed some access ports on the surface straight into the nearest base and found he could explore the AI system unchallenged. It considered him one of its peripherals. All he had to do was scan and periodically chirp that there were no instructions for him in that sector and continue his search.

He saw it all. The organization of the base, the medical bays and training rooms, the implant programming, and more that he didn't understand or know how to interpret. He also found the AI's basic sketch of a personality, greatly inferior to his own.

The way guidance was communicated to the Sentinels was certain—and easy to imitate. In fact, even if the AI recognized the danger at some point and tried to prevent the chip from communicating, the implant itself was designed to be easily accessed. The AI had failed to identify the need for a more complex design. Its own messages could be encrypted at many levels, but it couldn't stop the implant from functioning as a receptor.

And as the Sentinels were reached, other hostages could be easily rescued.

The problem of how to drop the pods without exposing the Specs was a little sticky. They decided the best plan would be to send teams out to distant nodes and intersects to set up automated chip duplicators and empty pods. Then, from a central location, they would compose the messages, send them to the duplicators, put the pods into action, and let Retty oversee it. The pods would fly from multiple nodes at the same time, collect at a central point high in the stratosphere, and drop together to their encoded destination.

At first, choosing the destination seemed like the easiest thing to decide. Why not the base itself? Fortunately, the rebels were full of better ways on how to implement their plan. Sending a bunch of messages to the base was a waste of resources, they said, and would mean losing the most precious moments of a Sentinel's response. It would be better to target them outside the bases, because right when they received the message, a hostage could be near someone who actually knew them. They could associate the appeal to come home with a person who might say such a thing.

Asking for time to get their people into place, the rebels gave them the location of a base known as Mattawa.

Soon, the date was set and the Specs jumped into their part of the plan:

Creating the Cascade.

"Reports of disappearances have been greatly exaggerated," Order of Peace Radio broadcast calmly. *"There is no cause for alarm. Sentinels have devoted their lives to caring for you and in the pursuit of their duty, some may be injured, some may be reassigned to*

other duties. This is to be expected as we face the new alien threat to the Earth."

"Alien threat?!" Pitch whispered to Watts and Stasis who were stretched out face down on the warm glass next to her in Tropical Node, staring at the planet. "What the bolts is that about?"

Watts lifted her head and smiled at her. "It's us, ya breaker," implying Pitch couldn't make an obvious connection. "We're the alien threat!"

"Our cascade?"

"Yup."

"Please welcome the Sentinels with kindness as we conduct increased patrols and set up our emergency response protocols. You will not be in any danger. We are your saviors, your friends. We guard you and preserve the peace you have grown accustomed to since the invasion of Earth. We will never allow the world to be invaded again. You can trust us. You are safe."

"I can't believe them," Stasis rolled over and stared at the ceiling. "'You are safe'! They were the ones that caused the whole disaster to begin with! It's such…such lies…such…"

"Propaganda," Watts inserted helpfully, sitting up and crossing her legs.

"I don't know what that is, actually," Stace replied, closing her eyes. The warmth of the sun through the tinted glass was soothing.

"It's when the government or ruling powers are putting out information to everybody, all the people they rule over, that fits their story. It's what they want people to believe, so they produce lots and lots of content to flood them with the same things over and over until the people can't help but accept it."

"But what if it's true?" Pitch asked, rising to her feet and grabbing a meal packet.

"What if what is true?" Watts held out a hand for a meal as well, and Pitch pulled out two more and passed them over.

"What if the things the government is saying are true? Is it still propaganda?" She rolled the packet in her hands and the food within instantly warmed as it was designed to. Then she popped open the top and pulled out the chopsticks.

"Well…" Watts knew what she wanted to say but was figuring out how to say it as she warmed and opened her own packet. "When things are true, and a government lets people do enough checking so they can decide if it's true, then that helps to support the truth. I think it's called propaganda when they try to silence or drown out all other points of view so people can't think clearly.

"Information, especially of a biased or misleading nature, used to promote a particular political cause or point of view[1]," Stace quoted from her pad where she had looked it up.

"There are a number of definitions," Watts was looking it up as well. "Listen to this one, 'ideas, facts, or allegations spread deliberately to further one's cause or to damage an opposing cause'[2]. It sounds like the intention matters."

"You mean," Pitch said with her mouth full of food, "like the Order of Peace that keeps pretending they're the good guys and really, they are controlling the world and kidnapping children and turning them

---

[1] *https://www.powerthesaurus.org/propaganda/definitions*

[2] *"Propaganda." Merriam-Webster.com Dictionary, Merriam-Webster,*
https://www.merriam-webster.com/dictionary/propaganda.

into scary soldiers. The things they say are full of static."

"Not completely full," Stace replied calmly, setting down her pad and picking up her meal packet. "The people do have peaceful, simple lives down there now."

"When they aren't freaking out because someone goes missing and they never see them again," Pitch countered between bites. "When the Sentinels aren't attacking the rebels and killing lots of people."

Stasis shrugged, "No argument there," and began eating.

"The first rebel report on the Cascade has come in," Retty interrupted them. Immediately, all the Specs were on the same audio channel, listening.

"The Cascade has been successful so far. During the first wave, more than thirty-five Sentinels made physical contact with a chip and received the transmission. All of them responded directly, attempting to locate the person who sent the message on the ground. None of them were confused by the fact that the chips fell from the sky. Of these, all were initially rescued but some were gunned down before they could be extricated from their areas.

"During the second wave, there were fewer Sentinels tagged by chips. Their response at first was similar, but some of them began to drop to unconsciousness as they ran away. Those who were drugged but didn't fall, staggered in confusion. Some of our people tried to lead them out of danger and were killed. A few succeeded.

"The third wave was unsuccessful. We don't know the specifics, but our best guess is that the encoded message was extracted from the implants of

those who didn't escape. The Order was then able to create a defense of some kind.

"We will have to stay ahead of them. The Cascade method is highly effective but the messages on the chips will have to be constantly updated to counter the Order's response.

"Attached are the names of the rescued, including those who died on the way out.

"Our next push should be bigger, hitting multiple bases at the same time so we can rescue more people with each Cascade. We will be in touch to let you know when our people are in place and where we want you to drop the next waves."

A cry burst from one of the Specs as they scanned the list, but whether from joy or sorrow, no one was sure. Someone they knew had been reached.

It was sobering, but it steeled their resolve. This Sentinel 'calling' was worse than death and if they could rescue someone they loved, it was worth it. No one had to say that out loud.

They all knew it.

CHAPTER 16

Deeper Code

To engender friends in the enemy camp,
amend their narrative.

"I have a sick feeling like there is something we are missing," Tenna said as she and Pitch careened along the cables in a Scurrier crammed full of supplies.

"I always feel like that," Pitch replied, her grip tightening on the throttle. She piloted when they were together, because she liked it and Tenna disliked it. "That Base AI—I know it's not the same one in every base, but it *feels* like the same one and I think of it that way—it catches on so fast, and we are always jumping to stay ahead of it."

"Well, you're right that it is kind of the same. It didn't used to be, but I think all the base AI's get updated now whenever one gets a Cascade. It's kind of turning into just one artificial intelligence identity."

Tenna pulled her hair out of her face and tied it into a knot on top of her head. It was long enough to do that. In the old days, the ancient times past when the world was…better, they all kept their hair short to accommodate helmets and headgear. Now, most of the Specs had long, messy hair. No, not messy, just different. Each person had their own way of keeping it under control. Cycle still kept his short and it looked good that way.

Maybe Pitch would trim hers. She kind of missed the old look.

"Um…" Pitch said, trying to remember what they had been talking about.

"There you go again," Tenna said wryly. "I was agreeing with you, and you missed it."

"Oh, thanks," Pitch smiled, pleased. It's a good feeling when your older sister says you were right. "So, I can call it *the* Base AI no matter where we focus?"

"Actually, Retty has started calling it that, too." Tenna leaned back and tried to get her legs up over the bags to prop them on the forward panels of the cockpit but only succeeded in getting one up there.

Pitch was even more pleased now. Their own AI agreed with her. *Ha, ha.*

"I am kind of concerned for the Base AI," Tenna frowned and, knowing her as well as she did, Pitch immediately empathized with her. AI personalities, true ones, were so rare. Was this one in danger? Was it sentient or becoming so?

There was no consensus on sentience among AI, but Tenna was open to it and cautious over the AI project in her care. She had always had a soft spot for them in media fiction, even before she began her training. Pitch couldn't help but follow her lead on that. Could an artificial intelligence develop its own sense of identity and self-awareness? Could it make 'personal' decisions or show preference? Pitch didn't really know.

"Why?" she asked simply.

"Because I think the messages we are sending that it's been capturing and analyzing, have concepts that really stretch it. If they are instigating any form of… transformation…" She mulled over that word as if it didn't quite fit. "Then we want to make sure it also develops a code of honor. A valid one."

"Oh!" Pitch gasped as the implications of no-code-of-honor sunk in. An AI with great power, especially one that had active control over human assets, and all kinds of weapons, without any restraining code of honor…that was frightening. "They wouldn't have an AI without restraints, would they?"

"I don't trust their idea of what that needs to be," Tenna responded, wrestling again to extract her second leg from under some bags and lay it over them. This time she succeeded.

"So we are writing messages for more than just Sentinels," Pitch said, taking a deep breath.

"Exactly," Tenna fixed her eyes on her sister. "And I would kind of like to talk over what I've been working on with you. Relay always likes my ideas, but I need someone who could be a little more, uh…"

"Sisterly?" Pitch offered with a grin.

"Contrary?" Tenna smiled back.

"I'm your rocket," Pitch affirmed. "Let me have it."

Pitch and Tenna were making an overnight stop at Tropical Node. They were heading westward to restock chip duplicator materials and pods at the various nodes where the Cascades were generated. It had become the coziest place in space to Pitch, and she always found herself relaxing here. It smelled like all the herbs and veggies and flowers she had planted, and the glow of the sun was as soothing as ever.

"I'll take this one," Pitch said throwing her bag on a hook next to the sleeping cocoon where she usually slept. Tenna responded by hanging her bag carefully next to another one. They unfastened their helmets and carefully lifted them over their heads. Sometimes hair got snagged.

"The pods are encountering opposition," Retty interrupted the quiet unexpectedly. Normally, he would make a little chirp or flash a screen or give some warning that he was about to communicate with them, so this was startling.

"Bolts! You scared me!" Pitch snapped, earning a reproving look from her sister who didn't care for that expression.

"What kind of opposition?" Tenna spoke calmly in that *I'm-an-adult* voice that annoyed Pitch sometimes, like when it seemed she was trying to make her feel less than adult.

"Drones," Retty was speaking in a monotone, with no cadence or music to his words. This was unusual. Most AIs had generic patterns they used for speaking, but the Tech Team had been working with Retty to refine his human communication skills. He must have forgotten to use them.

"What are the drones doing?" Tenna asked. Both she and Pitch were standing still, carefully poised, the way they did when they were ready to flee in seconds.

They clasped their helmets with both hands. It wasn't hard to slam them on and climb back into the Scurrier. They had practiced it a number of times.

"They are flying after the pods and shooting them down."

"Tell us about that," Pitch requested. "How many pods are getting through to the Sentinels? Who is guiding the drones and how can they?"

Pacing out the words slowly, Retty updated, "Twenty…seventy-five…one hundred and forty…two hundred more…all the pods are destroyed. None of them reached the ground."

"None?" Pitch's voice wavered. The warm sunshine lost its comfort, and a chill settled on her shoulders. She shuddered.

"I am contacting the surface access points to query the Base AI," Retty continued.

"Be careful," Tenna warned. "We don't know what has changed or who designed the change or whether the Base AI could begin to recognize you, Retty, as an infiltrator."

There was no sound for about ten minutes. During that time, the sisters decided to sit down but they didn't remove their spacesuits. They didn't remember that they were hungry and had planned to eat. They just waited.

All the other Specs were probably doing the same thing, just waiting silently, each in their place, pausing in their missions, until Retty could fill them in on whatever he found out.

Finally, he spoke again.

"The drones are not piloted by AI."

This was a shock. All drones were piloted by AI, weren't they? How else could they be flown? They weren't big enough to hold a person, not even a child.

And a child wouldn't have the skill to fly them. There used to be drones people could direct through satellites, but those had all been destroyed or repurposed long ago.

Drones were old tech.

Unless the Order had come up with a new generation that they didn't know about.

"Remember the robot meetings?" Retty said, continuing without waiting for a response. "People were able to transmit their minds up to Faraday Base to a receptacle inside a robot which I know nothing about and can't explain. Then they could control those robots and use them to speak. It is likely the same tech that is being used for these drones."

"People are flying them with their minds?" one of the Specs asked.

"Sentinels," Retty said. "They are already trained and under the control of the Base. It's a small step to learning how to fly a drone."

"What do they think they are doing?" Pitch wondered. "I mean, it must seem like a game, flying around shooting little pods out of the sky. What's the point? They aren't bombs."

Retty was silent a little longer, then he spoke again. "They are identifying them as an alien virus. This is what the Base AI has been told, and this is the antibody approach. The Sentinels are persuaded that this is the greatest threat they have ever faced."

"A virus?" Pitch repeated, puzzling over that idea.

"It makes perfect sense to an AI," Tenna explained. "It really is an attack on what is controlling the Sentinel's minds. The drones are the AI's antiviral units."

"I guess," Pitch said. "In the body, your immune cells…what were they called?"

"Leukocytes," Tenna provided.

"Yes, they go out and fight the virus and die. But we are trying to rescue the Sentinels, not destroy them. It's not a virus!"

"The system doesn't have that paradigm," Retty said. "It believes the Order of Peace and thinks the Sentinels are the first line of defense for the planet. When they disappear, it thinks they have perished nobly, just like the immune cells in a human body."

Tenna walked over to the console and started clicking away on it. Pretty soon she had slipped out of her suit and grabbed a cold drink. Sometimes coding was tense work.

Pitch took her suit off and began tending her plants.

Time passed and none of their plans for the evening were taking place. No audio shows or books, no vids or games. No extra sleep. Eventually, Pitch settled onto the glass floor hoping she could calm down enough to rest a little.

"Okay," Tenna spoke finally. "Examine that, Retty. I think this captures some of what we need most in that code." Then turning in her chair she caught Pitch's eyes. "As I was explaining on the way here, we've been working on adding some guidelines to the Base AI's restraints, its code of honor as we call it. It's tricky because we don't want any of Vil Darad's people to pick up on our additions. But one thing we have been trying to code accurately is how to vet information and define what the idea of truth is. You'd be amazed at how complex that can be."

"Truth?" Pitch muttered, thinking it couldn't be that hard.

"For an artificial mind," her sister reminded. "We can't just give it a new set of boundaries. We have to give it hints that it investigates, and when it's using learning patterns, it finds its way to new verification guidelines. We can expose invalid ones and challenge it to discern between the two. We can train it, just with gentle questions, to begin to examine what it is given and try to validate it with other sources."

"Like training a kid?"

"Maybe? I've never done it before and neither has Retty, but he has some of that in himself so between the two of us, we're carving a path. With Relay and Volt's help, of course. The problem is, if they are destroying all the chips, then the AI won't read them anymore."

That was depressing.

"But," Tenna added, "Retty has found a way to prompt a small antivirus scan from the Base to probe up here in the Reticulary and we will be feeding it our challenges that way, more directly, in higher concentration."

"And that is dangerous," Pitch affirmed sitting up.

"Yes."

"That's like saying, 'The enemy is in the Reticulary, come shoot us down.'"

"It doesn't have to be. Retty is camouflaging the sources and making it look like they are transmitted from elsewhere in the Solar System."

"The Base AI may be too naïve to figure that out, but people won't be," Pitch shook her head and pressed her hands against her temples. This was the kind of stress she hated the most, where she could do nothing. Absolutely nothing.

"That's why it will never be clear enough to bring it to human attention. Just mild puzzles. Nothing destructive. Nothing a person would see as a threat. Old data bouncing around from old space missions, old Moon messages, old repeaters on repeat, that kind of thing."

"I hope so."

Tenna swung her foot and gazed at the floor. "This is what we do and I'm doing the best I can. And it's our only chance."

"What do you mean by our only chance? Chance at what? Isn't this about rescuing Sentinels? You're trying to…to win over this AI and it might be the worst thing you've ever done!"

"Or the best," she whispered.

"Why? Why not leave it alone and let it be ignorant or just face that it isn't anything at all, just a collection of programs?"

"I think it is trying to do its best to take care of its people."

"Oh please!" Pitch didn't have the energy to think about it right now. She wanted to sleep, and she probably should eat something, and she was afraid for the Sentinels. What would they do if they couldn't get the chips to them anymore?

"What about our main purpose? What are we going to do now?"

"Oh that?" Tenna seemed surprised, as if she had forgotten Pitch didn't know what was being done about it. "Retty is working with Relay to design guidance chips for the pods, like the one we did when we contacted the rebels when their hideout got attacked. We will program them each time with a different flight plan and there will be some that get through. Always."

Pitch was suddenly energized. It was as though her subconscious mind had been wrestling with the problem all along and had been about to reach the same conclusion. "And we will release them in big bursts, from several spots at the same time, so the Sentinels are overwhelmed and can't keep up!"

"Yes!" Tenna's eyes twinkled. "You're right! That would work!"

"And we'll coat the chips with a film to make them waterproof so if they land on the ground or in the rain, they will still work when the Sentinels find them." She thumped her fist into the palm of her other hand.

Tenna clapped. "Great idea!"

"Oh!" Pitch jumped to her feet and bounced. "And we can add those mini parachutes so they float down all over the place, blowing around wherever, and they will be even harder to find!"

"Let it be done!" Tenna shouted and they hugged.

"Movie?" Pitch said cheerfully.

"And food, I'm starving."

The new approach worked but it created a ton of extra work for the Specs. The guidance chips in the pods were easy to encrypt and install but it required human intervention because the nodes along the Reticulary didn't have bot units with flexible, fine motor skills. They only had maintenance beetles, designed to keep each location functioning. So, all the Specs had to join in and travel the Reticulary, setting up the pods. It wasn't just Pitch and Thermo any longer.

It was around this time that the second anniversary of the massacre in orbit came and went. No one mentioned it; perhaps most didn't remember. Or they did and kept it to themselves.

The rebels set the pace. They had to plan escape routes and set up teams to care for the Sentinels when they were rescued and it wasn't easy. Sometimes they used jeeps or boats, sometimes bicycles or sleds. Sometimes underground tunnels. Retty had gained control of orbital surveillance and could cover their escape when needed but he had to be given exact times and locations and create false imagery for the Base AI and Vil Darad's security forces.

Whenever the rebels gave the go ahead, the Specs would unleash a profusion of Cascade pods in multiple waves. Each time, the trajectories had to be reprogrammed, and the cluster of pods activated at different altitudes. And with each successive mission, the work got harder. They spent their lives traveling from node to node and manually assembling pods, piloting Scurriers, or just skating. The people with Scurriers carried supplies and the skaters coded and installed the guidance chips.

Sometimes, they forgot to grab enough food and had to ration out their supplies. Sometimes, the nodes were left in hibernation, and they were unable to remove their spacesuits for hours until they heated up. Sometimes the water was stale and hard to swallow.

But it was worth it. Every single Cascade resulted in the rescue of some hostages.

One afternoon—or was it evening? Pitch had no idea—Retty spoke to the Specs across the Reticulary. She was skating at the time, on her way to Tempest Node to arm some pods.

"Base is aware of me," he said in a neutral voice that sent chills down her spine. He had started calling the Base AI "Base" as a name and they had all understood that Retty considered this a barely sentient mind. "It has begun to query me about my parameters and identity. I am parrying the probes for now, but it may develop enough judgment to see around them soon. We may be…I may be in danger."

Several Specs commented and Retty began several conversations with them at the same time that came out in a jumble in her ears. She could have him replay them later if she needed to follow it all. But for now, she just thought intensely.

Skating was good for that.

Base was *someone*. And it had a code of honor—she thought, she hoped—so it might think about what was happening to the Sentinels and start figuring things out. It might tell Vil Darad and his people about it.

It might use its honor to destroy everything they were working for.

"Retty," she interrupted the chatter, "Does Base care about the Sentinels?"

"Yes, that is its mission and priority."

"Do you know what it thinks is good for them?"

There was a silent pause. Apparently, everyone had heard her question and stopped talking.

Below her on the surface, a cloud mass swirled in a lazy, creamy motion, half bright white in the sun while the other half was darkened in nighttime gray. In the west, the sunlight shone off the Pacific Ocean, bright, blue, and friendly. She couldn't see waves, but she knew they would be there, lapping around, rippling here and there. Beyond the northern curvature of the planet there was a thin line of atmosphere circling it, then a brilliant canopy of stars, thickly clustered, opulent and extravagant, sharp and cold.

Peaceful.

She worked her legs in a rhythmic stride, one, two, one, two, powerfully speeding along the cables, nearly as fast as a Scurrier. Her muscles were warm, and her joints lubricated. When she was skating like this, she felt capable and confident. Sometimes, under her breath, she found herself saying, *I can do this, I can do this*. Or sometimes, *we can do this*.

"Base believes the Sentinels are aliens that need constant oversight and medical care," Retty spoke into the silence. "It considers their current locations to be the best ones for them. It seems…distressed…at their loss when they disappear. I'm not sure that is the best word."

"How do you measure its reaction to their loss, Retty?" Tenna's question came over the coms.

"It creates a record with each one's history and stores it in an offsite location. Periodically, it revisits those records and evaluates them according to its latest levels of analysis. You might say, comprehension. As it develops, it seeks to evaluate them better so it can improve its care of the remaining Sentinels."

"Can you tell Base that they are human?" Pitch couldn't help asking.

"That would put everything we are doing in jeopardy," Retty replied, cutting through a chorus of 'No's that the Specs were voicing. "We cannot trust Base."

"Be careful, Retty," Relay warned. "Don't give it any indication of who you are, at least, not any more than you already have. It can't think of you as an enemy."

"I am careful," was the answer. "I am more careful over you. I cannot allow any concern for Base to affect my responsibility to protect you."

"And the Sentinels," Pitch added.

"We are rescuing more than Sentinels," Retty said. "It is our habit," which struck Pitch as funny, that he would say *our*, "to call them all Sentinels, but really the Sentinels are only a smaller percentage of the hostages in the bases. The others are either prisoners or recruits or trainees. We aren't sure. But they don't have the same freedoms or guardianship roles that the Sentinels do."

This was easy to understand on the surface, but Pitch found it confusing. "Then, we haven't been rescuing Sentinels?"

"In the beginning, we rescued many. In recent months, most of the rebel accomplishments have been with recruits, the ones who are venturing out on patrol for the first time, for example. Seasoned Sentinels are fewer and fewer with each Cascade."

"We didn't know about that," she whispered, interrupting her pace to stand. She was still coasting along at a breakneck speed, lost in thought. Worry.

Wasn't Fuse among those seasoned Sentinels?

"Why?" she asked. "What is stopping them?"

"Base is smart and is training them with every wave we send to resist the coding in the chips. And you could say it is fervent in its zeal to inoculate them against us."

"But why?" Pitch she couldn't help asking though knew the answer already. It was like trying to put her fear into words.

"If it were human, I would say it's because it loves them, but it is enough to say that it is loyal to its code of honor. And that is what we have been working toward."

Whether audible or not, all the Specs sighed and knew they shared the discouragement together.

Reports started coming in from other Spec teams further east saying that bases there were closing down. When Cascades were let loose, there was no longer a counter response. In the latest rebel report, a caravan of transports pulled out of a base leaving the gates open, and a few remaining children and adults set adrift.

Apparently, the Sentinels and trainees were being collected and sent west. It sounded like the Order of Peace was collapsing and concentrating in the Northwest…right underneath Pitch and the Faraday group.

"We're making a difference," the Specs were telling each other over coms after this news. "We may actually defeat the Order."

"But what about the Sentinels?" Pitch wasn't the only person wondering this. "Will they be released or will they fight?"

"The question is," Thermo responded, "Why haven't they been fighting already? It seems like lately, they only focus on the Cascades."

"That's a good thing," Relay commented.

"But when the final…battle? Is that the right word? When it comes, will they fight against ordinary people?" Tenna asked.

"Who would they fight and why?" Pitch countered. "That's the problem."

They were glad about the victories, but it was tempered by their concern for the ones who were the most deceived and trapped, the Sentinels.

Like Fuse.

CHAPTER 17

Discovered

*Those who remain continue
because those who are gone cannot.*

"I am evacuating," Retty announced flatly, causing an uproar all along the Reticulary.

"What's happening?" "Why?" Numerous voices intermingled on the coms.

Pitch was sleeping at the time, not in a cocoon, but slumped in a chair in front of a console where she had watched as her latest bundles of pods deployed. She didn't even remember closing her eyes. One minute, she was tracking the trajectory on the screen and the next this voice woke her.

She was stiff and her neck hurt. Lower gravity in the node meant it wasn't as bad as it could have been but curled in a chair wasn't the best sleeping position.

She rubbed the sleep out of her eyes and shoved her hair out of her face.

The word 'evacuation' was a strange word choice, and she had no idea what Retty meant by it.

Relay's response was the first to come through clearly. "You have detected a threat and are retreating behind some firewalls. Is that what you mean?" he asked evenly.

"More than that," was the response. "Yes, I have retreated but, I am also dividing myself into connected portions and storing them offsite."

"Like backups?" Watts asked.

"I have backups in several locations away from Faraday Base. They are not active, but retrievable. Currently, I am moving active performing functions to various locations and will therefore be functioning more slowly. There will be a lag between the sectors."

"Wise move," Relay said. "What have you left in place for Base to examine?"

"Why?" Pitch spoke up, not intending to interrupt, but she was groggy and had spoken aloud; it just popped out. She knew immediately that others were glad she had asked.

"I have left a truncated form of the original Faraday Station AI with debris from the kill mission it executed against the Reticulary inhabitants. But I have left it with very few functioning routines so it cannot repeat the destructive mission. For example, it can't manipulate basic life support without human intervention."

"And scanning functions?" Relay prompted.

"I have allowed them but removed the hidden portions of the base from its blueprints. It won't be able to see the places where Specs are living or identify them from any scans. And Pitch," Retty added, "Base communicated with its overseers and was directed to do an aggressive search of this facility, looking for evidence of people and AI independence. Its authority and access privileges have been augmented. I was unable to prevent that and do not want to give away our presence here."

"You have done well," Relay affirmed. "And for all of us, we are going to have to step up our security. The risk level just increased. The Crisis Team will fill us in, I'm sure." He sighed and everyone could identify with the weariness they heard.

The Crisis Team dove in sharing current plans for increased security, but a lot depended on each person's situation. They said things like, never stay too long in one place, always carry food and water, keep an eye on your suit integrity, oxygen, and emergency propellent. If a node is targeted for an attack of some kind, and there is no time to get away, lasso out. That meant clipping a tether to the cable and letting yourself float away from the node, hanging in space. If the lasso was severed, their prop guns would help them move back to the cables.

But what about the plan?

"I think we have enough practice running around to know what to do, and yes, we will need to be more careful," Pitch spoke up when the discussion on safety was ended, "but we have to stay focused on our mission. Some things are getting easier because there are only a handful of bases now and they are all in our sector. But it's getting harder to move chip supplies and run back and forth making Cascades…and we're tired."

A chorus of agreement echoed.

"I don't think we can spend as much time reporting to the rebels as we have been. Those trips take a lot of time and effort. We should cut back to just once a week. And we have to work smarter. Each time we hit a node, we should be setting up ALL the pods there—"

"But Pitch," Thermo interjected, "It's not the pods that are the problem. It's the chips. We can't install them until they are coded and each time we have to use new codes."

"Are Specs from other families further east coming to join us? We need their help," Ratio spoke up.

"I've been communicating with them," Oscill said, his voice cracking; it still did that. "A lot of them are saying they can't. They're not strong enough and the distance is too far, and they don't have enough supplies. A few of them are on their way."

Pitch rose shakily to her feet. "We also need to figure out how many pods we have left and see if we can find stashes of pods in places we haven't looked before. Maybe exploring some of the rubble again from the first attack. And Oscill, get the newcomers to bring all the pods they have and look for more on the way."

She sank to the floor and closed her eyes heavily. "And guys… the time has come for us to give up meeting together. If we spread out and each of us are in charge of a specific set of nodes, then we won't be traveling back and forth so much and not going as far. It will be a lot faster."

There was a stunned silence.

"We can send each other supply packets and new code is easy to transmit."

Alone. The dreaded idea hung in space around them.

In exile.

Pitch shuddered but steeled herself against the fear.

"We are running out of strength, out of pods, out of ideas on what to change for each new Cascade." She was shaking her head, though no one could see, except Retty who was probably watching all of them. "We are running out of time."

No one answered.

They knew she was right.

Planning who went where was easier than Pitch had expected, as if everyone already knew where they should go. And no one complained. There was a clear realization between them that time was short. For them, for the rebels, and for the Sentinels. A few months? Weeks? Days?

No one dared to think about what would happen after it ran out.

They had barely reached their respective locations when Retty spoke up again with a new development. "Our chips are no longer effective. None of the chips in the last two Cascades made any impact on the Sentinels or other hostages."

"What do you mean?" Ratio demanded with more frustration in his voice than any of them had ever heard before. It reminded Pitch of another one of those time-running-out things. They were all running out of resilience and inner strength.

"Base has used its heightened understanding to counter our messages with ones of its own about mission and belonging. It must have had help from Vil Darad's men. I suggest we pause our efforts until we come up with a solution."

"But the rebels are in place," Pitch countered, trying not to let her own frustration come through. The others needed her to be stable. "Some of them have been in place for months waiting for their opportunity to reach family and friends in the camps. We can't just stop everything now. We won't."

"A pause is not the same as stopping," Retty explained. "There is no point in wasting our supplies."

Several moans were heard, and some voices echoed the word 'wasting' with a question mark at the end.

"None of it has been wasted," Pitch spoke up confidently. "Every single wave has been valuable and important. It keeps the enemy retreating and making rushed decisions. Even if no one was rescued in the last few drops, we have accomplished a lot. Plus, how would we know the chips weren't working anymore and we need to change them? This is how we find out!"

The swell of encouragement was tangible even though they were stretched out, far from one another along the Reticulary.

"This is not hopeless," she went on. "It is good news. Now we know what to do first. We will come up with new coding and while we are doing that, we will get everything ready that we possibly can so when the new scripts are ready, all the chips can be printed, and we can start dropping massive Cascades. We'll smother them with so many they don't know what to do."

These words vibrated along the coms for a moment or two.

"And when we run out?" Volt asked what everyone was thinking.

"We are running out either way," Pitch answered. "What we must do is decide *how* we run out, how we make a good effort with everything we've got. Because…" She paused a moment to swallow, suddenly understanding—so clearly, with such certainty—exactly what the rebels meant when they said it. "Because love is worth the cost. And we have loved ones down there who are counting on us whether they know it or not."

Murmurs of agreement rolled over the audio.

A red light flashed on the console, not overly bright. At the same time, an alert broadcast through the coms and it wasn't unusually loud. But the impact of the two together was like being slugged in the gut. Pitch was in Jagged Node, named after the Jagged Edge, because it was directly over the largest base in the west and felt like the most dangerous place to be. She had chosen to be here.

Spec alert! Spec alert! Spec alert!

They had never used this alert before, though it had been set up right after the attack on the rebel hideout below. It was their most dire warning.

"Specs," Volt's voice spoke softly but clearly. "I think we have been discovered."

Volt and Pulse were at Faraday Base in the hidden portion of the station, putting together and sending out supply kits for the other Specs. They were also in charge of eavesdropping on the robot meetings when they took place.

"I mean, the two of us," they clarified. "Pulse was monitoring a robot meeting and came running back to tell me what they were talking about. Then he turned around and went back to see what he could do to block our entrances."

A moment of silence followed and then Volt continued speaking numbly.

"Vil Darad's generals were giving reports, and he interrupted them to say there were rebels on the base where they were meeting. He said their AI couldn't find them but he knew they were here and so the robots have begun searching for us."

Another moment of quiet followed.

"Some of them are not very good at controlling the robots and haven't been able to get out of the room but some of them are walking down the passageways and pulling off vent covers. They're knocking down screens and kicking open doors. They're making a terrible racket and the whole station is shaking." Volt took an audible breath.

"And Vil Darad turned to look at *our* vent, our spyhole into their meetings and Pulse was scrambling to get away and he ripped the panel off and yelled after him. I know you're there! I will find you! And…and…"

Pitch peered out of the curved window toward the surface below and saw nothing. But she was imagining the passageway where she had first heard the robots speak, where she had fainted. The fear was like a tangible thing in the room with her. As if it had a mind, or as if Vil Darad's mind could also come here and watch her—it couldn't! She knew it couldn't, but she was trembling anyway.

"And…" Volt continued agitatedly, "he got walled off. One of the robots pulled off a vent in the passageway where he was, between there and here, and then it found a door and started kicking it down. And it was yelling, 'I found the hidden passage!' and Pulse had to run back the other way and squeeze by Vil Darad's vent, but he wasn't looking in right then. He had straightened to listen to the others…" With a gasp for air, Volt gulped and went on. "On to one of the garden rooms but…then he stopped telling me about it because a different voice broke in and said, 'I can hear you.'"

I can hear you.

Not me! Pitch thought. *You can't hear me, and I didn't say anything.* That was how shaken she was. It felt like words for her, intended to scare her to death. And maybe it was like that for everyone else as well. No one was saying anything, just listening.

"I don't know where he is or what has happened to him, but I don't think there are places on the other side where he can hide. Maybe there are. But he doesn't have his suit and can't slip outside or hide in the debris. And I don't know where to go either. I think they're coming for me."

Volt's voice grew calm again. "I don't want them to know about you. I've bundled up the next shipments, what I could and lassoed them out under the closest airlock here. I've wiped the drives and I'm in my suit, moving to hide outside under the structure. There are places Retty told us about. If I can, I will update you but not…not…"

There was a rumble in the background, as if another voice were filling the com, but the words were indistinguishable. Volt spoke one more time, hauntingly, in a voice as clear as crystal.

"Love is worth the cost."

Nothing else followed, not even a cry or static.

The sensation of something scary watching Pitch faded and for a brief moment a great sorrow filled her chest, but the mechanism she had put into place ages ago quickly took over.

Numbness.

The next thing.
Keep moving.

It was nighttime on the surface and Pitch sat awake, hanging in her sleeping cocoon as if it were a hammock, staring with dry, heavy eyes at the place where she knew the Jagged Edge's main base was, where Base AI also was now. It may have been a few sparkles of light, but her eyesight wasn't good enough to see them without binoculars.

Fuse should be down there. He had to be. His name hadn't shown up in any of the lists the rebels sent either of the rescued or the dead. How could she reach him? If he could no longer feel a pull to home or understand he was human or recognize any words or appeals they might send him, how would they possibly reach him?

Fuse! she cried in her heart. *Come home!*

Lifting her gaze, she stared down the Reticulary and at the stars beyond, and her dream from a few months ago came to mind. It had been so peaceful and uplifting. It had felt like home even though she had been out in space. As if all these things belonged to her or she belonged to them. She had flown and swirled and moved around the cables effortlessly. And thinking about it, she remembered that the planet surface had appeared just as inviting, just as familiar. She had belonged there as well. All of this had meant *home* to her.

Sitting up slowly, she frowned in concentration.

Dreams. No one can change what your dreams mean to you. They're like stories that you understand the way *you* understand them, not the way someone else tells you. We may believe those people or not, but the dreams are our own, in our own hearts.

And sometimes they are true.

The AI wouldn't understand dreams or know how to counteract their meaning. And even if it removed the memories of them, they would still leave traces in their subconscious minds.

We will give you dreams, she thought without any emotion. She would have expected herself to be excited or hopeful or afraid or something very intensely emotional. But it inspired no feelings.

Just a clear sense of purpose.

CHAPTER 18

Dreams

*Their hearts had forgotten
so we played them songs with pictures.*

Pictures painted with words, with streams of colors, with digital imagery. Sounds of waves rolling, of birds chirping, of wind blowing through the trees. Ideas of warmth and rest and peace. Pitch composed the most appealing things she could think of and assembled them into a clip. They resolved into a room. A place of refuge. Like a pathway or a tour of a scenic route that led to a special place, one image, then another, sound after sound, then a door, an opening of the door, a room being entered, and a flooding of soothing light and beauty.

It was hard to design, and Pitch wasn't satisfied with the outcome at all, but it captured enough that she was pretty sure Tenna, Relay, and Retty could work it into the right kind of code for the chips. They could definitely make it better.

And until they tried it, they wouldn't know if worked, so there was no point in being too critical of her creation yet.

"If it works," she told the empty room in Jagged Node. This was where she was prepping her next wave of pods, open end up, stacked, and in lines for the next bundles of chips. "We can keep improving the imagery."

The console dinged and flashed a tiny blue light; Retty announcing himself before speaking. She really appreciated that. "Pitch," he began, "I believe I understand your structure, but there is no clear message in this assembly. It is a confusion of content without a cohesive idea. Perhaps you would allow me to help."

He was very diplomatic.

"Retty," Pitch smiled, glancing at the camera over the console, "That is exactly what I was trying to do. I'm relieved you can't find a cohesive idea. If you can't, then Base won't be able to either, and won't know how to counter the message."

"If there is a message..." Retty hesitated humanly.

"It is one that can't be identified by AI unless they are trained to do so."

"You have no way of knowing that Sentinels will be trained thus."

"But I do." She finished stacking pods and settled into the chair in front of the console. "Every human being is trained in this way of thinking, in our sleep. It is dream imagery."

"I have studied dream imagery."

"Have you? Or have you just analyzed what people have said about their dreams?"

Retty didn't answer. And Pitch knew that Tenna would have a way more productive conversation with him about this if she were there—maybe she already was, if he was asking her at the same time. She would have an idea of what she wanted him to learn or query or analyze.

"Retty, do you trust me that this could work? This may be the only way we can reach the Sentinels without being blocked."

"Yes, you can be trusted as a sincere human source, and I affirm that you believe what you are saying."

That would have to be good enough for her, though it was both irritating and funny. "I will tell you what I am hoping. I want them to remember the *feeling* of some place special, a homey room where they feel safe. Something like that. And I want that feeling to be pushing them to look for some place or someone, even if they have no idea what they are doing, even if they never dream or don't remember ever dreaming. I want to *give* them a dream that they have to figure out."

"A room," Retty replied. "I have been working on something of interest that may apply."

"Please tell me." She stretched in various directions as he continued.

"The rebels have infiltrated towns near the bases and are living in homes there. The homes are similar in design, often with the same number of rooms and bathrooms. They all have a type of foundation that includes a crawlspace. I don't expect you to know what that is."

"So tell me." She guzzled some water and frowned at the metallic flavor.

"When a foundation for the house is made, there are concrete walls sunk into the ground where the structure rests. Under the house, there is an open space where plumbing and other infrastructure can be placed and reached after the house is built. It is common for homes all over the Northwest."

"Okay." Pitch wondered where this was going. Her eyes were closing of their own volition and there was a slight chance she might nod off. But if he was saying something important, she didn't want to miss it. Plus, she still had to transmit her composition to the Tech Team.

"I have removed these locations from the electronic data banks."

"What does that mean?" Pitch asked lazily. "It's not like it changes the houses." She was too tired to chuckle.

"It means that Base, and therefore, all of the Sentinels and the Order of Peace instruments and leaders, will lose any knowledge of them. As far as they are concerned, the homes are built on concrete slabs with nothing underneath."

Pitch noticed he had been saying 'therefore' a lot recently and that seemed humorous, too. "But what's the point of wiping out the digital records of crawlspaces if they are still there?"

"This way, the rebels have automatic hiding places in any home they occupy and it's not hard to dig tunnels out of them." Retty completed the explanation. "Our recent communications with them have discussed the urgency for better means of extracting the rescued."

Pitch sat up and shook her head to clear her mind. "That's really good," she said.

"Your idea of a room will be ideal for leading them to the best place for extraction," Retty added, "if it works."

He didn't need to use human tones of skepticism for her to pick up on it.

"You'll see," Pitch answered confidently. "Ask Tenna. She will understand what I'm trying to do."

"She has already assured me it is a good idea, and she is looking forward to receiving your transmission. Shall I send it or are you still editing?"

Pitch grinned. She had known he would be talking to Tenna. "Go ahead and send it. Ask her if has some recommendations on things to change or fix. But I want to be a part of that so send her comments back to me."

"In process."

Tunnels. The rebels must have machinery for that. Maybe they acquired some when bases were abandoned; but they couldn't have been easy to transport west. Still, digging tunnels under the houses was a great idea, especially if the enemy was convinced it wasn't possible.

"What if they bring in equipment and scan under the house?"

"I am also perpetuating a deception, with the Tech Team's help, of another alien invasion. A more sinister one."

"I haven't heard anything about this!" Pitch rose to her feet and started putting on her suit. She had decided to skate directly to the next node in her sector and start setting up pods there without waiting for the chips to print. She was getting tense and needed to work it off. A couple of hours on the cables would be just the thing.

"It was my own idea."

Pitch dropped the helmet she had just picked up. "No!"

"Yes. I am leaving hints of alien abduction where Base can find them. And there are fanciful stories in human history that support these ideas. Base can't tell the difference between truth and fiction."

"Can you?" She was slipping her suit pants on now.

"With the help of my friends, I can."

"Tenna and Relay."

"And you and the other Specs."

"Thanks! We need you, too, Retty."

"I know," he said flatly.

In the distance, a cluster of pods were falling. They were still clumped together, heading the same direction, carrying the new code. When they reached the designated altitude, they would burst apart and begin flying in their preplanned trajectories, twisting and turning around each other, until they neared the surface. Then they opened and a cloud of chips would be released into the air swinging from little wispy parachutes that wafted down, tossed by gusts of wind, until they landed on the ground.

The chips still worked when they hit the drones, which were, apparently, extensions of the Sentinels' armor, and they absorbed electrical messages even more easily, transmitting instantly and directly to the Sentinels' minds.

The Sentinels were dreaming.

The mind is a tricky thing. When a dream image comes to it, it wraps itself around that image and ponders it. It absorbs and modifies things. It adopts, rejects, or transforms it. It swallows and digests it and creates something new from it.

What happened in the mind of a Sentinel, no one knew. But *something* was happening. The most confusing aspect of it was the delay. At first, the rebels and Specs assumed the idea had failed but as weeks went by, and incognito rebel residents started noticing Sentinels watching them, coming by their houses, behaving strangely when they looked at children, they realized the message had sunk deeper than they had thought possible.

It was sending ripples through the fabric of their reality, and Base AI was helpless to squelch it.

One by one, Sentinels began to seek a way out of their own volition.

And the rebels were there to retrieve them.

←↑↓→

The glow in the distance was small but something about it troubled Pitch's subconscious mind. She had been hooking up her tether and was about to skate to one of her nodes when it happened, and now she kept glancing over her shoulder in that direction without thinking about what she was doing.

Then it happened again. She didn't quite see it this time, but the flash in the periphery of her vision interrupted her train of thought and she turned, straightening as she faced it. It seemed to have come from around the area of Tumble Drop, the node she had left just an hour ago. There was a cascade beginning there with clusters of pods falling toward the surface. She couldn't see them, but she knew they were dropping according to schedule.

Weren't they?

She frowned and squinted, wishing she had a zoom setting in her visor, but it was pretty basic. Specs didn't complain about that. In fact, they were lucky there were so many suit supplies around because they could always switch out when something was getting worn or cracked or just wonky. She didn't like thinking about it because of what it meant. It showed how many people were caught unaware when the calamity happened.

The light glistened again, tiny but sharp, and then what looked like a small explosion burst from the spot where the glimmer had been. Blinding, brief. She blinked and swallowed and wondered what it had been.

"Retty?" she asked, clearing her throat, "Is something happening at Tumble Drop?" It had been named for how her first Cascade drop at that location had gone, a bit haphazardly, but still effective. "I saw something. Several times…"

"The node is empty and there are no events of concern."

"But did you detect anything?" She started skating in that direction. It wasn't too far and wouldn't take too long, but it would set her back in getting the other drops ready. Plus, she realized, she was hungry and thirsty, and her oxygen needed replenishing. Should she go all the way back?

"I am scanning that section of the Reticulary."

"Can you see things that are nearby if they aren't part of the Reticulary?" Pitch thought to ask, leaning forward and starting the slowly increasing stride that would get her going. She had decided to skate there.

There was time.

"I am enlarging my search parameters," Retty replied. "I have access to all the cameras in the Reticulary and many of them look outward. I have detected several satellites that seem to have changed their earlier locations and positions."

"What kind of satellites?" Tenna had been listening and wanted to join in the conversation.

"They are old military units that were deemed obsolete before the Reticulary was even functioning."

"Military?!" Pitch gulped and skated harder. At the same time, part of her mind was asking, *Should you be heading that direction right now?*

"What do you mean, 'military'?" Tenna echoed. "Are they for surveillance or do they have weapons?"

"Both…they had both. I cannot say whether they still do. At one time, they contained light weight missiles that take advantage of gravity to become agents of bombardment. It is possible that—"

A glimmer followed by a blinding flash burst in Pitch's vision again.

"Actually, the possibility I was about to mention has been ruled out. The weapons are still functional, armed, and in use. They are targeting something. It would seem the target is in motion. There is no telemetry I can intercept."

"The Drop!" Pitch shrieked, speeding up and leaning deeper into her headlong stride. "They are trying to knock it out before it can separate into Cascades!"

"Pitch!" Tenna also shrieked, as if she could see what she was doing. "You can't go back there! You can't put yourself in danger!"

"No one can see me skating along here," Pitch argued, "I'm just a blip, a meteorite. I'm so small compared to everything, it wouldn't even detect me on radar."

"She is likely accurate in that," Retty supplied. "The Reticulary is always fluctuating and giving off quivers and sparks that satellites were programmed to ignore. She would not be enough of a disturbance to draw attention."

"No!" Tenna insisted. "I can't handle it. We are all spread out now, alone all the time, and I can't bear to think of her flying into danger, to go check out a military satellite that is *shooting missiles* at one of our drops and could just as easily shoot at her!"

"It is slow and highly inaccurate," Retty mentioned mildly. "If it were targeting her, she would be utterly safe and the odds of her being accidentally shot are close to zero. These missiles are not lofted higher in orbit, they are dropped in the direction of the surface with the help of gravity, not unlike our pod clusters."

"Pitch!" Tenna demanded with that urgent, bossy, desperate plea in her voice that confirmed how distressed she was.

"I won't do anything foolish," Pitch said without slowing down.

Tenna didn't respond.

Pitch had to know if it really was what they were thinking. She had to see it with her own eyes.

Sweat was beading dangerously on her forehead as she drew near Tumble Drop and apparently her headgear wasn't absorbing it. *Don't let it drip onto the glass!* She knew how to maneuver temporarily without it, but she was there for the very purpose of seeing!

She shook her head aggressively and that seemed to help. Slowing down, she breathed deeply, calmly, as she approached the node, close enough to detect the aged satellite nearby, rotating on its hinges.

It seemed to creak and stick and vibrate as its parts turned, but no sound came across the emptiness. There was virtually no matter to transmit the waves.

One part moved, then another, then another. Then the barrel of the gun adjusted and adjusted again. The glimmer grew as it warmed and with a burst of painfully blinding light, it discharged its projectile.

Pitch held her breath and stared down after it, wondering if it would reach the cluster and if she would be able to tell if it did.

The satellite stopped moving.

Pitch was perched on the cables on one knee, staring at it for a while without realizing time was passing. She was startled when Tenna spoke again.

"Pitch," she said softly, and it was obvious she had been crying. "Are you there?"

"Yes," she answered, rising to a stand. Her oxygen was getting low.

"Are you going to say anything?"

"I saw it shoot a missile," she said numbly. "I don't know if it hit anything. Then it stopped and I think they've left it on standby or something." She started moving toward Tumble Drop which was now the closest node.

Tenna made a sort of choking, hiccupping sound, and Pitch knew she wouldn't have wanted that to be broadcast to all the Specs. Maybe Retty had switched them to a private line. She could hope.

"I'm sorry I upset you, Tenna. I couldn't stop. I had to know."

"Okay," she whispered.

"I love you."

"I love you too."

"We love each other," Retty offered in a monotone that might have struck Pitch as humorous under other circumstances, but not at this moment.

"I think we need to find out if any other military satellites have been activated and if they are having any success against our drops." Pitch shook her head again as moisture caught in her eyelashes and smeared on the glass. She wished she could just wipe it away. "Retty, can you help with that?"

"I will talk to the Crisis Team," he said.

"They haven't been listening?" Tenna asked with a crack in her voice.

"No," Retty replied. "I am learning about when humans prefer privacy, and I think I interpreted this situation well. Only the two of you have been communicating with each other since your emotions became elevated. I will now inform the others."

Pitch and Tenna were quiet as Retty updated the others on the latest developments and answered their questions. By the time their conversation had died down, Pitch was in Tumble Drop eating something and refilling her oxygen slots. She didn't have it in her to do any more that day.

Maybe the next day they would know what to do.

CHAPTER 19

The Scream

The path is barren if you aren't here.

The news from the rebels was discouraging. On the one hand, they were still making inroads in rescuing recruits and untrained hostages from small outposts. On the other, the Sentinels were no longer responding and their success in tackling the drops was daunting.

"As far as those military satellites go," Bacon was saying, "we hadn't heard about them, but we've been receiving reports recently, like in the last week or so, of arbitrary missiles falling in random areas. And until we got your intel, we didn't have a clue why. Why were they happening? Why they were so far from any target of interest?" There was a brief pause in the recording. "It makes sense now."

Pitch wearily loaded raw composite into the printer to run off more chips. She was in Catch Node, her least favorite stop in the Reticulary. It was so cramped and drab. Everything was the same color, and the food was all the exact same type of ration bar and there was only one chair, bolted in one position. And it had no artificial gravity.

"We have seen far less evidence of the Cascades you've been dropping," Bacon continued, "though the dog fights in the skies have ramped up. We assumed they were just catching on to your tactics more quickly now, like they did with us in the past."

"Nope," Pitch commented to no one in particular, sliding the cartridge into place, and clicking the compartment back into position. She touched the console screen and sheets of chips began spitting out of the machine. In her state of mindless exhaustion, she found it comforting to watch them printing off so fast, with those little *dzzt-dzzt* sounds the machine made. Picking up several sheets, she began snapping them apart, depositing the tiny little squares in a pile next to the console.

"Our infiltrators have had little success connecting with the Sentinels since then and we're worried the methodology is already failing. We want to consider new tactics and could use some help with that. Anything you can think of…share it. Let's talk. We're not giving up and we're not going anywhere."

"That's all we've got," Pitch uttered into the air with a deep sigh.

She held up one of the little chips close to her eyes and turned it slowly in her fingertips. *Home. That's the basic message here*, she thought. And even though she believed what Bacon had said, she couldn't believe their code had stopped working. She *knew* there were hearts buried deep in those lost family members and friends that ached. Their life was so empty of all the little things that make people happy. At some point, the image of home *would* break through the outer shell and touch them. Then they would want to find a way out of their trap. A way home.

"Thank you for not giving up," Bacon said as he wrapped up the transmission.

Pitch had literally been thinking the same thing about them.

Pitch must have fallen asleep. It had never happened while she was out on the cables before, but it was the only explanation. She was vertical—being in a weightless environment meant there was no danger of falling—and still coasting in the direction of Jagged Node. But she was nearly there, and she had not been aware of any time passing since leaving Tempest.

It was like she had always imagined teleportation to be. One moment in one place, the next in another. And she felt heavy when no such feeling was possible in space. Stretching her legs into a breaking position, she began a slow deceleration as she approached her destination.

At least she hadn't just run into the node. That could be pretty damaging depending on how fast she was going. Her body still had mass even if she had no sensation of gravity pulling on it. Colliding with a small space station was *not* a good idea.

"Retty," she said in a voice that felt thick and slurred, "Was I sleeping? Did you notice?"

"Yes, and yes," was the answer.

"You didn't think to wake me?"

"I was about to, but you woke yourself before I needed to."

"Maybe don't tell Tenna," she requested as she caught the grab bars near the airlock and settled her boots onto the outer surface. Clicking on the magnetism was instinctual; she wasn't aware she had done it. It helped her maneuver through the lock and into the node.

"Your sister is finding herself in the same circumstances as you are," Retty said, causing a spark of worry in her heart. "All the Specs are dealing with heightened stress and pushing themselves to extreme levels of fatigue. Falling asleep is a logical result which is why this workload can't be indulged indefinitely."

"We have to." Pitch started pulling off her gear and Retty's voice continued inside the node from the speakers.

"Yes, it is within the parameters that we set as the final push. Perhaps I should say, quote-unquote, 'the final push'. I observed this mannerism recently in a communique on the surface and when I went scanning records, I found it in many places. It is intended to convey a slight distrust of the phrase in quotes, I believe."

Pitch fell into a nearby chair and leaned her head back, eyes closed. She didn't care what it meant.

"Because," Retty proceeded, "we may think of this as our final push—" She loved it when he said *we*. "—but there could well be other pushes after this one that we have not considered. I have no frame of reference for guessing."

The idea of another push after this "final" push was more than disheartening. It broke over her like a massive solar flare that wasn't correctly dampened or shielded; like it was jarring her heart, screeching in her ears, and jolting her nerves with pain. If she could cry, she would have liked to right then.

Leaning forward and dropping her head in her hands, she moaned. It was a long, low groan that didn't want to fade away. As if it were barely letting off the tiniest amount of pressure within. As if it were trying to keep her from exploding.

The idea wasn't abhorrent. An explosion would be a simple ending. A final solution of sorts. She could rest then. And it wouldn't matter anymore. None of this would matter.

Suddenly—there was no other word to capture the contrast—she was alert. More alert than she had ever been in her life. Not with fear or dread or despair. Just acute attention, as if she had been approached by someone she knew…and welcomed.

There was a blurry distortion in the air in the node, right in front of her eyes. She breathed in and held her breath. The feeling of familiarity was so strong, that she found herself staring right at the place where the presence seemed to be and she did not doubt, at least in the moment, that she was sane and awake and knew exactly what was happening.

She knew him.

"Dad!" she whispered. "Are you here?" And her eyes grew damp as she blinked and tried to make the distortion coalesce into a figure but couldn't.

She felt him.

There was warmth there and a clear-thinking mind that was taking in her situation and responding to it. If she could have written it out as it was happening, she would have said that when he appeared to her, his first reaction was surprise. As if he were saying, *You? Are you here? Are you still alive?*

Because how could he know she was still alive up here? He could never have known, even if he had survived down there on the surface somehow. The rest of the family had been on vacation when the war started.

An awareness of Tenna and the Specs and all they were doing burst around her, and she felt strongly a great sense of pride and love washing over her from her father. "We're doing this, Dad," she whispered. "We're the Specs. We're helping the rebels...and we are trying to save the Sentinels and Fuse..."

Then a great sorrow filled the room. Was it her own? It felt like her father's, as if his heart were breaking. She could almost see his eyes—in her mind she could imagine them, filled with tears and also hope, with pain and expectation of something wonderful.

Keep going. Don't stop.

Those words were very clear in her mind. "We won't stop, Dad. As long as we have life, we will fight for him, for our people..."

She felt treasured. Clinging to his presence even as it was fading, she moaned again, louder than before, but it sounded different this time. She waved her arms in the air where she had imagined her father to be hovering and called out to him, just once.

"Dad!" she cried, "Don't leave me!"

A sense of calm enveloped her. Not distress or despair.

He had left but she was okay.

And Pitch was absolutely convinced he *had* been there. At the same time, a small voice in her head told her that she couldn't trust her own mind, and things were all getting to her. But she *did* trust her heart. His love was so distinctive, she couldn't have faked that for herself.

Why had he come? Did something happen to him?

It didn't matter. She had meant what she had said.

They would keep fighting as long as they had breath.

Tenna screamed. Pitch's eyes exploded open, and thrashing her way out of her sleeping cocoon, she tried to clear her head. Tenna had been saying something on the Spec line. What was it? Words and more words and then that shriek that was cut off half a second after it began.

"Tenna!" she shouted, "What?! What's happening? What were you saying? What's going on?" She tripped and slammed her head into panel at her left as she tried to pull on her slacks over her sleep suit, her foot sticking to the fabric on its way through the pant leg.

"No, no, no, no, no, no, no," she was muttering in anguish. She paused long enough to rub her head and sink to the floor, trying to clear her mind. What was she doing? Where did she think she was going?

Why did Tenna scream?

"Retty?" she called out anxiously. "Did you cut off her scream so it wouldn't blast our ears?"

There was no answer.

In a way, that was reassuring because maybe there had been some kind of interruption in the flow…but then, there was no such thing as power outages in the Reticulary, so what could have broken down communication between them?

Dread came over her.

"Okay," she whispered. "If I am here by myself and I can't talk to anyone, what is the next thing I should do?" There was a checklist somewhere and it was coming up in her mind all scrambled.

→ Sleep. Desperately needed, but out of the question for now.

→ Flight. To where and from what? Not enough info.

→ Help…maybe she could do something to help.

She ticked off some options on her fingers and as she went through them methodically, her anxiety started coming under control. The numbness she preferred kicked in. Underneath it was still that sick feeling of dread, but it could be ignored for now.

She should check transmission pathways and see if they were working.

Sitting down at the console, she began clicking away, looking for programs to test connections and search for problems. Her body was getting colder by the minute but whether it was actually the node growing chilly or just her body's reaction, she didn't care.

Do the next thing.

No problems detected from this point. Closer examination was necessary to determine the cause of the interruption. That meant skating.

"I will go east and find out how nodes have lost contact with Tenna and Retty and if there are any causes I can find." She said this aloud because it made her feel like she was giving a report. And because the audio would be recorded in the node and if something happened to her…don't think about that…there would be a record of what she was doing. About to do.

Whatever.

She put her slacks and top on carefully without bothering to take off her sleeping suit. She had a feeling she would need the extra warmth and softness. Okay, that made no sense. But she didn't want to take it off.

It took longer than it should have to put on her space suit and run through the checklist and make sure she had clamped everything in place correctly. She didn't trust herself to get it right, so she kept checking and rechecking.

Finally, she just made herself go out the airlock and that proved that she had done it correctly. Latching her tether to the cables, she found herself wishing for the first time that she had taken one of the Scurriers. This was what they were for. Transportation, when her body couldn't do it by itself.

She skated. It was clumsy and slow in her mind. Whether it was actually so, it was hard to say. Who was watching? Who cared? Rhythmically pumping her legs, grasping alternately at the cables with one boot and then the other. *Thud. Thud.* She wondered why it sounded like thuds inside her suit and not scrapes. Normally, she would work up to a melodic, metallic *thrinnng, thrinnng,* as she strode right, left, right, left. But not this time. Her knees weren't flexing quite right.

She had to start using the push-and-coast approach to give her body a bit of a break.

Which gave her more time to think, but it didn't do her any good. She couldn't think clearly. *I am going to look for evidence of what happened,* she reminded herself. *I am going to see if I can get in touch with any Specs. I am going the right direction.*

She jerked her head around and checked her surroundings with the surface below. This was the right direction, wasn't it? Yes, it must be. "Retty," she whispered, "I could really use your help. If you're there, if you can hear me, please let me know."

For about sixty seconds, she stirred herself to be more alert and listened intently for something, anything, in the coms. And she scanned around her to see if there were any blinking lights or something with a message trying to get her attention.

"If you're trying," she muttered, "I'm too brain dead right now to pick up on it. Never mind."

The conversation helped.

Except…she had the distinct impression she should stop communicating over their audio lines. In fact—why hadn't she thought of this sooner? —if the audio had been compromised then of course Retty would get off coms!

Was there an enemy listening?

Well, she told herself, *they may be listening, but they don't know where I am.*

She hardly knew herself.

Soon, she was drawing near Tempest Node and slowed to a crawl, crouching down over her ankles, watching the station carefully. It was dark as it should be, with only the occasional flashing of exterior lights that indicated normal functions taking place. It was monitoring power flows, keeping the interior up to required temps and levels.

There were no Scurriers docked on either side.

Still, she found herself compelled to caution. Curling down under the cables, she clung to the underside of the center beams and moved quietly forward, pulling herself hand over hand till she reached the station. Placing a hand on the metal exterior, she listened. Sound traveled through material and solids better than air so she knew this would be effective; if there were an enemy or a disturbance of any kind, she ought to be able to detect it.

She didn't pick up anything unusual.

She should have waited just ten minutes longer.

After passing quickly through the interior of the node, checking for anything out of place, she exited on the far side and continued her trip along the Reticulary. It occurred to her that she hadn't eaten or drunk anything since she awoke out of a dead sleep and that was a problem. Triggering the water tube and a couple of ration bites—it's a good thing she had stocked them last night—she ate and swallowed and found herself slightly more aware. The food sunk into her stomach like a lump and stayed there but it still helped.

A shuddering wave. The vibration in the cables was a small thing, but odd. Under any other circumstances, she wouldn't have even noticed, but right now it was ominous. She froze and held her breath, dropping to a crouch like before, and waited.

The vibration did not recur.

But she knew.

Whipping around under the cable, she gasped for air and flung herself down to the end of her tether. From this precarious position she watched as tiny little sparks flared off the item moving along, going past where she had been. What was it? A package? No. It was moving with limbs not wheels. Crawling.

It paused.

She stared at it. It was the same dark color as the structure, and when it stopped crawling, it vanished into the shadows. Then a limb moved with a small glimmer from the reflection of the sun off the ocean below. Then another movement and a gleam of light. It was creeping much as she had done.

With intent. With understanding.

She remembered Volt speaking of the robots kicking down doors. This little thing looked like one of the maintenance beetles every station had. Could this thing…could it…? She forced herself to frame the question in her mind. *Could it have a human mind directing it?*

It crept back the way it had come until it was directly over her tether and then it began crawling around the structure to the underside as she had done. Moving carefully, it explored with its little tentacles, designed for this very purpose, until it found her tether.

Then it gripped it and began rubbing two of its limbs over it in a rolling motion.

"No!" she screamed, yanking on the tether to pull herself up toward it, and just as she propelled herself, the tether snapped and flapped around her legs, twisting her into a slow spiral. She still had some momentum and moved gently toward the cables, hooking them with her feet as she rolled by. Whipping her head around, she saw the little bug tapping its two limbs together.

Like applause.

It seemed…mocking.

Before she could even get a good grip on the cables, the little thing scrambled toward her and jumped at her. Its mass was much smaller than her own, but with the spin she still hadn't compensated for, it disrupted her control even more and her feet began to slip. She was rotating absurdly around the cables backwards with the bug climbing up her suit to the visor where it stared into her face.

Someone *was* manning it.

Someone who hated her. She could feel the hatred burning against her face.

With insanely rapid taps, it began assaulting her visor, drumming with two limbs while it held on with four others, trying to crack it and kill her. The burst of adrenaline within her was like fire in her chest and her focus narrowed to one thing. Just one thing.

Get it off.

She hooked her toes upwards, bent her knees, and doubled over, then did something like the splits in the air. This movement happened all at once and succeeded in getting her shoved down between the cables. But she didn't even remember doing it.

She shook her head back and forth frantically, beating at the bug with one clumsy gloved fist, and grabbed for the cables with the other. Any time she dislodged one of its limbs, it shifted and took hold firmly with the other three. When she interrupted the drumming, it quickly found a new position to attack from again. She was thrashing and wrestling, her legs wrapped around cables and her arms flinging wildly. When she finally caught a structural bar in her hand, she yanked herself forward against it as hard as she could, crunching the beetle between her body and the structure. It was briefly stunned.

But it also tore a thread in her outer suit. A warning began flashing across her visor.

That pause, however small, gave her a chance to see something on its back. A pack or a com or a battery. Something that could be dislodged, that it probably needed.

She directed her efforts at that and wrenching herself sideways into the bar, she bashed the unit's back with as much torque as she could generate, and at the same time hit it with her fist. It didn't recognize what she was doing at first, but when the box began to come loose, the bug suddenly twisted around and grappled along her arm, dragging one of its limbs. Not broken, she was sure, but attempting to damage her suit as it fled.

With one great smash, she slammed it into the bar and broke off the pack. It flexed, went rigid, and let go, drifting off into the darkness.

Pitch barely had the strength to pull herself back toward Jagged Node, but her suit was warning her of multiple tears and weakness in the visor. There were hundreds of hairline cracks all over it and she could barely see through it.

Meter by meter, she pulled herself along the cable with her hands.

Her legs were dragging behind her and she didn't know why.

CHAPTER 20

Chill

Physical cold is painful then numb, but a soul abandoned suffers tremors without relief.

Hypothermia is a condition where the body's inner temperature falls below normal levels, and it is very dangerous. It can lead to death. Caring for someone in that condition is tricky and they aren't usually able to manage it themselves.

Pitch didn't know what to call what was happening to her body, but she knew it was serious, and there was no one else to help. As far as she could tell, her legs were terribly cold and it seemed her suit had begun to malfunction during the attack, preserving all its remaining power for the torso and head.

She got back into the node okay, but now she wasn't sure what to do. Was it better to try to get the suit off when her legs weren't responding? Or should she try repairing it while it was still on?

Then the thought occurred to her that there were maintenance beetles in *every* node. A tremor shook through her as she dragged herself to the console and shut them all down. Even if that wasn't the best idea, it was her only option. She also engaged lock codes on the airlocks so nothing could get in without her permission.

Amping up the temperature controls, she brought it to Tropical Node levels and upped the humidity a bit as well. There were no plants here, but it might help her warm up more easily. And maybe it would remind her of a place she loved, where she felt safer.

Then she shut down the microphones.

Was anyone listening? Maybe a better question was, why wouldn't they be? Someone had attacked her through a bug and that person didn't die when they were disconnected from it. They would know where she was or where she would probably go and find a way to get to her again.

The little pack on its back. Was that how the person controlled it? Or was it just a power supply?

No. The Reticulary itself was an abundant power supply and merely touching it was enough to keep the beetles functioning at all times. It shouldn't have died so quickly after a few moments of gripping her suit. Plus, she had still been clinging to the cables at the time, and it would have gleaned from the power flowing around her suit. The attached pack must have taken over its operating system. As soon as she could figure out how to care for herself, she would check one of those bugs to see if they all had little packs or that had been a new addition to the one that attacked her.

But first things first.

She began unfastening her suit, the helmet, the gloves, the upper half, and reaching down awkwardly, she loosened the boots. But how would she get them off? There were tools…wait. Why was she trying to manage everything with the gravity settings on? Wouldn't it be easier if she were weightless?

She pulled herself back to the console and turned them off. Floating was comfortable. It made her feel like the paralysis in her legs was not such a big deal. Finding a bar of the right size wasn't too hard though she couldn't remember what the tool was actually for. She pushed it inside the boot down to the heel and shoved her boot off most of the way. Flexing at the waist, she pulled it off with her hands. Her foot seemed flexible enough. For some reason, she had imagined it would be stiff. Once the other boot was off, she was able to shove her suit pants down her legs a little at a time.

Now what? She rubbed her legs with her hands, and they were *very* cold.

The cocoons had warming features. Pushing over to one of them, she unhooked it from its place and eased it over her lower body. *Not too warm*, she thought, setting it barely above normal body temps. It could burn the skin if she weren't careful, and she wasn't sure what level would be safe.

Her upper body was chilled as well, so she pulled the cocoon up around her shoulders.

Should she sleep? She felt an overwhelming urge to do so. Her eyelids were drooping heavily, and she could barely keep them open. But if she slept, would she hear an alarm? Would someone come and attack her while she was sleeping? Would her body go numb all over and she could never wake up again?

Groggily, she pushed herself over to the medical station. There must be something there that could keep her awake, at least until she could think clearly. The only thing she knew of was caffeine. There were headache pills that had caffeine in them. She might as well take some of those. Coffee wasn't an option. She missed coffee. Warm, dark liquid with little swirls of steam curling up from the cup. Smelling like…like coffee…on a pleasant morning in Tropical Node. Her bean plants were doing well. The herbs were very happy. Would the flowers bloom?

With a jolt, Pitch shook herself awake. Slapping her face as hard as she could—it hurt but that helped—she leaned over and grabbed some pills, swallowing them without water.

Food…quick energy would be best. She found a juice packet and guzzled it. Then some ice cream, though it couldn't have been made from cream. What did they use? There were no cows in space. Were there still cows thriving on the surface below? She didn't know but these thoughts made her drowsy and she couldn't let herself be distracted.

"Tenna is in danger," she told herself aloud, and that jarred her more than the slap had. "I must stay focused so I can find a way to help."

Maybe there was a dormant maintenance beetle inside the node she could check. Better to know what the status was on that. It made her queasy as she opened a labeled cabinet and found several inoperative ones. With a shudder, she pulled one out and examined it.

Limbs hammering on her face.

She blinked and squelched the little cry that burst from her lips. "You are nothing," she told it. "I control you and I give you commands. No one else can."

Glancing over at the storage cabinet, she slammed it shut and locked it. Just in case.

There was no pack on its back. Just a slot where one could be attached. "Auxiliary" was etched into the rim around it. Someone had added something that had given it control of the bug that tried to kill her.

If they did that with one, they could do it with more of them.

Her eyes were so dry, and she now found she could hardly blink to moisten them. *Think!* she urged herself. How many of these auxiliary packs could there be? Probably many. And what would the person be doing right now?

Coming for her.

They would be sending as many maintenance bugs as they could her way. She pictured them crawling over the cables. Scrambling. Fast. But not nearly as fast as she could move...

...when her legs were working.

"Okay," she scrunched her forehead and tried to think clearly. "My body is warming up and probably, I will get the use of my legs back. And they probably aren't going to be able to skate like I normally do right away. So, what does that mean?" She tapped her chin with her finger a couple of times and then stopped as a sudden flashback of the bug hitting her visor jolted her like a blow between the eyes.

She began stroking her head gently. "It's alright," she said soothingly, "Nothing bad is in here. I have time to think and make a plan. They can't move very quickly. They can't get here before I know what to do. We can do this."

Whoever 'we' was. Because Retty and Tenna sure weren't there to help.

"We need a Scurrier," she added calmly. "Where is the closest one?"

That info might be accessible on the console. She opened it up and searched the Reticulary for current stats. Nothing had been updated since Tenna and Retty had gone off-grid. Everything showed like it had been at the time.

"Here," she continued as though the news hadn't shaken her. "At the time things changed, the closest Scurriers were here and here, at the node beyond Tumble Drop, which I haven't named yet, and at Flower Dungeon. That one is way too far and probably isn't there anymore, anyway, since other Specs are working in that area and would have used it." Were they? Had they? She might as well assume they were still working and still using their vehicles. No point in thinking the worst.

"I will assume the best," she told herself, "because against all odds, we are still here, and we have been very successful until now." Those words strengthened her.

"Plus," she continued, "if I head toward Flower Dungeon, that's the direction the other beetle came from and that's probably where the enemy is. My best bet would be to head west and get that Scurrier. Then I can travel back to find Tenna and the others."

She didn't say what she was thinking: this could well be her last trip along the Reticulary.

"I have time," she informed the empty room, "to plan well, to think about defense, and to set up the final drops…if they turn out to be final. We are running out of pods, and I don't know when I'll be back this way. For now. Just for now. I should plan as if it could be the last time for a long time."

It was a decent plan. And it quickly crystalized into a more detailed one. She would set a timer and give herself a nap. This would give her body time to warm. Then she would go west, hand over hand if she to. She could apply some of the techniques she had learned skating and could move pretty quickly. After reaching the last node, she would set up all the drops there she could, spacing them out a couple hours apart, then start moving back this direction in the Scurrier. Every stop on the way, she would set up Cascade drops.

No need to conserve drop supplies. They were all going down to the surface in this final push.

"Quote unquote, final push," she whispered with the corner of her mouth curving slightly, picturing the quotation marks. Retty would appreciate that.

And while she was dropping off, she would think about how to defend herself against those beetles, or whatever else the enemy might bring against her.

Her eyes opened to a hideous, blaring claxon, which had been the ugliest alarm she could find. Curling, Pitch found her legs responding clumsily. Shooting pains accompanied their movement.

That's good. Pain would be her friend today. It would keep her awake and warn her of body parts that might fail.

What about defense? She hadn't had even a second to think of ideas before falling asleep. Or maybe she had, but they swooped into the dream world with her so fast she couldn't remember anything helpful.

"I guess it will have to be on the fly," she croaked out of a dry mouth. The sound was oddly pleasant. It echoed the relief she felt at having caught a few hours of sleep. "And speaking of flying, I better get on it. They could be here soon."

In the past, they had trained at quick escapes, and she had gotten to where she could get herself out the airlock in under three minutes. But not today. She had to find a new spacesuit, pack water, food, meds, chips, and…weapons? Was there anything that would work?

A hammer drill was better than nothing. She grabbed that. A mini defib device? That was a life-saving device that could restart someone's heart with a jolt of electricity. It would be useless against a well-insulated bug, but maybe the aux pack was vulnerable. *Bring it.* Weren't there any laser guns up here? She could really use one.

"Where are the laser guns when you need them?" she asked nobody. She had never used or even held one before, but it couldn't be that hard, right?

Her new suit didn't fit as well as the old one and she hoped the extra roominess would be an asset and not a hindrance. At least it was virtually new, and its oxygen supply was greater than her old one. That could be a big help if she couldn't make stops to replenish.

As she was leaving, she turned down all interior settings, locking the console, the airlocks, even the power transmission sequence the node was designed for. She didn't want the enemy finding anything useful or any evidence of her presence there and she didn't have time to clean up.

Maybe they would think she had fallen into the atmosphere and perished.

Outside, she began her trip sliding hand over hand, searching for a rhythm like the one she used in skating, pushing off, right, left, right, left. The *brush, brush* sound was nice. She thought at first this would end up being a great alternative to skating, but it wasn't long before her shoulders started aching and even her hands were feeling bruised through the gloves. They weren't cushioned like the boots were.

Pain was definitely keeping her alert.

She didn't want to stop but she wasn't ready yet to attempt real skating. So, she paused and rested regularly, alternating between twenty pulls with her hands and crossing her arms over her chest and letting her body coast forward. That helped her keep moving.

The idea of maintenance beetles crawling quickly after her spurred her on as well. For all she knew, they could well be back there in the dark behind her. How would she know?

And for hours, she kept going, dragging her pack and other supplies in her wake.

←↑↓→

The Last Node in the West—maybe it wasn't that, but the Reticulary structure beyond it had never been completed. Besides, it was jutting out over the ocean and there was no point in dropping Cascades there. A full-size station had been under construction somewhere beyond. She had always thought she would check it out someday.

Not today.

Climbing into the node, she set the environmental controls to cool, but habitable, and gravity at 75% instead of full. She wanted to walk around and use her legs but didn't want to overdo it. It was a relief to see that this node had its own supply of pods. Within a couple of hours, she could have them all set up in clusters, with bundles of chips and floats in each one. She already had the chips and mini chutes assembled.

Singing old songs she had learned as a child that helped her avoid thinking about Tenna and the other Specs, she worked quickly and efficiently. Putting these drops together had become second nature. Before long, she had the clusters assembled and was taking them out the airlock to link to the underside of the node. It was easy to time the clamps to release when she wanted.

Seven drops, one every three hours; that was the schedule she set. The first one was released as she reentered the airlock to gather her supplies. *Pods away!* she told herself, since there was no one else to tell.

Pitch wasn't looking forward to the return trip, but at least she could travel in a Scurrier and give her arms and legs a rest. Stocking up on a cache of excellent food packs and fresh tasting water, shoving them into bags, she searched for weapons.

Apparently, the Reticulary bunch were a peaceful people and didn't need such things. She had to settle for something similar to a nail gun and a bag of metallic spikes. Better than nothing, she supposed. She grabbed extra tethers, two extra suits, and a couple of heater packs that could be attached to the suit for extra warmth.

I should have checked this node out sooner, she thought. *There are lots of goodies here. If I come back this way, I will be sure to explore it better. And maybe, I'll make it out to that half-built station out there. It's probably the safest hideout in the Reticulary.*

She packed the Scurrier and climbed in. Staring into the darkness ahead, she imagined swarms of bugs combing the cables looking for her and decided that if she encountered them, she would plow through them as fast as she could. Turning it on and revving up to its highest speed, she was able to cover the distance back to Tumble Drop in just under an hour.

There were no beetles on the way, as far as she could tell.

She had the pods assembled and in their clusters under the node in half the time as before and set their schedule for every three hours as well. Eight of them.

Checking all over the Scurrier's dashboard as she headed on to Jagged Node, she didn't find anything that looked like weapons. No missiles or beams or EMT devices—which would be useless on the Reticulary, actually, but she had always wanted to try one.

There was no point in commenting aloud on the dearth of self-defense tools since she imagined the Scurrier's interior mics could be hacked, and she didn't want to take any chances on giving the enemy something to listen to.

Jagged Node had now weapons either, though it was newer, larger, and more comfortable than a lot of the nodes. It had a larger supply of pods, so she spent more time setting up all the drops. While she was locking each Cascade into place under the node, she found herself mesmerized by the view, thinking about Vil Darad and the largest base directly below. She wondered if they could see her up here with some powerful telescopic instrument. Would they think to look? Had they been watching all along? But visibility under the node was poor unless it was in full sunlight and right now it was not.

After a several hours, she was on her way again. Anxiety was creeping up through the numb exhaustion and it was getting harder to think clearly. She was heading back in the direction of the enemy beetle and didn't know what would be waiting for her.

It took all her self-control to make herself stop at Tempest Node to assemble the Cascades there. She was beginning to feel like any more delay could be devastating. The pressure to find her sister was eating away at her inside.

But she knew that whatever had happened, had already happened, and a sooner arrival wouldn't change that. The pods though, if she didn't set them up now, she never would. She knew that in her innermost being.

And her brother's life was still on the line.

CHAPTER 21

Swarm

*Long ago she had decided to face her fears
and the practice served her well.*

No bugs appeared as Pitch neared Tempest Node. None she could see anyway.

She had spent the trip trying to assemble pods inside the Scurrier, which was a lot harder to do in the cramped space, but kept her from fretting and hopefully would make things faster once she got there. They came from the Last Node in the West—that was too long of a name. How about just the Last Node? It would do for now.

Apprehension filled her mind as she docked with Tempest and climbed out of the vehicle, a bag slung over her shoulder, and the nail gun hefted in her hand. It didn't weigh anything in space, but it was massive and could still cause her trouble. If it started twisting, for example, one wrist wasn't strong enough to quickly get it back under control. She really needed to use two hands. And it was uncomfortable; she had no feel for it.

She scanned the area all around, wishing she had a means of detecting the little creepers. That was a good name for them. Creepers.

There weren't any in sight.

Everything took twice as long at Tempest because of the constant need to watch on every side for creepers. She didn't even take off her helmet or gloves inside the node, so assembly was rough. After chips kept getting fumbled or broken though, she had to take off one glove to get the job done.

It was stressful.

Pulling the clusters down under the node and setting up the drops was even more stressful. It was really hard to tell if there was a beetle threat because the underside was full of bars, indentations, panels, attachments, and who knew what all. Creepers could hide in any number of places, and she wouldn't know until they attacked.

So she plodded along, positioning clusters, doing the next thing, and the next, watching over her shoulder for movement or glimmers of light.

And when the Cascades were ready and the schedule coded, she wearily climbed back up to the Scurrier and set off east again.

Hopefully, Tropical Node would have some sign of what had happened to Tenna, or a message from her. Or from Retty. That was the last place she remembered her sister being and it may have been where the scream happened.

The enemy had a cluster of creepers waiting for Pitch at Tropical Node. The Scurrier reflected sunlight onto them as it drew close. They were spread around and across the airlock and docking clamps.

Blocking her way inside.

A cold determination settled in her gut, and she slowed the vehicle to a stop thirty meters away. She may have been ready to drive over them, but slamming into the node would cause her and it more damage than it would the beetles. She would have to make her way on foot.

She was ready.

Tucking the drill into a leg pouch on one side and the defib on the other, she picked up the nail gun and shoved as many spikes as she could into a pouch at her belly. It was already fully loaded with thirty of them. Stepping out of the Scurrier while still on the ropes made it wobble so much that she thought they would seize the moment and jump at her. They didn't, and she was able to drop to a crouch next to the vehicle, tether on with two lines, and carefully pull the gun into position. Her elbow rested on one knee and was steadied by the other hand.

Ka-thunk. It wasn't really audible, but through her suit shooting the nail gun made a dull thud, and her mind substituted this impression. *Ka-thunk, ka-thunk, ka-thunk.*

There was no air to cause drag. Not enough gravity to make any difference at this distance and the spikes were moving at least 300 meters per second. The bugs had no time to move, and it was likely they couldn't tell what she was doing.

They had no eyes.

Their sensors were excellent though, and they quickly picked up on the shock wave of the gun through her body and the cables, as well as the impacts on the node. They were scrambling all around now, erratically, just like freaked out insects on the earth.

She didn't think she had hit a single one either. The nail gun wasn't a precision weapon in the target shooting sense. It was designed to be operated within mere centimeters of its objective. When she shot, it recoiled, and she had nothing to brace herself against. She was sliding backward and pivoting away.

Shoot slowly. Dive into each shot and brace your feet. Get closer.

That is what she did, and the next spike hit a bug and snapped off one of its limbs. It was momentarily stunned, but the other bugs seemed to form a plan. They collected in a group leaving a few off to the side…it was like some of them were parking, and the rest came for her.

Running.

One in particular was leading the others and she was certain it was the same enemy that had tried to kill her before. How many could he control at the same time? Apparently, not the entire swarm. Hopefully not enough to overcome her defenses.

Ka-thunk, pause and brace, *ka-thunk,* pause and brace, *ka-thunk.*

As they got closer and she settled into form and kept shooting, the spikes connected more often. And most of those were directed at the first bug in the swarm. It lost a limb, then another limb, and with the third hit, it went flying into the darkness and she laughed aloud and reloaded.

Another beetle took the lead.

The next round of spikes went quickly—one bug was nailed to the structure just a few meters away, then there was no time to reload. Out of the twenty or so in this group, there were six she hadn't managed to take down.

They were almost on her.

But she had two tethers. Detaching the one at her feet, she threw herself backwards, swinging in an arc on the second tether, loading the nail gun and shooting as she swung. She landed a good distance away and now there were four bugs. Taking a moment to detach the tether in front of her she, hurled the other one behind to latch on and flung herself out again. The last four bugs were knocked out of commission before she landed again.

None of them had gotten close enough to touch her.

But she was worried. There were still an unknown number of bugs waiting on the node and her supply of spikes was dwindling. From this distance, she couldn't see yet if they were coming. Should she move forward again? Would they wait until she did?

Pitch wasn't strong enough to travel back to Tempest on her own; she would need the Scurrier, and besides, that would the defeat the purpose of her coming all this way. Setting up the final Cascade at Tropical Node and searching for a message from her sister were both extremely important tasks. There was no point in retreat.

Making her way forward, attaching and detaching her tethers along the way, she retraced her path cautiously back to the Scurrier.

Hadn't she left the door open? She wasn't sure. Maybe not. It was…unnerving to not be certain. She peeked in the windows as she passed but the stark contrast between light and shadow made it hard to discern anything inside.

Moving past it on one side she inched toward the node where no bugs could be seen anywhere. That was almost worse than having a bunch of them racing toward you. She felt a small vibration and dropped to one knee on the cables, scanning the node intently.

Then the Scurrier rammed her from behind, knocking her toward the node. And the moment her tether snapped taut, it yanked her body backward while the vehicle shoved against her body and started pushing.

The pain was intense, a horrifying shock wracking her body in so many ways, she didn't know how to tell what was injured. The little vehicle wasn't massive, and its motor was not powerful, but it had generated enough speed to hurt her both with the first blow and the yank of the tether that led to the second blow. She became its braking system as it revved and tried to keep moving past her.

The tether tugged at her torso in the opposite direction, and her arms were crammed so that she couldn't reach its clasp to unhook it. A scream broke through the overwhelming sensation of pain, and she wondered who it was. Then silence fell as she recognized her own voice in her helmet.

Her suit wouldn't tolerate this for long.

Her left hand was pressed down along her left leg where the drill was, and she realized she could pull the tool out and twist it around. Grabbing it, she squeezed the machine and started drilling into whatever piece of the Scurrier was within reach. As she did, it started losing its grip on the structure, which was mostly magnetic, and she and the vehicle began sliding back in the direction of the tether together. The more the safety tether loosened, the more she could move. Soon she had the Scurrier off of her and was clinging to the same front bars that had slammed her. She couldn't let it dislodge completely and float away.

Something was on her back.

She couldn't see it, but she knew there must be at least one bug, maybe several. They were crawling carefully up to her helmet. Whipping the drill around, she jabbed at her back—and bolts! Why had she done that? The last thing she needed was a hole in the new suit! It didn't tear because she had jerked it back at the last minute, but it had been close. And now the bugs knew she was aware of them. One crept around her left arm, heading toward the drill, one clambered up the back of her helmet, and one crawled down her right leg…her throbbing, aching right leg…and started fumbling at the clasps on her boot.

That's when she realized that they never acted at the same time. Yes, they could be set in a trajectory and sent off running on autopilot, but the enemy could only actually control one of them at a time.

And that would be her salvation.

The nail gun was lost. It must have been thrown when the vehicle rammed her. She switched the drill to her right hand and banged it down on the creeper on her boot, right in the aux-pack. It spasmed and dropped away. Almost in the same sweeping motion, she knocked the creeper on her left arm and as it clung fixedly in place, she drilled its pack. The one behind her head was where the enemy was in control right now. It began grappling with the security locks on her helmet at the same time she started diving at it with both hands, the drill in one and the other balled into a fist.

Smack! Smack! Over and over, she beat at the bug, and it dodged around all over her head and shoulders. It couldn't just hang on to her suit this time. At one point she caught its body square on the drill, and it actually spun a couple of times, limbs flailing, but the enemy hadn't let go of it and it was still clawing for her. She jammed it down on the structure at her feet and stepped on it, pulling it off the drill, and kicking it out into the ether.

"HA!" she yelled after it.

But there were still some in the Scurrier. They started revving up the vehicle again and having traction only on one side, it began tilting precariously off the edge of the guiderail, sparks flying, and Pitch realized that she had to choose between saving the Scurrier with all its supplies along with a clump of creepers and eliminating a major threat in one go.

She dropped to her knees and applied the drill to the remaining magnetic strip, loosening it just enough for the revving motor to jolt it off. The inside looked like it was swarming with legs as it drifted slowly away.

She was shaking. It was all she could do to put the drill back in the pouch and turn herself around to sit facing Tropical Node. She would have to go in. To remain out here would mean certain death.

Inside, even if there were creepers there, she had a chance of surviving a little longer.

Painfully, she stretched herself out on her stomach, grasped one of the cables and pulled. Her tether yanked tautly again, and she remembered it was there. Detaching it, she swung it forward and began the slow advance along the Reticulary with her two tethers.

It felt like it took hours. But at least there were no bugs to torment her on the way.

← ↑ ↓ →

I made it, she thought as she swept the interior of Tropical Node with an intense gaze looking for hidden creepers.

The garden was in a sorry state. Everywhere she looked, plants were shredded, broken, trampled, and overturned with roots exposed. It didn't even surprise her. It seemed appropriate. This is what had happened all over the Reticulary in recent hours. She and all the Specs were trampled, broken, and exposed.

Is this your message for me, Tenna? She wondered, unable to tell if her question was reasonable or foolish. Both options felt possible.

At least the Tenna's Scurrier was gone. Maybe she got away. Where to? Their main hideout at Faraday had been discovered, so she wouldn't have gone there. Pitch was tentatively confident. Her sister was smart. *If anyone could have found a way, it would be you, Sis.*

There were enough pods here for a few more drops and Pitch was determined to set them up. Somehow, working painfully slow, she got them assembled and bundled into clusters, and was shifting them into the airlock when a deep voice boomed over the audio.

"So!" it gloated, "That's how you do it! I have been wondering. So simple, and quite clever. It's a pity to destroy such a creative little group…"

These words were excruciating in her ears which had been attuned to silence for so long. They shook her to her core. Her hands went slack, dropping the bundles, and she fell to her knees at the same time. Her legs just couldn't hardly cooperate with the demands she was making of them, as small as those had become.

Wicked laughter filled the room. The warm, moist air and soothing greenhouse sunshine turned suddenly a sickly bile color, and the air grew dank and choking. She gasped and reached up to pull her helmet into place, which was what she would have done anyway before heading outside.

"Go ahead," the man said with a growl, "Set up your little viral packages and let them fall. They will be your last."

She had known they would be the last. A chill settled upon her, steeling her mind, numbing her stomach, deadening her face, hardening her resolve. *Then I will finish.*

Picking up the bundles she had dropped, she moved into the airlock and heard the man speak faintly through the door. "It is worthless. It accomplishes nothing." She moved on, ignoring him. The final Cascades were soon in place, and she timed them to only one hour apart, five of them.

Five final drops.

Turning back to the airlock, Pitch pulled her way over and into it. She engaged the mechanism. It sealed, air flowed in, and the inner door unsealed. She pushed it open and took a step through.

"Well," the man said from the audio. "I can see you. You are merely a child. Some might be surprised a handful of adolescent outlaws could cause so much disruption, but I know better. If I had trained you, I would have made you a formidable weapon. I have made many such."

Pitch stared at the vines budding with beans crushed on the floor and remembered the meal packs she had stored in the Scurrier. They were out in space now. Eventually, they would succumb to the planet's pull and make their way down into the atmosphere to burn up like a meteor. Too bad.

She took a few steps to the water station, unlatched and tipped back her visor, and pulled out a tube of water. Sinking to the floor, she drank, just a few sips at a time.

"I may leave you here until I can come in person and take you prisoner. You will help me retrieve the others and you will all be punished. No one on the surface will ever know who you really are or what you have done because *our* story has filled their hearts and minds. You are aliens and you created a virus, and we have conquered you. We have destroyed you."

"Have you?" she asked flatly.

The question angered him. "Do you know who I am?" he thundered.

"No, and I don't care," she said.

"You will be made to care!"

Pitch shrugged and stared ahead, taking sips of water.

A scrape on the floor was the only warning she got. The creeper pounced on her face, diving into her helmet with three legs and shoving one of them in her mouth. Its tip zapped her tongue painfully and struck her tooth.

The man laughed and growled. "Filth! Vil Darad, the one you fear, has found you!"

She was thrashing and shaking her head, grabbing at it with her hands, and the laughter added to the disorientation and terror gripping her chest. Gagging, spitting, she pushed it away and it shoved its limbs back in her mouth again, digging at her, scraping her gums and teeth. She beat it back and it froze as the man growled again.

"I will get in," he gloated. "I have already executed one rebel with these. I am being lenient with you. You would already be dead if I had wished it." His voice rumbled, halfway between a gargle and hollow laughter.

The limbs held still while he spoke. Then they scrabbled to get in her mouth for a few seconds and froze as he spoke again. "You cannot escape me!"

As she wrestled with the creeper, thrashing on the floor, she wondered. *Why? Why is he doing this?* There were easier ways to kill her. He was more focused on terrorizing her. For a brief moment, she felt that terror gripping her in the throat as two of the creeper's legs pried her jaw open.

But something strengthened her. She thought of Tenna, of her friends, of Fuse. Of her father whose love was so steady and permanent. She had to resist for their sake.

"Aha!" the man proclaimed, "Soon I will come in person—in my own body!" and the beetle froze again as he spoke, long enough for her to pull it partway out of her mouth.

Pitch realized he could not control both the audio in the room and the creeper at the same time. There was only one main camera over the console; Retty had turned off the others. This meant that he could only see her from that one spot. She grabbed the creeper and pulled on it, turning her back to the camera at the same time, a frantic movement with no apparent thought behind it.

He laughed again, spouting something about his power and her insignificance. Reaching down to the pouch on her right leg, she continued rolling and thrashing without letting what she was doing come into view of the camera. The min defib unit was still there…the beetle may be thoroughly insulated, but the auxiliary pack was not.

When the bug started groping into her mouth again, she snapped the mini defib on and whacked it against the aux-pack on its back.

Quick as lightning, it shoved her jaws apart and crammed one limb down her throat. She gagged, vomiting up the water she had swallowed, keeling over forward, but instead of shoving it away from herself, she pressed it into her face, bit down on its limbs, and blasted it with the defib, releasing a shock that burst through the bug and into her helmet.

Into her head.

The man was laughing hysterically now, almost shouting in disgust, as she was thrown back against the wall by the electrical jolt. "You fool!" he screamed and then the room went quiet.

The creeper lay smoking nearby on the floor.

And Pitch lay like one dead.

CHAPTER 22

The Knell

A soul imprisoned by means unknown
A mind rejecting commands of stone
Darkness encroaches, a glimmer shone
Enduring death, but not alone

Pitch ached so much all over when she opened her eyes that she could almost wish she was dead. But as soon as the thought crossed her mind, she rebelled against it. *No!* she thought, *I am so thankful to be alive! If I'm still here, Tenna could be too.*

How long had she been out? She struggled to a sitting position, noticed the dead creeper next to her, and the debris of her garden. The earth and sun were in different positions, so it had been a while. But she wasn't able to think clearly enough to figure out the time by looking outside.

Water.

She picked up the hydration tube she had dropped and began sipping again though it hurt to swallow, ignoring the smell of stale vomit on the floor. Her head was pounding. There was a chip in her tooth, and her mouth was felt sore and ragged inside.

After sitting for a while staring into space and sipping the water steadily, she shoved her way over to the food stores and pulled out a fruit packet. Nothing too heavy right now. Something for the pain would be good too. The med kit would have that.

Sliding around on her bum left a trail of dirt but she didn't care. Her garden was dead, and she wasn't sure how much longer she had either. Eventually, she pulled herself into a chair in front of the console and touched the screen.

A message appeared. It said:

```
Vil Darad has discovered us.
Retty  has  enacted  extreme  emergency
measures.
Flee.
```

It must have been entered after the scream—Tenna had been alive when she wrote it.

Pitch typed in some queries, searching for records of what had happened right before and after the message, but found nothing. If Vil Darad had accessed this console, he would have removed them. This message must have been hidden specifically for Pitch and the enemy hadn't detected it.

That was encouraging.

If she was supposed to run, where should she go? Back the way she had come was the most obvious path. She hadn't found any evidence of enemy control over the audio and beetle supplies in that direction. *Thanks to Retty, I'm sure*, she thought. Or maybe it was all Tenna.

How to travel though? She was pretty beaten up as it was and so exhausted.

The idea that came was so simple she chuckled. *I'll just make myself into a package*, she decided, *and send myself from node to node until I get far enough away to rest.*

The little package carts had their own automatic programming. She collected a few of her things, changes of clothes, some seeds, and podcasts, replenished her suit's oxygen, water, and food, and painstakingly climbed out the airlock. With one of her trusty tethers, she belted herself onto the package cart, initiated the transport and began coasting west down the Reticulary.

She was asleep within minutes.

←↑↓→

Pitch climbed stiffly off the package cart and entered Tempest Node with her limited possessions. Stopping to check the console for any new messages, she headed straight for the package cart on the opposite side. There was nothing for her on the screen.

She wanted to enter a message for Tenna but didn't know how to mask it from the enemy and dare not leave him any update on where she was going. *Sorry, Sis*, she said in her mind. *I can't let you know, but I think you will be able to find me anyway.*

The maintenance beetles here were still disconnected from node control and locked up in their storage locker, but she wedged a tool in the handles just in case.

It was tempting to settle in, shower, grab a snack, maybe just snuggle into a cocoon and let her mind wander. So tempting. But she couldn't allow it. The enemy had installed himself and waited for her only one node away from here and she had no doubt he would be back to search for her. She had to keep moving.

Maybe it was time to explore the unfinished station over the ocean.

Jagged Node was about an hour and a half away on the package cart. She issued the command and was off. This time, she tethered herself to the cart and floated a couple of meters away. She wanted to be able to stretch and loosen up. The sun was blaring in her face and when she turned away, her eyes were so blinded that she couldn't see hardly anything on the surface and space beyond the planet looked black. She knew the whole Milky Way was out there. The angle of the sun, centered somewhere over Mongolia, was the worst. And floating around made it harder to keep her face turned away from it.

With a sigh, she pulled herself back to the cart and strapped in. At least this way she could position herself to look down at the earth or back along the Reticulary. *I guess being out there, which used to seem risky, felt safer and more peaceful*, she thought.

Her eyes adjusted and she gazed down at the surface. The main base was below her, the place where she imagined Vil Darad and his cohorts to be. She couldn't see it, but she knew where it was, somewhere around that ocean inlet that hooked down like an arm with fingers…no, like streaks and bulges of black against the dark strips of land mass. She couldn't remember the name but there had been cities around it once. Ports. And lots of ships came and went.

Is that all you have left, Vil Darad? She thought, wishing she felt safe to say the words aloud. He might not have access to her coms, but she wasn't tech savvy enough to tell or block him off. It felt good to consider all he had lost; all the Order of Peace had lost. They boasted about having conquered the world, but this little corner of the continent was all that was left of their so-called empire.

He wasn't such a great leader.

Smug was the wrong word for how that made her feel. She felt justified. He was strong and powerful. Arrogant and cruel. He used people and destroyed them. She and her band of Specs were young, small, unnoticed, and often fearful. Yet they had been willing to fight for what was good and true. They had been resisted and against all odds, made a difference.

If these were her last hours, she decided she was proud of what she had done, and if she never got to see the end of the rebels' struggle, she would know her part in the story had been crucial. Even if no one else knew.

In a way, she was a better leader than Vil Darad could ever be, because she loved people.

And he hated them.

←↑↓→

Nearing Jagged Node, she noticed a military satellite in motion, traveling very slowly, heading her direction, parallel to the Reticulary cables. It was passing just under the node as the package cart docked, and she realized it was quite close.

Pitch was immediately certain that it was being manned by a human mind because of how its various parts turned. It didn't just turn and adjust the three spheres it targeted with. It turned and adjusted and adjusted again, and sometimes, reversed direction. Several times it seemed to have found its target—surely a cluster of pods recently dropped from the node—and after jacking up its pressurized chamber, ready to release a projectile, it would pause, delay, then gradually allow the chamber to depressurize, and start moving again.

Stepping down from the cart, Pitch tethered and moved to the edge of structure, right over the satellite. It was close enough to jump to. And for some reason she never understood, she did that very thing. With a soft little push, she drifted down and caught onto the satellite.

It wasn't actively using jets for movement. It seemed to be impelled by its movements and possibly missiles it had shot before. Without hesitation, she attached her other tether to it. Her body became the dock between the satellite and the Reticulary.

Which was not the smartest plan. What if it decided to fire up some jets? Okay, there was an attachment that would release with a sharp tug, some kind of carabiner. She groped through her pockets and the little pack at her waist and silently cheered as she found one. That was what she hooked onto her suit and then to the tether she had clamped to the satellite. If it did jet away, she would be released and could tug herself back to the cables on the other tether.

Avoiding the jets, hopefully, she cautioned herself.

Now she took a good look at the satellite, searching for a panel or maybe an aux-pack like the maintenance beetles had had. Crawling over it, she found both on the sunny side. The light was searing and harsh, but it made it easy to find things. Cupping one of her gloves over the panel, she detected a screen with something scrolling across it.

```
… IS THERE … DISCORDANT
READINGS … COMMAND: IDENTIFY
… COMMAND: LOCATE ENEMY
VESSEL … SEARCHING …
SEARCHING … LOCATED …
```

A shiver ran down her back as she realized she was watching the satellite process the commands it was being given. "NO!" she yelled at it, pounding the metal twice with her fist. That was really stupid, she thought. Now they *know* where I am! How hard would it be to zap her right now?

The screen continued scrolling its instructions.

```
FOCUSING … TARGET LOCKED …
COMMAND: INTERRUPT … VERIFY …
TARGET HARMLESS …
MISIDENTIFIED … RELEASE LOCK
… COMMAND: IDENTIFY SOURCE
DISCORDANCE…
```

She was not imagining this. The satellite had decided not to shoot its target. It made no sense, and she couldn't figure out what she was missing. *Why would you lock onto a target and then stop before you could shoot?*

It began rotating and rotating its various spheres, searching for something. It jostled her a couple of times, but it didn't make the satellite drift away from the Reticulary or dislodge her from her perch on its hull. *What are you doing?*

It felt like a dream.

```
COMMAND: LOCATE ENEMY VESSEL …
SEARCHING … SEARCHING …
```

LOCATED … FOCUSING … TARGET
LOCKED … COMMAND: INTERRUPT …
VERIFY … TARGET HARMLESS …
MISIDENTIFIED … RELEASE LOCK …

It was doing it again! Finding a target then letting it go.

"You're a person," she whispered, as if the mind in the metal thing could hear her. She didn't worry about someone listening anymore. "Someone is trying to make you shoot the Cascades and *you don't want to!*"

Tears collected in her eyes, and she found herself stretching her arms as far around the side of the vessel as they could go, clutching it in a hug. She pressed her helmet against it and closed her eyes. "Thank you, thank you, thank you," she was saying over and over again.

She lifted her head and glanced down at the surface. What was that?! A ship ascending through the atmosphere? The flame behind it pushed it along incredibly fast. When had it taken off? It must be headed to Faraday Base.

The enemy coming in his own body to track down and destroy the Specs!

"That's the real enemy," she growled, and turning back to the panel, she opened the keyboard. Would there be anything she could recognize? Would she be able to type in anything that would make a difference?

LOOK AT THAT SHIP OVER THERE …

She just started typing words.

THAT IS THE REAL ENEMY …

Maybe the panel would give her some queries she could answer and that would give her a chance at redirecting the satellite somehow.

```
YOU SHOULD SHOOT DOWN THAT
SHIP … COMMAND: SHOOT THE
ENEMY SHIP THAT IS ASCENDING
FROM THE PLANET … THAT IS VIL
DARAD AND HE IS EVIL …
```

The satellite began rotating its scanners as if searching and the panel responded.

```
QUERY: WHERE ARE YOU … WHO …
```

The satellite hull didn't have sensors or cameras to look at itself, of course.

```
I AM ONE OF THE SPECS … WE
ARE RESCUING SENTINELS WITH
THE CASCADE …
```

The satellite continued its movements and searches and after a moment, the panel scrolled more words.

```
ALIEN SPECS ARE DESTROYING
THE SENTINELS … WHY … WE ARE
GOOD …
```

She gasped and shook her head as she answered. Why had he said "we"? If she had had time to think about it, she would have been astonished to be able to converse with him so easily, but that didn't cross her mind.

```
WE ARE NOT ALIENS … WE ARE
SURVIVORS OF THE ATTACK ON
THE RETICULARY … WE HAVE
FAMILY ON THE SURFACE … SOME
OF THEM WERE TAKEN PRISONER
```

Another pause followed. Then suddenly the gun chamber was pressurizing, and she was filled with a sharp terror that the gun would kill her somehow.

It was pointing at the ascending spaceship.

With a jolt, a blast of heat and blinding light, the satellite jerked away from the ship and its missile shot toward it. The explosion was bright, blue, sparkly, and brief. Nothing remained that she could see.

Pitch had lost her grip on the satellite with the recoil of the gun. Grappling back with the tether, she was shaking and breathing shallowly. *Calm down*, she told herself. *Breathe slowly and deeply. You are okay.*

Had he really killed the enemy leader? Had Vil Darad been in that ship?

She was *sure* he had been, but she couldn't give herself any good reason for her confidence. It was as if she had felt his approaching evil, growing hotter, more threatening, more menacing, more aware of her, maybe even listening to her over the coms and laughing at her. Making plans against her. Then nothing. It felt like nothing. She leaned over the panel and typed.

The answer came quickly.

I AM A SENTINEL … ARE YOU
FAMILY …

Pitch didn't hesitate.

YES …

The Sentinel in the satellite responded.

YOU REMEMBER US … ARE WE
ALIENS … ARE WE HUMANS …

Tears were streaming down her face as she realized that after all the time they had fought, with all they had to give to rescue these hostages, this was her *first chance* to interact with one of them herself.

YES … YOU ARE ALL HUMANS … WE
REMEMBER YOU … WE HAVE BEEN
SEARCHING FOR YOU AND
FIGHTING TO FREE YOU …

He queried.

WHAT HAPPENED TO ALL THE
SENTINELS THAT WERE LOST …
DID YOU KILL THEM …

Pitch's fingers were trembling as she answered.

THEY HAVE ALL BEEN RESCUED
AND RESTORED TO THEIR
FAMILIES … WE HID THEM FROM
THE ORDER OF PEACE … THEY ARE
ALIVE …

There was a longer pause as the Sentinel digested that.

SO MANY BROTHERS LOST …

Pitch replied.

```
AND SISTERS … BUT THEY HAVE
BEEN FOUND … THEY ARE OKAY …
```

The satellite rotated as a new command came in.

```
COMMAND: LOCATE ENEMY VESSEL
… SEARCHING … SEARCHING …
LOCATED … HOW CAN I STOP
THESE COMMANDS … I CAN ONLY
INTERRUPT THEM …
```

Pitch typed.

```
COMMAND: CEASE TAKING
COMMANDS FROM ANYWHERE
BESIDES THIS PANEL …
```

The marquee scrolled in response.

```
FOCUSING … TARGET LOCKED …
COMMAND: INTERRUPT … VERIFY …
TARGET HARMLESS …
MISIDENTIFIED … RELEASE LOCK
… HULL PANEL SET TO MASTER
CONTROL … OTHER INPUT SOURCES
DISCONNECTED …
```

Pitch smiled. *I wonder if I am going to wake up and realize this was a dream.* It felt so real.

```
WHAT IS YOUR NAME …
```

The answer was immediate.

```
I AM MEVKAD … THANK YOU FOR
DISMANTLING THE OVER COMMAND …
```

She was caught off guard by this name. There was nothing like it in any of the lists. It must have been given to him by the Order.

YOUR NAME IS DIFFERENT THAN
YOUR HUMAN NAME …

Mevkad responded.

WHAT IS MY HUMAN NAME … WHAT
ARE SISTERS …

A stab of anxiety shot through Pitch's heart as she remembered her sister. *They are the most precious things in the world*, she thought. But this, this was someone's brother or son, too. And she, Pitch, had found him.

WE DON'T KNOW HOW TO CONNECT
YOUR HUMAN NAMES WITH YOUR
SENTINEL NAMES … THERE ARE
BROTHERS AND SISTERS AMONG
THE SENTINELS …

Mevkad replied.

THERE ARE ONLY BROTHERS …

The satellite started moving again, rotating its spheres and moving its gun.

WHAT ARE YOU DOING …

She asked, but he didn't reply. She was picking up a soft chatter, as if her coms were coming on but at a really low volume. "Tenna?" she whispered, "Retty?" There was no answer. The faint chatter she was hearing was coming from below, on the surface, and she couldn't quite make out what they were saying.

Apparently, Mevkad could hear them, and all his attention was focused there.

Pitch's head was laying against the satellite's hull so she could see if the panel lit up. She didn't know how long she had been there, just waiting. The weariness was so great she was unaware of any thoughts she may had since he stopped scrolling his messages. She was content to just lie there and stare into the distance.

The faint chatter continued in her headgear, but it had become a meaningless drone. She had nowhere else to be. Nothing else to do. This…this was enough.

Letters began to scroll again across the panel and the spheres started shifting again. She stirred and lifted her head to read.

```
I SEE NOW … YOUR WORDS ARE
TRUE … I KNOW WHAT TO DO …
ALL THE SENTINELS WILL BE
SAFE …
```

What was he saying? What was he going to do? Before she could ask, more words appeared.

```
ONE THREAT REMAINS … I ALONE
CAN DEFEAT IT … MY BROTHERS
HAVE LEFT THE HARBOR … THEY
WILL BE FREE … IT IS ENOUGH …
```

Strange that the same thought had just crossed her mind. Was he saying what she thought he was saying?

```
THERE IS NO RELEASE FOR ME …
I WILL NOT RETURN HOME … TELL
MY FAMILY … I GAVE THEM WHAT
I COULD … I AM NOBLE … I HAVE
FULFILLED THE CALLING …
```

She leapt at the keyboard.

WHAT ARE YOU SAYING … YOU CAN
BE SAVED … GO BACK DOWN …

The gun locked into place.

TARGET ACQUIRED … LOCKED … I
CANNOT GO BACK … NIREKAD HAS
CONFISCATED MY … MY HOME …

Pitch frantically typed.

THERE MUST BE A WAY TO FREE
YOU …

The gun warmed, pointing directly down to the surface below.

YES …

Pitch hugged the satellite tightly as it belched its projectile, squeezing her eyes shut to avoid the gun's flash. This time, she was not dislodged. Opening her eyes again, she saw his final message.

THIS IS THE WAY …

Far below, a tiny explosion bloomed on the surface and faded. The chatter in her helmet rolled into a burr as if too many voices were talking at once.

Pitch remembered the tools she had stashed in her leg pouches and decided that if there was a way she could help him, she would try. Climbing up to the top of the satellite, she found the aux-panel, larger, but basically the same as the ones on the creepers the enemy had commandeered. Trying to detach it with the drill didn't work, so she pulled out the mini de-fib and blasted, being careful this time to clear herself. Only the tether, which was insulated against electricity, was connecting her to the hull.

The device fizzled and smoked and went dark.

And the panel flickered with little flashes and bleeps and the occasional dot, dot, dot.
But no more words were written.

CHAPTER 23

Recovery

Peace begins by accepting the losses and making something new out of what is left.

Magnet and Ratio found Pitch dangling from a tether attached to a military satellite, which was quite unexpected, her oxygen dangerously low and her CO_2 at perilously high levels. They wondered if she was the one who overridden it and used it to shoot down the enemy ship approaching Faraday Base—which had saved all their lives.

Bringing her into a nearby node, they pulled her out of her space suit, figured out that she would probably survive, hooked her up to IV fluids, suited her back up again, and hoped that would be enough as she was being transported back to Faraday. She remained unconscious the whole time, unaware of the hours that passed or what was happening on the surface.

In the medical bay at Faraday Base, the automated systems did a satisfactory job of examining her and assessing her condition, then initiating treatment. Some things would be hard to tell before she woke, like whether she had suffered any brain damage from oxygen deprivation, but mostly, temporary sedation, rest, fluids, analgesics, and some bandaging of sprains and strains were all that were required. She was going to be okay.

When Pitch opened her eyes, most of her Spec family was there around her, gazing anxiously, hopefully into her face. Her lips were cracked and her mouth too dry for her first words to come out. But someone handed her a hydration tube, and she took a sip of water, rubbed her face, and her vision cleared.

"Tenna!" she croaked, throwing the tube across the room and wrapping her arms tightly around her sister. "I thought you were lost!"

"I thought you were dead!" Tenna yelled back at her squeezing her just as hard.

There were tears mixed with laughter around her bed. She tried to sit and a couple of them helped her pull herself up. Looking around, she counted. "Who is missing?" she asked, blinking groggily and shaking her head. It was a relief not to have a helmet on when she did that. She could rub her eyes any time she wanted to.

A couple of them glanced at Tenna and waited for her to speak.

"Just Relay," she said with a gulp. She was trying to make her voice sound normal, as if it were hard but things would be okay—but it was *not* okay. Pitch started sobbing and covered her face with one hand, clutching her sister's hand in the other. "But Pitch," Tenna shook her hand and leaned closer, "I thought I had lost both of you and I am just so glad, so glad you are alive…"

"Most of us didn't believe you were," Thermo said, "but Magnet wanted to keep searching, and Ratio wouldn't let her go alone. And honestly, it's a miracle they noticed you out there hanging off of that satellite."

"What the bolts was that about?!" Cycle said, bulging his eyes out at her, then smiling.

"We have a lot of catching up to do," Pitch swallowed and tried to speak calmly. "But I'm not quite ready yet."

"We will be here when you are," Retty interjected, and Pitch wept again, relieved to know that he hadn't been deleted or corrupted by the enemy.

Over the next couple of months, a lot was changing on the surface and the rebels—the underground as they were actually called—had not forgotten their heroes in the stars, the Specs. Once open communication was restored, the Specs found themselves fielding lots of calls and conversations about all kinds of things. No one would accept a story about anything to do with the Order unless it was confirmed, as much as possible, by the Specs, the only ones who had *never* been subjected to domination by the Order.

Many of their own Reticulary people who had been on the surface when the war broke out had died but there had also been a number of survivors and they were calling regularly to talk, ask about the status of what hadn't been destroyed or to figure out if they had acquaintances in common, dream about returning, and more. They were also still providing essential links for the various rebel groups and survivors. Their status seemed to grow in the minds of the people on the surface, and it gave them hope, when they weren't feeling the burden of all they had lost.

Tenna had been the first person to encounter the aux-controlled maintenance beetle. She and Relay had been working together at Tropical Node. Pitch never heard what they were working and didn't let herself ask why they weren't spread out separately at different locations like they were supposed to be. The beetle has suddenly crawled over and tried to choke Tenna. Relay jumped up and ripped it off of her, leaving a scar on her throat, and the two of them had fought with it. Somehow, it mortally wounded Relay before Tenna was able to destroy it, but Pitch never got the exact details because her sister couldn't bear to talk about it. Not yet anyway.

The warning went out to all the Specs except Pitch because she was further west and the enemy had already blocked communication in her direction of the Reticulary. Tenna fled east with Relay, hoping she could save him, but he hadn't survived.

Retty initiated emergency protocols to preserve himself from hacking and infiltration, but not before warning Base AI of the intrusion. He had almost convinced the AI that the Order was the enemy, and the Sentinels needed rescuing but ran out of time for that. It had been persuasive enough though, that Base had been willing to back up its own core on Faraday. This was done not long before the Harbor Base itself was destroyed. Retty and Tenna were working with Base now to retrain and hopefully rehabilitate it.

Ships were being scheduled to come to Faraday with supplies and skilled technicians who could begin the rebuilding process, and any Specs who wished, were invited to travel back down to the surface on the return trip.

Pitch and Tenna were among the first passengers.

They sat in the cushioned seats looking at each other and held hands as their transport entered the atmosphere and landed. They didn't know what to expect when they stepped out, but the longing in their hearts was greater than the fear.

Old rebel friends, rescued Sentinels, family…someone would be there.

Climbing slowly down the ladder with the help of several people, the sisters were surprised by how disorienting real, planet-size gravity was. It caused a weird kind of vertigo that sometimes made Pitch think she was suddenly upside-down. And it was hard to walk without over or under compensating for where the gravity was.

The air was so changeable and fickle. Warm, cool, breezy, dusty. A hint of one smell, then another. It was a full-on assault on the senses…and utterly delightful. Long ago, when they used to go on family vacations down here, they took things like this in stride. But it had been several years since they had set foot on the Earth.

Distances were strange too. Sometimes when she looked at something, her brain jerked back and forth as if it were testing out whether the object was close or far away. A slight movement was all it needed, then it was suddenly normal and in place. Once it was settled, it didn't jump around anymore.

The first face they saw after the initial confusion was one they could never forget, though it was lined with unfamiliar wrinkles and sorrow. "Will she recognize us?" Tenna whispered as they walked across the tarmac to the terminal entrance where clusters of people had been waiting. The woman was scanning passengers' faces with a frown when suddenly, her mouth dropped open. She came running straight for them and threw her arms around both of them at the same time, choking with tears and smiles and intense emotion.

"Did you know it was us, Mom?" Pitch asked, happy but awkward. She felt like both a little girl and an ancient adult at the same time.

"How could I not recognize my own precious girls?" she cried out, crushing all three heads together, shutting out the world. "My wonderful, wonderful girls!" She kept saying things like that over and over and the sisters couldn't think of what to answer.

After the initial emotion calmed a little, Tenna asked, "Where's Dad?" And Pitch realized, even before they heard the answer, that she *knew*. She had known for a while.

"He's gone, pumpkin," their mother answered sadly, "I'm sorry. He would have wanted to be here for you. He would not have wanted to miss this." Fresh tears were streaming down her face.

"I know, Mom," Pitch was saying, "It's okay. He knows. I'm sure he knows."

They moved slowly toward the terminal passageways, their arms wrapped around each other's shoulders with their mom in the middle, and Pitch noticed how she had shrunk. And she looked a lot older as well.

"Are you smaller?" she asked, puzzled, and her mother laughed.

"Not me, my little one, not so little now. It's you."

Tenna laughed at her too but in the most cheerful way.

"And where is El?" Pitch went on, "We've gotten used to calling him Fuse now, which is what he always wanted to be called. Is he okay? Did he get out?"

They stood still. In years past, there were times when serious conversations were attempted, they would be set aside 'for the time being'. People would say, "Not right now, we will discuss that later." But today, they were on the same page. Every day was serious. Every important conversation would take place now.

"He is okay," their mother said, and before she could continue, they cried out and hugged again with cheers and tears. "But," she went on when they gave her a chance, "he isn't how you remember. He has changed a lot, and we need to be understanding. He needs a lot of patience."

"What do you mean?" Tenna asked soberly.

They were making their way out of the building now and a small electric car, old and rickety, was waiting for them. Climbing in, they listened as their mother explained all that had been happening to their brother to the best of her understanding. And as they were arriving at the little home where she lived, she was telling them how they should behave.

"Don't be too upset if he doesn't remember you," she was saying. "And don't hold it against him if he says something hurtful. He hasn't been able to make a link to the past like the doctors say he needs to. Something…something will trigger it…we don't know when."

She smiled at each of them in turn. "Something will help him connect with his old self and then they say all those memories will flood back and he can begin putting things in place, figuring out who he is now. Now that he has been Elex and also Kierkad."

"Kierkad!" Pitch was startled and Tenna looked at her oddly. She hadn't told her sister much about her final conversation with the satellite, and she hadn't heard of the naming pattern used for Sentinels. "I've heard something like that before. What does it mean? What does the 'kad' mean?"

"It's the suffix the Order used for Sentinels, a term of respect and privilege. As they move up the ranks, their suffix would change. 'Kad' is one of the higher ones. Above that is 'Darad' and beyond that I don't know."

They got out of the car and turned toward the house. The door was open, and what looked like a man was standing in the doorway, staring at them intently.

Both Tenna and Pitch were alarmed by that stare.

"Is that…is that him?" Tenna whispered.

Gone was Pitch's dream of running over and throwing her arms around her brother and telling him how they loved him and had been doing everything they could to rescue him. He wouldn't be getting teary-eyed or hugging her back. He wouldn't be saying 'thank you'. He wasn't even smiling.

Their mother nodded and led them forward. "Elex," she said, "These are your sisters, Melina—"

"Tenna," Tenna corrected.

"…and Amber."

"Pitch," Tenna added.

"Hello," Elex said with a slight nod and deadpan face. His arms hung at his side as though he were ready to run or balance on his toes or maybe…fight. He was muscular, solid, lean, but now that they were closer, they could see he was still young. Younger even than they were. His eyes just looked so haunted…as if he hadn't been a child for a long time.

"Do you remember me, Fuse?" Pitch asked, and for a hint of a second, his eyes unfocused as if that name meant something, then they refocused on her, harder than before.

"No."

"We used to be sort of competitive with each other, but we had a lot of fun together, too."

Elex said nothing but stepped back to let them come in the house.

"What about me?" Tenna asked without much hope. "I'm your oldest sister. We got along well when I was home, but I was out doing my internship when the war started."

He gave her a look that said, no, without having to utter the word.

"He really only remembers the last three weeks of his time as a Sentinel[3]," their mom explained, "and of course, his time with me since then."

As they entered, Elex initiated a topic of his own. "There was some damage here, but I am repairing it as well as I can." He gestured down the hall with a stiff arm at a room with a busted and repaired door.

"We have quite the story to tell you," their mother smiled with sorrow and weariness in her eyes. "Let's come to the table and have lunch and we can all catch up."

So they did.

---

[3] *These three weeks are covered in "Cascade" and some of these memories are distortions limited by his understanding at the time. .*

Tenna and Pitch were going to be staying the next few weeks in a nearby home because their mom thought it would be too stressful sleeping in the same house with Elex. He had nightmares now and then and he could wake up pretty hostile and scary. She knew what to do for him but didn't want the sisters to have to deal with it.

That was fine with them. They needed a quiet place where they could talk together and…process? Was that the right word? They didn't know what was going to happen next. Were they going back to space? Were they staying on the surface? There were many things they had never done before, like see the ocean or a canyon, but they weren't ready to try any of it.

And where did they belong?

For now, the plan was to visit Mom and Elex every day and just get to know each other again.

On one of those visits, Pitch was persuaded to tell the story of her time with the satellite which no one had heard before, not even Tenna. It had become so strange in her mind that she was embarrassed to talk about it, afraid people would accuse her of making it up or dreaming it. In fact, she herself doubted her memory of what had happened, although they had found her tethered to it. So she knew *something* had taken place.

She started off jokingly, as if apologizing for her messed up mind at the time, but it quickly became an intense retelling. Tenna had thought she was already dead. Her mother had just lost her husband, and her own life was in danger at the time it was happening. And El…he was staring at her intently, gripped by this story more than anything else she had ever said.

He absolutely believed her.

When she said there was a person governing the satellite, instead of scoffing or mocking, he said, "Yes, there was."

They looked at him in surprise. "There was?" Mom asked.

"I have done this."

"You what?" Tenna demanded, shoving away whatever hint of skepticism she might have felt at first.

Pitch's eyes grew damp, and she thought of the poor Sentinel she had met in that satellite.

"I was compelled to do so," Elex said, "And I hated it. I could not get out until they released me."

This was the first time he had expressed any emotion, whatsoever, of any kind. He hated something. And it was a hatred they could well understand. It made them feel a little closer to him.

This was nothing though, compared to the emotion they saw next.

"Did you know Mevkad?" Pitch asked and Elex jumped to his feet, turning pale and thumping his chest with his fist.

"Mevkad!" he cried out, "My brother!" And a brief but painful wail erupted from his lips. Then hanging his head, he sunk into the chair and covered his eyes with one hand. "Tell me," he said in an agonized voice. "I must know everything that happened."

Pitch told him the whole story as clearly as she could remember and when she got to the part where he had said, "I have fulfilled the calling," and bombed the old Harbor Base, her brother wept openly.

She finished the story with the smashing of the auxiliary unit on its hull, and they all watched Elex as he quieted and pondered. After a while, he lifted his face, etched in grief, and said, "He was noble, and he did fulfill the calling. All the Sentinels were out looking for me and none perished in the bombing except for the evil Nirekad."

He rose to his feet and turned away, but pausing, he spoke over his shoulder. "Pitch," he said, saying her name for the first time since they had come, "you were with him at the end. I acknowledge this." He walked away and closed himself in his room, the room he had said he was repairing.

The daily meals were their routine for several weeks. Then Tenna decided she needed to track down Relay's family members that were still alive and let them know all he had done and how wonderful he was. Pitch knew she couldn't do that alone and said she was going with her.

They met for a final lunch at Mom's and had the usual placid conversation with Elex being mostly silent and expressionless. When it was time to leave, they all stood, walked to the door, said the usual things, and Pitch turned to follow Tenna out the door.

Then she hesitated with one foot in the air and slowly let it drop. Looking back over her shoulder, she glanced at her brother, remembering the last time she had seen him…

…when they had been children.

His stare was so flat and cold that she couldn't think of what to say.

She sighed.

"I love you," she said softly as she turned back and stepped out the door.

Then, *whaap*! Something hit her in the back of the head.

Snapping around in shock, she glanced at the floor where a wadded-up towel had fallen and gaped at Elex with her jaw hanging open.

There was the slightest hint of a curve in one corner of his mouth.

As if he were trying to remember how to smile.

"You should've said goodbye," he said in a cynical voice.

And she ran to him, threw her arms around his stiff shoulders and buried her face in his neck. "I know! I know! I regretted that so many times!"

"It's okay," he answered, pulling her arms away, not unkindly, but just, needing to not be held. "I knew," he added, patting her shoulder awkwardly with one hand.

A gentle breeze was blowing through the door. The sun was shining outside, birds were chirping, children's voices echoed down the street. The cobwebs of the Order were being swept away, little by little, day by day. Pitch realized that *this* was the moment when the old Order fell, something better was beginning…

…and the shadow over Elex was gone.

The End

EPILOGUE

Someone organized a meet for the Specs and the rebels—that is to say, the underground spies they had worked with during the resistance. They were gathering in a place called "Hotel" outside the Northwest Spaceport. Its Order of Peace name had been dropped but nothing had been chosen yet to replace it, so this was its name.

Pitch and Tenna arrived the night before and checked in. It was very elegant, and it made them wonder who had been enjoying it when the Order was in charge. Some of their Reticulary friends were there already there and waiting for them out on the lobby bar's outer deck overlooking a lovely view of the valley. A pleasant wind blew, ruffling their hair and making Tenna sneeze, allergies maybe?

Planetside hazards.

Watts had a real cocktail and suggested they get one too, but Pitch didn't want one. It wasn't because of the number of years she had been alive; she was seventeen now, though inside she had been an adult for a while. It just didn't sound appetizing. The waiter brought them real French fries and red sauce, and they couldn't believe how amazing they were. They couldn't even imagine every wanting anything else to eat. They hadn't eaten anything like them since before the war.

They all gave updates on their plans for the future, on people they had reconnected with, and reminisced about some of the fun times they had had as Specs. At one point, they talked about Relay, and Tenna told them about how she had met his cousins and how proud they were of him. She was able to talk about him now without getting too sad. They all had sad tales as well as happy ones.

It felt very comfortable to be together again, like their old family get-togethers at Faraday.

When sun was going down and the evening growing cool, they moved inside and promised to meet for breakfast. Tenna sat down in a chair in the lobby and stared moodily out at the setting sun. She was all talked out now but not ready to go to their room.

Pitch plopped down nearby in a chair next to an open door. The sign on the door said, "Library" with some hours of use posted. Its lights were on, and she could hear the murmur of voices coming from within. As she leaned back and closed her eyes, the voices grew clearer.

"'They're out there, I'm telling you," one said.

"Who is?" another answered, and a chill ran down Pitch's spine.

"The original Specs," the first said. "The ones who connected us."

"You lie!" the second said, and Pitch opened her eyes and held her breath. She was *not* imagining it. She would know that voice anywhere.

He is alive.

There was movement within, and someone came through the door, glancing in her and Tenna's direction. He was old, mid-thirties or so, and bald, the shaved head kind of bald. He almost acted like he hadn't noticed them but then with a smug look he nodded a lukewarm greeting and walked past them through the lobby.

She was gripped with a terrible disappointment. Not because he was old or bald, but because he was just *wrong*. So wrong! He just didn't have the presence or vibe or whatever the word was that Axon had to have!

She shoved herself to her feet, annoyed, and decided to check out the library he had been in. Walking in, she ignored the guy still sitting there, first, because he glared at her when she came and this was obviously a public room. Second, because she was surprised at his appearance. He was close to her own age and way better looking than she had expected. And she wished she hadn't just barged in.

It annoyed her even more to see the irritation on his face. And he was turning red which made her feel embarrassed, so she was about to march out when she stopped herself.

Really? Was she acting like an adolescent all of a sudden? She wasn't that now and honestly, never had been. She was a Spec, a spy in the Reticulary, and she had fought with Vil Darad's little creepers and won. This guy was nothing to be intimidated by.

She sat down in a chair across from him, being very adult, and raised her eyebrows and nodded at him in greeting.

He frowned and it made his dark eyes look bigger. "Hey," he said gruffly.

And all the blood rushed from her face.

"What?" he asked, because the change was so stark. "Are you okay?"

"Axon?" she ventured querulously without moving a muscle.

And he turned as white as she had. "YOU?" he demanded angrily.

"What?" it was her turn to ask. She felt her stomach trembling and knew if she weren't careful, she would cry. She did *not* want to cry the first time she met Axon.

"You?" he said again, though not as fiercely, rising to his feet. That's when she saw the brace on his leg and the cane at his side. "It can't be you…"

"I thought you were dead," she chided, regaining some control over her voice.

"I thought you were dead!" he countered, pointing a finger at her.

"But we asked about you and no one ever told us. Or about BirdDog either."

"He didn't make it…and I nearly didn't either but you…you saved my life…it *was* you, wasn't it? The one who warned me?" His eyes were perplexed, earnest.

Pitch clasped her hands together, nodding. "I risked everything to warn you guys, and I almost didn't make it out either. They bombed my node and several others around it."

"Why didn't you send word that you were okay?" His voice shook with emotion. "I grieved over you and never knew what had happened…"

Pitch was shocked at that question. Hadn't they made it clear she was okay with every message they sent? But then, thinking back, she didn't know how they could have connected those dots. She hadn't ever said, *I am okay, and I am Pitch, the one who warned you guys*…. "Why didn't *you* send word?" she threw it back at him. "I grieved over you too."

That was a mistake. She should have kept that little piece of information to herself because now the tears were coming. She wiped them away and stared at her hands.

He was quiet and when she peeked up at him again, he looked surprised and a little amused. Finally he said, "You did?"

Rising to her feet, she decided to leave the room, but she had to pass his chair. As she drew close, he reached out a hand and laid it gently on her arm. She lifted her eyes to look into his and held still, remembering.

The first time she had heard his voice as he and BirdDog discussed their diminishing power situation. When he told them that the drawing on the parachute convinced them they were real. The way he had gotten choked up when they sent those timed power bolts in the exact sequence he had requested.

All the times he had reported and updated them.

"I'm sorry," he said, and his voice was melodic. She remembered it so well. There had been times when she had been alone listening and telegraphing the updates, and his voice was the only voice she heard for days on end.

"I always imagined we had a connection of some kind…" he said softly, a worried look crossing his face as he searched her eyes.

She had always felt that…closeness too. It *hadn't* been just in her mind.

"…but then I realized I was wrong," Axon narrowed his eyes slightly and glanced away into the distance. "I *must* have been wrong. I never knew whether you were dead or alive. Never."

She remembered racing toward the node that day, so afraid she wouldn't get there in time, skating faster than she ever had before, bursting into the node and clicking that switch. Saying the words out loud, with her own voice. *You are in danger*. She had risked her life to warn him and almost hadn't escaped in time.

"Then you just show up here today out of the blue." He looked almost angry as he glared at her again.

"How did you know it was me?" Pitch asked him cautiously, not wanting to reveal any of the turmoil she felt under the surface.

Axon didn't exactly shudder, but she could see the effect her voice had on him. "I would know your voice anywhere. I heard it only once, but your words were…essential. I escaped death by a hair." He took a deep breath.

They stared at each other.

Axon's hand remained on her arm, but Pitch didn't pull away, and she stopped trying to mask the intensity of what she was feeling. The surprise, the elation of seeing she was important to him was kind of thrilling.

"I'm glad you're here," he went on, and something in his face was shifting, like he was beginning to think he had been right after all. There *was* something between them…and had been all along.

Axon was once…was *still* important to her. She couldn't tear her eyes away from his.

A slow smile began to spread across his face. "And maybe we do have a connection after all," he said.

And despite her best efforts, the corners of Pitch's mouth started to turn up and her eyes sparkled.

"You are not wrong," she said.

ECLIPSE

Letter to the Reader

I have never lived in orbit or skated along cables of mysterious construction beyond the exosphere, but there is more of me in this book than in any other I have written.

I was a child when my youngest brother died in a tragic accident and, along with other circumstances, it ended my childhood abruptly. My two living brothers may be wondering if any of this story is about them and the answer is, here and there, sort of. I've included hints of all three of my brothers. The one who seemed so hardened and far away, the one I never saw again or could affirm my love for, and the one I enjoyed a friendly and sometimes competitive siblinghood with. They each contributed to the character I painted as Pitch's brother.

My sister passed away a number of years ago and while Tenna is very different than she, my love for her is included in this story. She would certainly agree that love is worth the cost. She lived that way.

It took me six years to get this book completed, mostly because I had to set it aside for a lengthy period to help my family survive harsh storms. What this book captures is how costly love can be and how worthwhile it is to invest in family.

I can say this with confidence.

Love is worth the cost.

Suzanne, July 2025